For my cousin, Stefan Luetolf, and for Auntie Pat and Uncle Werner.
This one's for you, with my love.

SHOOTING STARS OVER BLUEBELL CLIFF

DELLA GALTON

Boldwood

First published in Great Britain in 2021 by Boldwood Books Ltd.

This paperback edition first published in 2022.

I

A CIP catalogue record for this book is available from the British Library.

Paperback ISBN: 978-1-80415-290-4

Ebook ISBN: 978-1-83889-135-0

Kindle ISBN: 978-1-83889-136-7

Audio CD ISBN: 978-1-83889-235-7

Digital audio download ISBN: 978-1-80162-724-5

Large Print ISBN: 978-1-80162-782-5

Boldwood Books Ltd.

23 Bowerdean Street, London, SW6 3TN

www.boldwoodbooks.com

1

Poppy Allen took a gulp of the fresh, brine-scented air and shielded her eyes against the winter sunshine as she looked out across the strip of pale sand. It was warm for February and the sea was flat and calm. She wasn't the only one making the most of the stunning early-morning weather. Out in the bay, a small boat towed a waterskier in a black wetsuit past Old Harry Rocks. He bounced across the navy sea and Poppy could hear the distant drone of the boat's engine beneath the mewling cries of the gulls.

Her ankle boots sank into the powdery sand as she twirled slowly around. Wow, this was a beautiful location to film. In her mind's eye, she saw a pair of chestnut horses cantering in slow motion through the surf into a sunset that painted the sky pink and gold and turned the sea all around into a mirror of rose-tinted glass.

Which way was west? She checked her smartphone. Oh God, it was perfect. The sun would set over Brownsea Island. They might be able to use this very stretch of beach for that part of her show.

People raved about Dorset's beaches. Bournemouth drew the

crowds, but, in her opinion, Studland Beach was better. It was wilder, with no neat prom and no pier. Just a backdrop of sand dunes dotted with scrubby grass that stretched away into the distance. It was so much more romantic than its staid sister, Bournemouth, certainly for what she had in mind.

Date for a Day, a new kind of dating show, was Poppy's brainchild. Billed as a cross between *Take Me Out* and *It's a Knockout*, it involved seven contestants participating in challenges to win the attention of the picker. Netflix had commissioned a pilot that would be shown in the autumn. Poppy was determined to make it a hit. Being a producer was all she'd ever wanted to do and she was passionate about her work.

Poppy turned back towards the chain ferry, which was docking again. It came from Sandbanks three times an hour and the crossing took four minutes. From her flat on Poole Quay, it was quicker to come by ferry. The alternative was a very scenic forty-minute drive (on a good day) through Wareham and the Isle of Purbeck.

The ferry disgorged a handful of cars from the 9 a.m. crossing. She had got the one before. She never slept much past dawn anyway. Dave would probably be on this one. It had been tricky to get him to agree to such an early start, especially as he was – technically – working for nothing today. This was a pre-recce excursion, prior to bringing in her full crew. She could have done it by herself, but she wanted a sounding board and Dave had agreed to keep her company after she'd caught him in a weak moment last week following a shoot.

She'd known Dave Blackwell for a lot longer than he'd been her preferred director of photography – they had worked for other production companies together before she'd set up her own, Beauty Spot Productions, eighteen months ago, and they'd become good friends. There was no one she trusted more to help her bring her dream to life.

Poppy felt a prickle of excitement run down her back as she looked around her. It might be too busy to film here, but there were other more secluded, even more beautiful, beaches in this bay.

She glanced back towards the National Trust car park and saw Dave's old black Mercedes pulling in and parking beside her metallic-silver Jeep Renegade. Too impatient to wait, she set off to meet him.

Dave was frowning as he negotiated sticks of driftwood and the odd bit of dried-out seaweed, scattered by the breeze blowing off the sea. They met halfway.

'Hey, honey. You been here long?' He yawned and wrinkled up his nose. 'That seaweed pongs a bit. I'd forgotten that smell – it takes me straight back to childhood: lobster pots, seaweed and fish and chips.'

'You surely cannot smell fish and chips,' she challenged, knowing his fondness for them.

'No, I can't. It's wishful thinking. I missed breakfast.' He had a camera slung over his shoulder and was wearing the dark chinos, polo neck and windbreaker jacket he always wore when he was working. The beginnings of a stubbly beard were just starting to speckle with grey, in contrast to his hair that was still a dark brown. Not that there was very much of it – he wore it close-cropped.

Dave was thirty-seven but looked younger. Boyish was a word that could have been invented for him. Poppy was thirty-three and looked younger too and she secretly hated it because she felt people didn't always take her seriously. They often pointed out she had a passing resemblance to Taylor Swift. It was true she had blonde hair and delicate features, but Poppy did her best to offset her ultra-feminine appearance with biker-style boots and chunky jackets and she wore barely any make-up.

Calling someone a dumb blonde was a sackable offence these days, so no one ever tried it, but she knew it was still there – the blonde preconceptions lurking beneath the polite smiles. Her looks could be a disadvantage in her profession. She was aware that she worked twice as hard sometimes to compensate for any possible blonde prejudice.

'Cool boots,' Dave said.

'Thanks.'

Dave was the kind of guy who noticed details. He noticed everything. Part of a cameraman's job, she'd often thought. Being observant had to be second nature.

He looked around them. 'Stunning bit of shoreline.'

'Welcome to the Jurassic Coast. A World Heritage Site. This is the only place on earth where 185 million years of the Earth's history are sequentially exposed. You can literally walk along the coastline and see rock formations from 250 million years ago.'

'You sound like you're quoting from a travel brochure.'

'I am, as it happens. But I'm really proud of my home. Have you really never been here before?'

'Bit far off the beaten track for us. I was brought up in Portsmouth. Our nearest beach was Weston Hard. Or Calshot if we wanted to be posh. To be honest, my parents weren't big beach fans.'

'Mine were. We used to come here a lot when we were kids. I have the most brilliant memories.'

'It's pretty. Looks safe too.' He glanced at the waterskier. 'Lots to do, I'm guessing. I've always fancied a go at that.'

'Have you really?'

'Yeah. I have, as it happens. Don't look so surprised.'

'I thought you preferred watching sport on a big screen in the pub to doing it.'

'I go to the gym.'

'You've got a gym membership. That's not the same thing.'

'Isn't it?' He sucked in his breath and patted his stomach. 'You know me so well. But I would like a go at that waterskiing lark. How hard can it be?'

'Once you've mastered the art of standing up, it's not that hard. The boat does all the work.'

'You never said you waterskied.' There was admiration in his eyes.

'I know how to do it – I'm certainly not an expert.' A gust of sea breeze lifted Poppy's mane of tawny blonde hair, which had escaped from the collar of her jacket – she should have tied it back. 'I was really lucky to grow up here.'

'I bet it's gorgeous in the summer.' He rubbed his hands together. 'It's not that warm today, though, is it? Shall we go and check out the rest of these beauty spots then? As the one with the local knowledge, is there anything I need to be aware of?'

'There's a naturist beach further along.' Poppy pointed. 'But it's well signposted.'

'Excellent. Shall we have lunch there? I'm fine with a picnic lunch on the beach. In the interests of saving money, of course.' His eyes sparked with humour.

Poppy gave him a mock-stern look. 'Get your mind out of the gutter, Dave Blackwell. No, we shall not. It's too cold for shedding clothes.'

'True. We can save that for spring. I've heard there's going to be a heatwave in April.'

'In your dreams.'

He laughed and she knew they were both comfortable with the banter and flirting that had become second nature in the five years she'd known him. Sometimes she wondered what would happen if either of them tried to take it further, but this had never been put to the test. Partly, she suspected, because she saw him in much the same light as she saw her elder brothers, Micky and Lennox, and she was pretty sure he saw her in a similar way.

Once, on a drunken evening out after a shoot about a year ago, they'd been the last two in the pub and Dave had leaned towards her, clearly having trouble focusing, and said, 'I love you, Poppy Allen.'

She hadn't been quite as drunk as him and she'd narrowed her eyes. 'Is that so?'

'I do. I mean it. I'm not messing with ya. You're lovely, you are. You're like the beautifulisht, loveliesht little shister I never had.'

'I love you too,' she had said. 'In a strictly platonic, lovely-older-cousin kind of way.'

He'd screwed up his face and had one more attempt at trying to focus before falling off his bar stool. She'd called a taxi and poured him into it and sent him home. They had never got quite that drunk again and neither of them had ever referred to it either.

Now, Poppy cleared her throat. 'I only mentioned the naturist beach because I don't want you getting any untoward images in the background when you're shooting.'

'Right you are, boss. I'll look out for stray nudists.' He doffed an imaginary cap. 'Let's have a proper recce then. I'm assuming you don't want to film this close to the ferry?'

'You assume right. This beach runs all the way round to Old Harry Rocks. It's called different things depending on which bit you're on. Further round, there's Knoll Beach, South Beach and Middle Beach. They're mostly sandy, from memory.'

'How's the access?'

'There are National Trust car parks so we won't have too far to lug equipment, but some are closer than others. That's one of the things I want to check.'

'So, to be clear, today we are looking for picnic locations, horse-riding locations and waterskiing locations.'

'Precisely.'

She led him back towards the ferry until they were standing a short way from the strip of road. The sea tucked into the bay on the other side of them. 'The beach over there is beautiful too. There's not much of it, lots of marsh grass and dunes and there are a few houseboats moored up, but it's picturesque and quieter than this side.' She pointed. 'You see that little island out there covered in trees? That's Brownsea.'

'Isn't that something to do with the scouts and Baden-Powell?'

'Yes, I think the Scout movement actually started there. They first camped there in 1907. Apparently, Baden-Powell wanted to test out his ideas for a book, *Scouting for Boys*. These days it's owned by the National Trust.'

'You're very well informed. What's the posh castle?'

'That was originally built in the sixteenth century by Henry VIII as a fort. By the time the National Trust bought Brownsea in the mid 1960s it was in quite a state and they leased it to John Lewis, who restored it.'

'As in John Lewis, the department store?'

'Yep. I think they use it for staff. It's not open to the public. Anyway, you need a licence to land at Brownsea and permission from the National Trust to film there. Getting the kit across would be dependent on the weather.'

'True, but a castle's a great backdrop for romance.'

'Brownsea also has a reputation for midges. I got eaten alive last time I went.'

'Hmm, not so good, a romantic picnic on the beach with midges taking chunks out of you.' He rubbed his arms. 'They always get me as well. Tides, midges and weather would make for interesting risk ass forms.'

The risk assessment forms, or 'risk ass forms' as Dave always called them, were going to be interesting enough already.

'What are the other options for the picnic?' Dave asked.

'Corfe Castle. It's just ruins, but it's spectacular – a pile of monolithic grey stones high up on a hill. It's an iconic landmark. But you can't see the sea from there. I really want the sea in the background. Durdle Door's a strong possibility. That's a 200-foot-high arch that's been eroded into rock. The sea whizzes through it and hurls spray everywhere and every so often it makes the news because crazy teenagers tombstone off the top. You must have heard of Durdle Door?' Poppy shot him a questioning look. 'They've made some classic films there.'

'I'm aware of Durdle Door. Although I haven't been there for a while.'

'We can check that out later. Shall we have a closer look at these beaches first? I think we'll have our couple riding along one of them. You have to admit that would look great, wouldn't it? Very romantic – a pair of horses in slow motion, splashing through the surf.'

He rolled his eyes.

She already knew he had reservations about the riding part of the date, but then he wasn't yet privy to all of the information she had.

'You're the boss.'

* * *

As they strolled along the shoreline, they chatted about the job in hand.

Film had always been Poppy's passion. After taking a degree

in media and journalism and nine years of doing various jobs – from runner to series producer for broadcasters and big production companies – she had set up Beauty Spot, but the Netflix pilot was her first big break.

It had taken a lot of determination and a lot of calling in favours to get it this far. A reality dating show wasn't exactly an original concept. But, in its favour, dating shows were eternally popular and they did pull in the ratings. Plus, Poppy was excellent at her job and very persuasive.

The pilot would be a low-budget production. The only reason she could do it at all was because she knew so many people who were willing to provide their services for next to nothing on the understanding they'd get future work on the series.

The premise for *Date for a Day* was simple. One man or woman chooses a date from seven hopefuls who are narrowed down based on a series of challenges they have to perform. The date itself would also involve challenges. On the pilot episode, the couple would take part in two seaside activities: waterskiing and a beach ride, the idea being that they got the chance to see each other under pressure. It wasn't all hard work, though. In between challenges, they'd be treated to a picnic on the beach and a slap-up meal at a clifftop hotel, at the end of which they'd announce live on air whether they wanted to see each other again or whether it really had been just a 'Date for a Day'.

When they'd been walking for a few minutes, Dave said, 'Did you say it's a female contestant choosing a date for the pilot?'

'I did. Yes.'

'So she'll be picking from seven guys?'

'Not much gets past you.'

He shot her a mock-injured look. 'To be fair, that's not always the case these days. Women don't always pick guys.'

'Well, it is the case in my pilot. Even *Naked Attraction* didn't mix it up too much until series two.'

'Didn't you say one of the challenges was cooking their signature dish in ten minutes? You can barely boil an egg in ten minutes.'

'You can boil an egg in three minutes, Dave. Fact.'

'Well, OK, an omelette then. You need time to prepare the ingredients.'

'That'll be done in advance. Look, I know it's tight, but it's doable. I've done a lot of research. And it'll be hilarious to watch.'

'Yeah. That's true. I'm guessing there are plenty of contenders who are up for being humiliated in public.'

'Yep. People will do anything for their fifteen minutes of fame. Well, it will be more like two minutes in the final reckoning, but I had no shortage of takers.'

'Have you got all the contenders lined up?'

'Almost. A lot of them came through social media. But I also ran an advert on StarNow. That closes this week. I've already picked the girl who'll be doing the choosing for the pilot.'

He whistled through his teeth. 'Respect.'

'She's someone I know.'

'So at least you know she's reliable.'

'Oh, she is. I'll tell you about her later.'

'Remind me what the other challenges are?'

'They're more straightforward. The first one is called 'Picture Me'. Each prospective date has to sum himself up in a sentence. My girl then eliminates three of them. They'll have time to do that one in advance. All they have to do is remember their sentence. The second challenge is the cooking – there'll be four guys doing that. This time, she has to eliminate two of them. Then we're down to the last two for the final challenge.'

'That's the one where they perform their party piece?'

'Exactly. They have ninety seconds to impress her.'

'You can't do much of a party piece in ninety seconds. What if they want to play *Moonlight Sonata* on a baby grand piano?'

'I was hoping they'd do something more fun – like – I don't know...' She pretended to consider it carefully. 'Some cartwheels and a couple of backflips or juggle some fiery torches or something.'

'Juggle fiery torches? Have we got enough insurance for that?'

'I'm sure we could get it. Don't forget we'll be filming all this at the Bluebell Cliff Hotel. It's quite a special venue. Unique, I think. Certainly on the south coast.'

'In what respect?'

'Well, the Bluebell Cliff's mission statement is, "We're here to help you make your dreams come true." Or words to that effect. They're good at it too if you look at all the press coverage they get. That's the reason I picked it. They're totally set up for people doing crazy stuff on their premises.' A beat. 'Actually, if someone wanted to play *Moonlight Sonata* on the grand piano for their party piece, they could do it. The Bluebell Cliff has a grand piano.'

'You've thought this through.'

'When do I not?' She slanted him a smug glance. 'They also have an amphitheatre, a lighthouse and a bluebell wood. That would be picturesque, although we might be a bit early for the bluebells as we're shooting at the end of March. But it's a fantastic location. On top of a cliff. You can almost see it from here.' They'd walked a fair distance around the bay as they'd been talking and now Poppy shielded her eyes against the sun and pointed towards Old Harry Rocks. 'You see those great chunks of white rock on the headland – sticking up out of the sea?'

'Yeah. They're pretty impressive bits of rock. Are they chalk? I'm guessing they broke off the cliff at some stage.'

'Yes, they're chalk and, yes, they broke off the cliff if you're a geologist. The more mystical explanation is that they're named after the devil and his wife, who once sat there for a nap. He's the big one and the smaller one's his wife. Wife number two. I think the other bit of rock might be wife number one.'

'The devil's had more than one wife?' Dave eyed her speculatively. 'How does that work then?'

'Don't ask me. I'm just repeating the legend.'

'A pretty cool legend.'

'It entertains the tourists. There's also a story that says the rocks are named after a pirate called Harry Paye who made a career out of attacking merchant ships that sailed in and out of Poole Harbour. Who knows?' She spread her hands. 'Anyway, if you go up from there you can just about see the hotel. The white building. That's the Bluebell Cliff.'

'Wowee. I'm impressed.'

'They have a state-of-the-art kitchen. That's where we'll be filming the cooking scenes. Clara's a sweetie. And she is definitely up for a bit of madness and mayhem. I managed to negotiate a really good deal because of the nature of our project.' She tapped her nose. 'What could be a better dream come true than meeting your soulmate? Not to mention the fact we'll be filming the happy couple there too over dinner for some old-fashioned schmoozing. What's not to like?'

Dave laughed. 'That's pretty romantic for someone who's sworn off men for the decade.'

'I haven't sworn off men. Just commitment and settling down.' She shuddered melodramatically. 'Because that ship's definitely sailed.'

'A very apt saying in our current surroundings.'

She shot him a look and he held up his hands.

'OK. No more romance gags. Vicarious romance suits me very well too. Is the Bluebell Cliff a romantic enough venue?'

'I think so, but you can give me your opinion later. We're booked in there for dinner. They do very good food, I'm told.'

'How early can we go? I'm starving.'

2

As they got closer to South Beach, Poppy thought she could smell coffee and frying bacon carried on the coastal breeze. 'Is that my imagination or is someone cooking breakfast?'

Dave sniffed appreciatively. 'You're not imagining it. Unless I am too. And I don't think there's quite enough sand around here for a mirage. Hey, it's a café,' he said in delight as they rounded a bend into a small cove and came across a row of modest-looking, ramshackle beach huts with grass growing in front of them, set back from the sea, up on an elevated ridge.

Jo's café cum beach shack turned out to have a tiny raised decked area housing a couple of wooden picnic benches and the driftwood sign proclaimed it to be open. They bought bacon butties and Americanos and took them back on to the small beach, where they perched on a slab of rock and looked out across a flat calm sea that was part grey, part silver, part turquoise. A smattering of gulls wheeled and circled above it, but there weren't many people about on this February Friday. They'd met a few dog walkers, but the waterskier had disappeared. Above the bay, the sky was blue, patterned with a lacework of small clouds, and there were no sounds but for the whisper of a breeze through the trees in the small wooded area behind them and the odd call of a lazy gull.

'It's not a bad job, is it?' Dave said, finishing his butty and resting back on his elbows on the rock. 'Sometimes I think about all those people hunched over their desks in offices, breathing in sterile air and looking at the clock, wishing their lives away.'

'They won't be working at 8 p.m. tonight, though, will they? They'll probably be in the pub.'

'I'm planning on being in the pub at 8 p.m. myself. But it'd be nice down here when it's warmer, having a barbecue outside your own beach hut.' He gestured to the ones they'd just walked past. They were all shuttered and boarded, but when they were opened up for the summer, they'd have one of the best views on earth. 'How do you get to hire out one of those?'

'You don't. They're owned and you'd practically have to be born into the family to get one. Or inherit one.' She spread her hands. 'Someone would probably have to expire before you got one.'

'I think that's just become my new ambition in life – getting to inherit a beach hut.'

'Yep, but you'd get bored if you weren't living in the hustle and bustle of a town. Studland would be too quiet for you.'

'Yeah. You're probably right. But I'm loving the view.'

Like her, Dave preferred the convenience of a town. He'd moved from Portsmouth to Poole when he'd gone to uni and never gone back. Now he lived at Canford Heath, a modern estate not far from her. His house overlooked heathland – she'd picked him up from there often when they were working.

Which was best? A full-on heathland view or a harbour glimpse? It was a subject they'd debated before. Her Poole Quay apartment had harbour glimpses. The estate agent had coined the description 'harbour glimpses' when he'd sold it to her – and glimpses was the operative word. You had to be standing on tiptoe and leaning out of the tiny bathroom window to catch a peek of the harbour. On a good day, you could see the flash of the sunshine on water. On a bad day, you twisted your neck and got cobwebs in your hair. On the plus side, the quay was only a few hundred metres from her front door and the apartment had also been tens of thousands cheaper than a place with full-blown sea views.

Poppy hadn't been able to resist. She adored the sea. She'd been born and brought up in Poole. Her whole family were still local. None of them had moved that far from the coast. The sea was like that – it got into your blood. When they were kids, her father had claimed he had saltwater running around his veins. Poppy had always suspected this to be true. He'd worked in the boatyard and at night he'd been a volunteer lifeboatman, like his father before him.

One of her earliest and most vivid memories was of going cockling with her dad and her brothers, Micky and Lennox, at Evening Hill, which was the section of sea on the Sandbanks side of this bay. When the tide went out at Evening Hill, it stayed shallow enough for you to walk out for miles. Or at least that's what it had seemed like to Poppy in those far-off golden days. She and her brothers would each have a bucket and spade and they'd forage for the cockles in the soft, wet sand. It was so exciting to find one and put it in the bucket and know they'd be eating it later for tea. Occasionally they'd come across a hermit crab too, scuttling away from their probing fingers, or a shoal of tiny fish scattering in the clear shallow water.

She must have been about six because she didn't remember Rose, her younger sister, being there, or her mother. They must have been back at home. Rose would only have been little – there were just over three years between them. But Poppy remembered feeling so grown-up and proud to be going out with the men, being trusted to get the cockles for tea.

When she got tired, her father, a stocky giant of a man with arms that were hard as rock from hauling boats around, would hoist her up on his shoulders as though she weighed nothing at all. It had felt like being on top of the world.

Once he'd pointed out a little orange boat in the distance skimming across the water with a crew of men in yellow high-vis jackets visible against the spray. 'That's the boat your daddy goes out in to rescue people,' he'd said, and she and her brothers had shielded their eyes to look, but she'd had the best view because she'd been sitting on top of the world.

Poppy was ten when she lost her father. He'd caught pneumonia after a lifeboat rescue and died in hospital a few days later from complications caused by a faulty valve in his heart. No one could have foreseen the tragedy. No one could have guessed that her father's heart, which Poppy had always thought must be as big and bold and brave as the rest of him, had been seriously faulty.

She had never blamed the sea for his death. Neither had Eleanor, her mother. He'd adored the sea. 'Your daddy lived his life to the full. He loved every moment. We should honour that,' Eleanor had said after the funeral as she hugged her young family tightly. 'And we should always try to do the same.'

Poppy knew her brothers still had the same love of the sea as she did. Or at least Mikey did. Lennox was less enamoured. He'd trained up for the lifeboat service, but after an unfortunate incident when he'd got tangled up in an anchor rope and knocked himself out, he'd withdrawn his services.

Despite all this, Poppy knew she would never go far from the sea. She would have felt landlocked if she hadn't lived near water, even if she did just have a glimpse.

She and Dave finished their breakfast and strolled back up to the café to find the litter bin. On the way, Dave paused to pick up a plastic bag blowing along the shingle. He rolled it up with his breakfast serviette and put that in the bin too. They had the same ethics, Poppy observed, glancing at him. They both cared. That was another thing she liked about him.

* * *

They took Poppy's Jeep to Durdle Door. 'It's senseless having two vehicles polluting the atmosphere,' she said, as they sped along Ferry Road back towards Swanage. She much preferred driving to being driven. 'And we've got to come back this way for the hotel. In the summer, this road gets gridlocked, but we should be all right today.'

'Will it be all right in March? When's Easter?'

'It's late. Not until the middle of April. So fingers crossed. Unless we really are having a heatwave in spring. Are we?'

He winked. 'Hope so. I could do with an all-over tan.'

'I thought you were planning on going waterskiing in your spare time. You may as well while we've got the use of a boat and an instructor.'

'Yeah, that's true. I might not have time to do any actual filming.' He clicked his tongue.

'On the subject of filming, I've been in touch with the owner of a riding stables who does beach rides and she's very keen to get involved.'

'What if your winning contestant can't ride or is allergic to horses or something? Are we hiring a stunt double?'

'No, because that would defeat the object. It's a riding challenge. Anyway, we won't need to because they can all ride. Or at least they said they could on the application form. I made it clear it was a requirement. They don't need to be an expert or anything,' she added, seeing his surprise. 'They just need to look OK on a horse. We can do some fancy footwork with the edits if necessary.'

'More nightmare risk ass forms,' he grumbled. 'I don't know why I was worried about fire juggling.'

* * *

Three quarters of an hour later, they were at Durdle Door. Poppy drew up in a huge car park that wasn't much more than a clifftop field. It was much breezier than it had been at Studland. The sea, far below them, was flecked with white horses.

'You're not scared of heights, are you?' Poppy asked Dave as they got closer to the unfenced edge.

'Course not,' he said, taking a cautious couple of steps nearer to the sheer drop and then reversing backwards sharply. 'But I take it we're not abseiling down?'

'The path's pretty steep. You can hold my hand if you get scared.'

'I'll bear that in mind.'

As they walked down the rough-hewn path and the famous arch-shaped rock formation came suddenly into view, she heard Dave's gasp of appreciation.

'Wow! Now, that really is something. I have been here before, but it never ceases to amaze me. The sheer scale of that arch.'

'It's impressive, isn't it?' she said, pleased at the admiration in his voice as they both paused to stare at the colossal arch in the rocks which jutted out from the beach a long way below. The sea was laced with foam as it washed through and around the arch and from this vantage point they could also see the golden curve of sand hugging the cliffs.

'Now that's what I call a picnic location,' Dave added. 'Forget Brownsea. Let's have the picnic here. That would be fabulous to film. In fact, I've seen it in a film. Hang on, don't tell me.'

She waited and a few moments later his face cleared.

'*Nanny McPhee*, 2005. Emma Thompson was in it if my memory serves me correctly.'

'Spot on. Produced by Lindsay Doran and Tim Bevan. They also filmed some of Thomas Hardy's *Far From The Madding Crowd* here.'

'So it's no stranger to film crews then. That should help with the paperwork.'

'Intrepid film crews,' Poppy said. 'Do you think Mike will get down there OK?' She pictured their sound guy, who at fifty-two was the most senior member of her team. Mike lived on a diet of Pringles, Doritos and jam doughnuts and was proud of the fact that he could use his belly as a shelf for a takeaway Costa coffee when he was sitting down.

'Mike's fitter than he looks. Anyway, it's not the getting down there that will be a problem. It's the getting back up again. Our happy daters will need to be pretty fit too.'

'Are we going down?' she asked him. 'Or are you OK to view it from up here?'

'Are you calling me a lightweight? Of course we're going down.'

He was ahead of her now, clearly inspired.

On the beach, he paced about, trying out various shots. 'Does the sea come right in? We'd better get a tide table. But it is perfect. There shouldn't be too many holidaymakers in March either. It's definitely not Easter?'

'Nope, we'll be done by the third of April. No midges either.'
She looked at him. 'Definitely here then. Picnic location sorted.'

'I'd say so.'

* * *

The rest of the afternoon was spent visiting various other beauty
spots, just to confirm they'd picked the best ones – they had – and
there was a lot of laughter.

Poppy had booked a table for 6 p.m. at the Bluebell Cliff Hotel
and they arrived there in convoy a few minutes early. Aware that
Dave was on the phone in his car, she took the time to make notes
in her folder. Today they had earmarked locations for the beach
ride and the waterskiing, Studland Bay (which beach depended
on tides), and the picnic, Durdle Door. There was plenty of time
to get the necessary permissions and licences and do the risk
assessments. Everything else would be shot indoors. The Bluebell
Cliff was perfect for the studio segments. They'd set up a
makeshift studio in the ballroom and the cooking section would
be filmed in the kitchens.

The banging of Dave's car door alerted her to the fact he was
done on the phone and ready to go.

'Nice bit of art deco,' he said, stepping back to take a look up
at the pale white walls of the hotel as they walked across the dark
car park. 'Very photogenic. Are we planning to do anything with
the lighthouse? Abseiling down it, climbing up it? Hang on, I'm
sure I saw some YouTube video about this lighthouse once on
Twitter and some bloke was doing exactly that.'

'It rings a vague bell. I'm not sure about using the lighthouse.
I haven't ruled it out, though. Maybe we could get it in the background when they have dinner. There's an outside terrace and a
lawn that runs down to the edge of the South West Coast Path.'

'Sounds cool.'

'Let's go and meet Clara King.'

The plush reception which smelled of vanilla was being manned by a pretty twenty-something girl who greeted them with polished professionalism and phoned to let Clara know they were here.

Poppy glanced up at a plaque over reception which said simply: 'We're here to help you make your dreams come true.' She really hoped that was true. This pilot was the pinnacle of a long-held dream for her. If Netflix green-lit the series, wow, the world really was her oyster – oyster being an appropriate metaphor for a show by the sea. She planned to sell the rights worldwide for spin-offs – it could be franchised.

The arrival of Clara interrupted her fantasy. Like the first time they'd met, she was immaculately dressed in a gorgeous, stylish pale-lemon suit and sported a huge smile.

'How lovely to see you again, Poppy.'

'And you, Clara.' She gestured to Dave. 'This is Dave Blackwell, our director of photography.'

Clara held out her hand. 'It's great to meet you, Mr Blackwell. We're all very excited to be involved with Beauty Spot Productions.'

'Dave, please,' he said, shaking her hand.

'Would you like to eat first or look around?'

Poppy knew the answer to that one and Dave confirmed it. 'I think we'd like to eat first.'

'Then let me take you both through to meet Phil Grimshaw, our maître d'.'

Moments later, they were being introduced to a darkly handsome man who was so attractive Poppy did a double take. It wasn't just the tall, dark and handsome bit, although that would have been enough, but he had that head-turning presence that you can't manufacture, however well you dress and however tall you stand.

'Good evening, sir, madam.'

Good grief, he had the voice too. Deep and smooth. He'd have made a great Heathcliff.

After he'd shown them to their table in a discreetly lit corner and left them to study leather-clad menus, Dave leaned forward and said in a stage whisper, 'Are you thinking what I'm thinking?'

'We've got to have him on the show,' she said. 'He's magnificent. He's got to be an actor, hasn't he? Do you recognise him?'

'No – but he might be a stage actor. He's got that kind of voice – Shakespearean. Reminds me of Patrick Stewart.'

'Patrick Stewart with a lot more hair,' Poppy replied.

'You know what I mean.'

'I do. I'll do some investigating. Did you notice if he was wearing a ring?'

'No ring. No white mark. Which doesn't mean he's single, of course. How can someone that good-looking be single. I almost fancy him myself.'

'I don't,' Poppy lied. 'But I suspect I'm in the minority. He's the archetypal romantic hero, isn't he? The camera would love him.' So would her intended audience. What idealistic lady between eighteen and eighty didn't love a romantic hero? She wondered if he could be persuaded to change his name. Phil Grimshaw wasn't the sexiest of monikers. She dragged her gaze away from the maître d' who was talking to a couple on another table. 'In the meantime, what do you fancy for dinner? It's on me.'

'In that case, I'll have a T-bone.' He shot a look at the prices. 'It's not too exorbitant either, is it? Why haven't you brought me here before?'

She laughed. 'We will definitely be coming again.'

They ordered soft drinks as they were both driving, steak for Dave and sea bass and samphire for her.

'It's the catch of the day,' she said. 'How can I resist? Anyway, when you're by the sea you should take advantage of the local produce.'

'It says in the menu that all their produce is sourced from local suppliers. So I reckon I am,' he countered swiftly. 'My steak was probably born and bred up the road.'

While they waited for their main courses, they talked shop. The date selection process would make up most of the fifty-minute finished programme. The actual date would take a day to film but would only take up the last few minutes of the show, the climax being when the happy couple announced live on air whether they had a future.

This was a tried-and-tested formula for a dating show, but there was nothing wrong with tried-and-tested formulas and what would make Poppy's show different would be that they were filming on location at some of the most fabulous beauty spots in the UK. She had named her company with that in mind. Her intention was to put UK coastal towns back on the map, starting with Dorset.

It was her home and she loved it. She adored everything about the seaside county where she'd been born and brought up. Her mother always said they had the best of both worlds: they had the sea on one side and the New Forest on the other – but Poppy felt more drawn to the sea than the forest. Like her father and her brothers, she felt as though she too had seawater running through her veins.

Dad had been on her mind a lot today. She guessed it wasn't surprising. He'd have been really proud and she knew there was a part of her that was doing this for him. Honouring his life and his love of the sea, as their mother had said they should.

'Penny for them.' Dave's voice broke into her thoughts and Poppy glanced at him across the snowy linen tablecloth.

'Sorry. I was miles away.'

'So I saw. Was it anywhere interesting?'

'I was thinking about my father actually.' She sighed and Dave's eyes softened. He knew the story. You got to know the important things about someone when you worked long hours alongside them.

'He was a lifeboatman, wasn't he? I'm guessing that being close to the sea must feel bittersweet?'

'Yes and no. Dad would have loved what I'm doing. He was a born romantic.' Her mother had told them all stories about their idealistic father all through their childhood, keeping his memory alive for his children, even though she'd found happiness with another man and eventually remarried. Poppy loved her for never letting the memory of her dad fade. 'I do wish he'd got to see us all grow up.' She shook her head, surprised at her own nostalgia. The past wasn't a place she went very often. Gathering herself, she said, 'Losing Dad was bad, but I couldn't have picked a better stepdad. You can't ever replace your dad, but Kenny's great. I've known him for as long as I can remember. He and my parents were next-door neighbours forever.'

Dave chewed thoughtfully and swallowed. 'Wow.'

'I was best friends with his daughter Alice when we were small. Alice is four years older. She was the ultimate older sister. Glamorous, clever, kind. I idolised her when we were kids. I used to copy everything she did. Hair, make-up, clothes. It must have driven her mad, but she never got impatient with me.'

'I felt like that about my brother. I was forever copying his make-up and pinching his dresses.'

She laughed. 'That's one of the things I like about you. You never let me wallow in the past.'

'To be fair, you don't usually do a lot of wallowing.'

'And as it happens, I'm telling you about Alice for a reason.' She put down her knife and fork.

'Is it that she's single and has a hankering to go on a date with a handsome cameraman?' He wiped his mouth with a serviette and sat up straighter in his chair. 'It's fine for you to give her my number. You don't need to ask.'

'You're not that far from the truth, as it happens. Alice is single... and looking for a date. Not necessarily with a handsome cameraman.'

His mouth took a downturn.

She decided she'd teased him enough. 'You will get to meet her, though. She's the star of *Date for a Day*.'

'Wow, this project really is close to home for you, isn't it?'

She blinked.

'We'd better make sure it's a stonking great success then, hadn't we, boss?'

'That's the plan,' she said lightly. 'I'll have got all my ducks in a row as far as contestants go within the next month.'

'Contestants and backup contestants.' They both glanced back towards Phil Grimshaw, who picked up on their combined gaze with some sixth sense and turned enquiringly as a good maître d' should.

'He's coming over,' Poppy said. 'Will you ask him or shall I?'

3

'Is everything OK?' Phil Grimshaw was now standing by their table, which gave Poppy the opportunity to study him more closely. He had dark hair that was just on the right side of unruly with the tiniest hints of grey at the temples and eyes that were almost black. His manner was coolly polite. She'd met a few maître d's on her travels and he definitely wasn't one of the obsequious variety. There was nothing remotely camp about him either. He was stern but not sneering, although she was picking up definite hints of bad boy behind that polished veneer.

Poppy had been intending to ask him a few leading questions, but instead she found herself blurting, 'My friend and I were just wondering if you can ride or, um, waterski?'

'I have ridden horses.' He was managing not to let incredulity slide into his voice, but it was in his eyes. Clearly he thought she was crazy.

'Are you an actor?' she continued.

'I am.' His face cleared a little.

There was the slightest of pauses and she jumped to fill it. 'I'm

Poppy Allen and this is Dave Blackwell. I own a production company...' She broke off because he was nodding.

'I know who you are, Ms Allen, Mr Blackwell. It's good to meet you.'

Of course he would know. Clara King was that kind of manager. She wouldn't have neglected to tell her key staff who was dining in their restaurant.

Before she had gathered herself again, Phil went on smoothly, 'I understand we will be hosting Beauty Spot Productions for an exciting venture in the spring.'

He hesitated and she was in charge again. 'You understand correctly and seem to know the details. What kind of acting do you do?'

'Mostly theatre. I do some voice-over work too. I do whatever pays the bills, if that doesn't sound too mercenary, and, of course, whatever fits around my work here.'

'Of course.' That was what every actor did. They all had day jobs with flexible hours until they landed that elusive role. Acting was like every other creative job – writing, painting, being a musician: there were thousands of people who dreamed of making it their career, but only a very small minority ever made enough money not to need a backup income.

'Do you have a card?' she asked him. 'Maybe I could speak to you when you're not working.'

'I will make sure you have one before you leave.'

'Thank you.'

When he'd gone, Dave said, 'Did I imagine it or did you get a teeny bit flustered then, Ms Allen?'

'You imagined it. Like I said, he's not my type.' She changed the subject pointedly. 'He'd be an asset to the show, though, wouldn't he? And he's local, so the expenses wouldn't be too high. And I do think he's Alice's type. That's a definite plus.'

* * *

The truth was, Poppy thought as she crawled into bed utterly exhausted at around midnight – it had been a very long day – she didn't really know what her own type was any more. Most of her friends from uni were now married with kids – at the age of thirty-three, some were even on their second attempt – but she hadn't dipped a toe in the water once, although with regards to matrimony she'd come close.

His name was Stephen Knight and she had given him five whole years of her life. She had loved him unconditionally and utterly between the ages of twenty-four and twenty-nine. In fact, she'd loved him a bit longer than that. She'd fallen for him the first time she'd ever seen him on a stage with a microphone in his hand when she was twenty-three and he was twenty-four and he had blown her a kiss across the hot, jiggling tousled heads of the crowd.

She and her best friend since year four, Serena Richards, had joked that Stephen was her 'Knight' in shining armour. And, against all the odds, this became a reality.

Stephen Knight was a postman by day and, by night, the lead singer of the Bandits, who did gigs on the local pub circuit. He was tall and pale – the latter mostly due to lack of sleep – and he was a hugely talented singer-songwriter. He also had a work ethic, passion and enough determination to persuade a minor record label to sign him up when he was twenty-five.

As it turned out, he lived at the end of her parents' road in Poole, or she might never have met him for real. She had recognised him and told him how much of a fan she was and he'd asked her for a coffee. They'd hit it off instantly. He'd told her later with his usual eloquence that he'd fallen for her smile and her golden hair. She'd told him with a boldness she hadn't known she possessed until that moment that she had fallen for his wonderfully talented lips. She'd glanced at them as she'd spoken and he'd leaned forward and kissed her. Poppy had known then with that total and utter certainty with which twenty-four-year-olds knew all things that he was the one for her.

For the next few years, they had dated in between his tours and on her twenty-ninth birthday he had proposed, and they had spent the next ten months planning a glittering wedding and a star-studded reception to be followed by a honeymoon in the Maldives.

Stephen had not become the household name his record label had predicted but he had made enough money to be wealthy and his father, who had a head for money, had set himself up as his business advisor and made sure it was invested wisely. This had meant that Poppy and Stephen would start their married life without the millstone of a mortgage. She would have married Stephen if he was a pauper, but he wasn't. He was a man of means. He was gorgeous, he was talented and she adored the very bones of him. Poppy remembered back then how on some days she'd had to pinch herself to believe it was all true.

It was one week before her wedding when it all came crashing down. She was on her hen night, arranged by Serena at Poole Quay. Poppy hadn't wanted a big do. She was an introvert at heart and had always preferred one-to-ones to parties. She'd persuaded Serena that a meal on Poole Quay at Il Pescatore, her favourite Italian, followed by a pub crawl – there were plenty of pubs within walking distance – would be perfect.

The evening had begun badly because Serena hadn't arrived.

'I'm sure she'll be here soon,' Rose had said, handing her a sparkly hat with an L-plate on it. 'She wouldn't let you down tonight of all nights. Not unless she was actually dead!' Her sister had a leaning towards the dramatic, but at the time Poppy thought she was right – Serena wouldn't miss her hen night for the world.

For the next thirty minutes, every time the door of Il Pescatore opened, Poppy's gaze flicked hopefully towards it, but Serena didn't appear. Neither was she answering messages or calls to her mobile.

Poppy was just wondering whether she should actually leave her own hen night and go around to Serena's house to make sure she was all right when the door opened again and she saw the last person in the world she'd expected to see. Stephen.

She leaped to her feet from her chair at the head of the long table of hens and threaded her way through the Saturday-night jam-packed tables – Il Pescatore had more than one party going on – to meet him. She knew that something bad had happened before she got there. His body language was all wrong and his face was serious. As she reached him, she saw that he wasn't dressed for a night out – tonight was his stag do too – he was in an old T-shirt and jeans and he was unshaven. He was too cool a dresser to go out anywhere like that.

Then she was standing by his side, just inside the door where they hung the coats, and he was beckoning her out on to the tarmac frontage of the quay outside. 'Sorry, it was too noisy in there,' he said, as they stood outside the restaurant and he closed the glass door against a waft of noise and warmth and food smells that had followed them out.

'What is it, Stephen?' She could barely speak. It was as if some part of her already knew what was coming.

'I can't marry you. I'm so sorry.'

She clutched hold of his arm. 'What do you mean?'

'There's someone else.' He was taking a step back, shrugging off her grip as he did it, and she felt so frozen that she couldn't do anything else but let him.

For a few seconds, she didn't believe she had heard him right.

He turned on the pavement. She realised he had his car keys in his hand, his knuckles white around them, and she finally found her voice. 'What do you mean there's someone else?' But as she moved to follow him, she saw that his car was parked up in one of the spaces on the other side of the quay and there was someone in it. A familiar silhouette in the passenger seat. It was only at that moment as she stood there, still wearing her silly, glittery L-plate party hat that she realised it wasn't just the man she loved who had let her down in the worst possible way. It was her best friend too.

Poppy pushed past Stephen, stumbling in the unfamiliar heels as she rushed blindly across to the car and yanked open the passenger door, which Serena hadn't had the foresight to lock.

'You utter bitch,' Poppy shouted in a voice she barely recognised as her own, it was so full of venom and pain. 'How could you?' She reached into the car, intending to drag Serena out and force her to explain herself.

Serena raised her hands in self-defence. 'I'm sorry. I'm so sorry. We didn't mean it to happen. We just—'

Poppy felt arms grab her from behind. Stephen's hands hauling her back. How dare he? She kicked out at him, thwarted and fuming as he forcibly dragged her away and dumped her unceremoniously on the quayside. She tried to get up, but hampered once more by the heels, she stumbled and ended up back on her bottom with the cold damp of the concrete seeping through the cotton of her thin dress.

Pain and humiliation replaced anger as she realised that a little crowd of people had gathered to watch the disturbance. She was sobbing now, her head in her hands. She couldn't stop and through the haze of pain she was aware of a door slamming and Stephen's car pulling away, his tail lights disappearing into the dusk, leaving her in a broken heap of hen-night finery and anguish on the cold concrete ground.

Slowly, she became aware of Alice's voice close to her ear and a gentle hand on her shoulder. 'Come on, honey, let's get you up, the bastards aren't worth it.' She must have witnessed what had happened.

Then there was Rose's more strident voice addressing the strangers on the quay: 'Piss off, you lot. There's nothing to see here.'

Shaking, she got to her feet, with Rose and Alice on either side of her, and they both agreed that, no, of course she didn't need to go back into the restaurant. She didn't need to face anybody until she was ready. They would get a taxi back to Alice's flat and they would sort everything else out later.

Alice and Rose stayed with her all of that first, dreadful night, mopping up her endless tears, supplying coffee, listening as she alternated between ranting and pain. They ranted with her, were in her corner 110 per cent. It was Rose who persuaded Micky and Lennox that beating Stephen to a pulp, satisfying as it might be, was not the best option. It was her mum and Alice and Kenny who helped her to cancel the wedding. Her whole family helped move her stuff out of the house she'd shared with Stephen. She hadn't had to see him again. She hadn't wanted to see him again.

She didn't think she'd have got through that dreadful, heart-breaking time without her family. It was awful enough that she'd lost her best friend and the man she'd believed was her soulmate, but she had felt as though she'd lost her entire future too. Thankfully, her family had put their arms around her both physically and metaphorically until she was back on her feet. But since the break-up she had avoided getting close to anyone else.

Dave was right – she had pretty much sworn off men. She didn't dislike them en masse, she worked with a lot of very nice ones. But it would be a long time before she risked being vulnerable again. It would be a long time before she trusted anyone with her heart again. It was just too damn dangerous.

Poppy sat up in her queen-size bed in her cosy, moonlit bedroom and wondered why on earth she was thinking about Stephen now. It had been nearly three and a half years since she'd seen him. He and Serena had got married and, as far as she knew, they were still together.

He wasn't in the Bandits any more, but he was still a recording artist. Every so often she would hear one of his songs played on the radio. In the early days, she would have had to turn it off, but it had been a while since her heart had given so much as a twang at the sound of his voice. He was, ironically in the words of another popular song, 'just somebody that I used to know', and she was determined that this was how it would stay.

Now she reached for her mobile, which was on silent on the bedside table. She clicked it into action in the dark and looked at the display. It was a quarter to one and there were a couple of new notifications. A late-night WhatsApp message from her sister. Rose was a night owl and did all of her messaging and catching up in the early hours of the morning.

'How did the recce go?' Rose had asked, just six minutes earlier.

Poppy decided not to answer the message now or she'd end up engaged in a long WhatsApp chat and she'd never get any sleep. But she was touched that her sister had remembered it was today. Rose was a personal trainer. She worked in a gym locally and loved her work almost as much as she loved her badminton-coach husband, Jack. They had just bought their first house, a two-up, two-down starter home on an estate in Baiter Park. Rose and Jack were blissfully happy and Poppy loved them both to bits. It was Rose's thirtieth birthday at the end of March – Poppy was helping Jack to organise a surprise birthday for her. They'd hired a hall at the Fisherman's Haunt in Poole and were busy asking everyone Rose knew.

A surprise party would have been Poppy's worst nightmare, but Rose would love it. She was a party girl through and through. She'd always loved dancing – even better if it was on a table. Dancing on a table was Rose's party piece – she'd made a habit of it when she was a teenager. When she'd been small, she'd gone to ballet classes and there had been a time when their mother had mooted the idea that Rose might want to become a professional dancer. They had the kind of mother who had, within reason, always encouraged them to follow their dreams, even if their dreams were impractical.

It was Rose herself who'd reined things in on that dream. 'I'd rather get a proper job and dance as a hobby,' she'd said. 'I think I'd enjoy that more.' Rose was very grounded, despite her love of the dramatic.

Poppy had occasionally wondered if she should have done the same thing. Kept film-making as a hobby instead of pursuing it relentlessly and making programme production her profession. Putting all your dreams into one basket could end up going badly wrong if things didn't work out.

Her mind flicked back to the beginning of the day when she'd stood on the pale golden sands of Studland Beach, waiting for the ferry to come in, and imagined them filming horses cantering through the surf and waterskiers skimming over the blue sea. It was ironic that it was a dating show that Netflix had wanted. It hadn't been her first idea for a series, but it had been her best. Dating was eternally popular with enough people on the planet to make it a goer. She didn't see it as a problem. When it came down to it, she was a professional. She knew how to separate business and pleasure.

She sighed. There was no question about it, though. Today had clearly stirred up the muddy memories of the past. Was it any wonder she couldn't sleep?

4

It was Saturday and Poppy had given herself a rare weekend off. On Thursday she'd finished a small project for a client with a commercial studio, who'd hired both her and Dave, which was why he'd been free too yesterday.

She wanted to spend some time with her family. She'd neglected them lately. She'd been up to her neck in work. Today she had plans to go into town with Rose for a spot of retail therapy and some lunch, after which they'd arranged to call round to see their mother and stepfather, Kenny. She texted Rose to thank her for her late-night message and to confirm their plans. Not that she expected an answer. It wasn't yet seven. Her night-owl sister would still be in bed. Poppy yawned. One day she would master the art of lie-ins herself.

There was also a message from her older stepsister Alice, asking how it had gone the previous day and confirming they were still meeting for lunch on the coming Tuesday. Poppy texted her back too. They'd invited Alice to their retail therapy morning, but she'd declined because she had a meeting with a client in London. Alice was an event organiser. She worked for herself and she worked very long hours. No doubt she'd be winging her way up the M3 already.

Alice's workaholic tendencies were a mystery. She certainly hadn't inherited them from her father. She couldn't have been more different from Kenny, who if he'd got any more laid-back would have stopped altogether. But as Poppy had told Dave the previous evening, she couldn't have asked for a better stepdad than Kenny. Nothing ever fazed him. He was kind, good-humoured and supportive. He made her mother happy too. They were clearly perfect for each other.

* * *

Poppy pulled up outside Rose and Jack's red-brick semi-detached home with its neat square of front garden. She was getting out of her car when Rose came out of the blue-painted front door and shut it behind her.

'You're keen,' Poppy called as Rose came dancing towards her down the path. She still had all the elegant grace of a ballerina, despite turning her back on it as a profession. 'I'm not late, am I?'

'You're bang on time.' Rose consulted her Fitbit. 'But you're right. I'm keen. It's not every weekend I get to go shopping with my sister.' She tugged her cherry-red coat around her willowy figure. They were the same height, five foot eight, but Rose was a tiny size ten to Poppy's size twelve, probably because her job ensured she burned vast numbers of calories and the fact that she was never still, even when she was sitting down.

They had different dress styles too. Poppy's was edgy. She lived in skinny jeans and short jackets and she was wearing the same biker-style boots she'd worn yesterday, which were black with silver statement buckles. Rose's style was more quirky. Beneath her coat, she wore a floral dress with tiny heels and beads and her long wavy hair, a similar dark brown to their mother's, was in a ponytail. She looked carefree and happy and she was wearing a pair of wacky red glasses, which were tinted and had thick frames in the shape of hearts. On most people they'd have looked OTT, but they suited Rose perfectly.

'I like the glasses,' Poppy said.

'Thanks. They're funky, aren't they? I bought them in honour of your dating show.'

'No, you didn't.'

'No, I didn't. They were in a sale. But I couldn't resist.'

They hugged before getting in the car. Rose smelled lovely and Poppy sniffed appreciatively. 'Is that a new scent?' Her sister was a connoisseur of perfumes and never went anywhere without a spray of her favourite.

'Yes. Wild musk with a hint of oranges. I forget the name. I got it from M&S. Do you like it?'

'Gorgeous. It suits you.'

'Thanks. Are we going to Poole?'

'We can start there. Have you thought any more about what you'd like for your birthday?'

'Not really. Don't go overboard. Surprise me.'

'Of course I'm going overboard. It's your thirtieth.' Poppy wondered if Rose had any idea about the surprise party which was happening on the last Saturday in March. Probably. Not much got past her sister. There were only five weeks to go. She'd been hoping to touch base with Jack about the finer details of the party, but they could do that at the next curry night at Mum and Kenny's.

They weren't the kind of family who did Sunday roasts. They were the kind who did Friday Curry Nights, which happened on the first Friday of the month no matter what. This suited their mother who didn't like cooking – having had four of her own children and inheriting Alice, she said she'd done enough cooking to last her a lifetime.

Curry night involved ordering fifteen or twenty dishes from Spice Nights, the best takeaway in town. The venue was the conservatory extension at Mum and Kenny's. It was informal, no one dressed up and it was utterly lovely. Even their brothers rarely missed a Friday Curry Night and Alice came as often as she could make it.

Curry night was where they caught up on each other's lives, teased each other, supported each other and very often announced plans for the future. Occasionally, they argued, but mostly curry night bonded them closer together.

* * *

By lunchtime, the sisters had three carrier bags each and sore feet and they had just got to The Dorset Diner, so named because it served up all things Dorset. It was on Poole High Street and was Poppy's favourite place.

It smelled deliciously of coffee and Dorset apple cake and was surprisingly busy for the penultimate Saturday in February, so Poppy was saving a table while Rose queued up at the counter to order their lunch.

Poppy tucked their carrier bags under the table. She felt as though they'd tried on every single thing in the shops. None of her family ever did anything by halves. 'If something's worth doing, it's worth doing properly,' their mother was fond of saying. She'd always encouraged them to throw themselves into things: 'It's better to make a mistake than to waste your life wondering.' Poppy had sometimes thought her parents would have had more children if Poppy's father hadn't met such an untimely end.

It was common knowledge that Eleanor and Kenny had tried

for another child when they'd got married. Eleanor had been thirty-eight and Kenny forty-five, but it hadn't happened. In some ways, Poppy had been relieved. She got on well with her siblings and, she'd learned across the years, this was unusual. In most families, there were fractures and cracks, sometimes serious. Dave had told her once that he'd fallen out with his elder brother when he was twenty-two (over a girl, apparently) and they hadn't spoken for four years, which had struck her as terribly sad.

The sound of chair legs scraping the floor broke into her thoughts and she realised that Rose was back.

'Flaming heck, that was hard work. I think the whole town must be in here for lunch. Well done for getting a table. I got us Dorset knob biscuits because you can only get them this time of year with that lovely creamy Cranborne cheese you like and some Coastal Cheddar and Dorset Blue Vinny soup on the side because it's so yummy in here.' Poppy's mouth watered as Rose paused for breath and sat down. 'You looked miles away. Were you thinking about your new project? Jack and I are really excited. We think it will be a massive success. It's what the south coast needs – a reality show that puts it on the map.'

'Thank you, sweetie.' Rose had always been brilliantly supportive, as had Alice. Micky and Lennox were too, but less so, they were both preoccupied with their own lives and men were never as forthcoming. 'I was thinking about families actually.'

'Ah...' Rose hesitated, her dark eyes clouding a bit. 'Have you spoken to Mum lately?'

'Not much no. Why? Is she all right?' Poppy sat up a little straighter, suddenly anxious.

'Yes, she's fine. Don't worry. I mean, she's not ill or anything. But I think she's behaving out of character.'

'In what way?'

'Well... do you remember a couple of months ago when she

got into that string art thing and made that garish pink and turquoise owl picture. And all those other pictures of purple flowers and things?'

'Yes. How could I forget?' She shuddered. 'Didn't she put one up in the hall?'

'That's right, and she gave Auntie Sheila one of an emerald-green cat for her birthday. Auntie Sheila was speechless, which takes some doing. She doesn't even like cats. Let alone bright green ones. Anyway, apparently they were all odd colours because Kenny bought her a job lot of wool. Typical Kenny. Trying to be kind. He wouldn't have noticed what colour the wool was, would he?'

'No, he wouldn't.'

A waitress arrived with a tray carrying drinks and cutlery and paper serviettes and they paused to thank her.

Rose removed the two sachets of sugar from her saucer and put them to one side. 'Since when has our mother been crafty? She's always been academic and more, well, I suppose you'd call it scholarly.'

'Maybe she fancies a change now she's not working at the library. When she got made redundant, she did say she was going to find a passion.' Poppy arched her eyebrows.

'I always thought books were her passion.'

It was true. For as long as Poppy could remember, their mother had curled up with a book at every spare opportunity. There were books everywhere in her house – piled up in the kitchen, the bathroom, the loo. She usually had more than one on the go. They hadn't just been her job; they were her hobby too. They had never had to worry about what to get her for Christ-mases or birthdays. Book tokens had always been her favourite presents.

'She hasn't been reading so much lately,' Rose added. 'I think she was more upset about being made redundant than she let on.' She took off her glasses, which had steamed up, and polished them with her napkin. 'I mean, I'd get it if she'd joined a book club or taken an interest in Latin or something. But craftwork isn't her thing. Last week, she told me she was going to try bead-work. She's never been remotely beady.'

The waitress arrived once more, this time with two bowls of deliciously scented, steaming Blue Vinny soup. Then the cheese platter arrived with the Dorset knobs and for a while they focused on the food.

'Another odd thing,' Rose suddenly said between mouthfuls. 'Is that yesterday Mum sent me a weird text.' She got out her phone, pressed a button and handed it over.

The text said:

Happy Frying day.

'What do you make of that?'

Poppy shrugged. 'It's probably predictive text for Happy Friday. She's got a new phone, hasn't she? Technology isn't her strong point.'

'Ah,' Rose said, her face clearing. 'Yes. I reckon you're right. Doh. Going back to the library, though, maybe she misses it more than she's letting on.'

'You could be right.' Poppy felt a sudden wash of guilt. 'I've been so tied up with Beauty Spot and getting *Date for a Day* off the ground, I haven't spoken to her much lately. But the library was a massive part of her life.'

'She could get another job, though. She's only fifty-eight.'

'Probably not in a library,' Poppy frowned. 'There isn't another local one, is there? And I don't remember her ever doing anything else.'

'We can raise the subject. Subtly, I mean,' Rose said, 'this afternoon.'

'OK.' Poppy shot her sister a doubtful look, which Rose interpreted correctly.

'All right – *you* can raise the subject. I'm not very good at subtle.'

* * *

Raising the subject of whether or not their mother missed the library, either subtly or otherwise, was harder than Poppy had anticipated because when they got to the house she wasn't in.

'She's popped out for half an hour,' Kenny told them, as they followed him down the narrow hall into the kitchen, where he smothered his oil-blackened hands with a green gunk and washed them in the sink. 'Sorry, I've been working on the truck.'

Kenny was a mechanic and he brought his work home with him. If he wasn't dismantling cars at Lawson's Garage, he was fiddling with one of his projects in his own garage alongside the house. His latest was a flatbed truck he was doing up to sell.

'How's it going?' Rose asked.

'More slowly than I'd like, but it'll be worth it in the end. Do you want a look-see at what I've done?'

'Nah,' Rose said.

'What? You don't want to come and see my big ends?' Kenny joked.

'Maybe next time.'

Poppy giggled. Kenny's family not being interested in progress on his pet projects was a long-standing joke between them all. 'I'll have a look next time too,' she promised.

Kenny harrumphed good-naturedly, dried his hands and put

on a pot of coffee. 'Your mother won't be long. She wasn't sure what time you were coming.'

'Neither were we,' Rose said. 'Retail therapy – you know how it is.'

He shook his head. 'I've never understood why they call it that. How can spending lots of money possibly be therapeutic?'

'Oh, it is,' they told him in unison as he steered them towards the conservatory.

'Have you girls had lunch? Can I interest you in a chocolate biscuit? Your mother's been shopping this morning, so we're fully stocked.'

'We've had lunch, but there's always room for a chocolate biscuit,' Poppy answered for them both as they went into the sunlit warmth of the conservatory, which was one of her favourite places in the world. It was huge and ran along the whole of the back part of the house and it was always warm, even in the depths of winter. This was partly down to the masses of glass and the underfloor heating.

Heat-loving plants in terracotta pots were dotted everywhere. Cream and pink orchids competed for space with ferns and spiky green succulents, and on a corner table there were three amaryllis lilies that sprouted displays of deep-red velvet blooms once a year, before dying back to simple greenness again.

The conservatory was also warm because of the décor. The hothouse plants were where tradition ended, and comfort began. There was no conservatory-style rattan furniture here, just two long, squashy, immensely comfortable sofas facing each other across a pair of low glass-topped tables. Their once vibrant floral upholstery had been faded almost to white by the sun and they were now draped in throws and cushions that were an eclectic mix of scarlet and orange and emerald and peacock blue, which somehow all worked together perfectly.

Each sofa could comfortably accommodate six people, but there were also a couple of armchairs at either end – both of the rocking-style variety. When they had their curry nights, it was here that they sat. Red wine could be spilled and mopped up from the Mediterranean-style tiled floor without a lot of fuss and once a chicken vindaloo had been spilled without any lasting consequences, although Poppy knew from personal experience that a chicken vindaloo could take the colour out of a navy Barbour jacket if you were careless enough to spill it over one.

Kenny came in with the coffee and the promised chocolate biscuits and put them on the glass table with a clunk.

'Where is Mum anyway?' Poppy asked him.

He tugged his neatly trimmed beard – something he always did when he wasn't quite sure of himself – and cleared his throat. 'Your mother has nipped down to the community centre to get some information about bell-ringing.'

'Bell-ringing,' Poppy echoed in amazement, and she and Rose exchanged an incredulous glance. Poppy couldn't have been any more surprised if Kenny had announced she was getting some information on sumo wrestling. That was definitely out of character. Their mother hadn't been a fan of the local church ever since she tripped over a loose paving slab outside after a carol service one Christmas and broke her ankle. Neither had she ever shown the slightest interest in anything musical, least of all bell-ringing.

'She thought she might like to give it a go.' As he spoke, the front door banged. 'But I'll let her tell you about it...'

Their mother appeared in a flurry of long, brightly coloured scarves and fresh air. 'Hello, girls,' she called from the doorway. 'Is there hot coffee still or shall I put on some more?'

'There's plenty,' Kenny told her. 'I've only just made it and I've got you a mug. Sit down and relax.'

'Yes, sit down and tell us about the bell-ringing,' Rose ordered. 'Since when have you been interested in bells? And what happened to the beadwork? I was looking forward to you making me some funky beads.'

'I'll sit down in a minute. Let me get this coat off. Gosh, it's hot, isn't it? Is anybody else hot? Have you turned that thermostat up again, Kenny?'

'No, love.'

She disappeared, presumably to go and check. They all exchanged glances, but before anyone could say anything, she came back into the room, minus the scarves and her cardigan. She was wearing one of her no-nonsense, utilitarian brown tweed mix skirts and a custard-coloured blouse with gorgeous gold buttons. Their mother wasn't a fashionista, but she did know what suited her.

'That's better. I'm sorry I wasn't here, girls. Have you had a nice morning and, Rose, before I forget, have you decided what you'd like for your birthday? Was it the earrings?'

'I'm edging towards the earrings. Are you sure that's not too much?'

'Not on a big birthday, darling, no. We shall have a word with that husband of yours. Make sure we get the right ones. Is Jack all right?'

'Jack's fine,' Rose said.

'So how are *you*, Mum?' Poppy said pointedly.

There was the tiniest of pauses while their mother gathered herself. She was always much more comfortable talking about other people than herself. Then, almost unwillingly, she got a leaflet out of her oversized, squashy black handbag and handed it to Poppy. She opened it up and Rose, who was sitting on the same sofa, shifted up close enough so she could look over her shoulder.

It said 'Piano Lessons for the Terrified', and there was a logo of a distinguished but friendly-looking man sitting beside a piano.

'I changed my mind about the bell-ringing. I've never liked churches.'

'But you fancy learning to play the piano.' Rose's voice was edged with disbelief.

'I do, yes.' Their mother folded her arms. 'I've always wanted to learn an instrument, as it happens.' That was news to Poppy and, by the look on Kenny's face, it was news to him too.

'Have we got room for a piano?' he asked. 'They're quite big.'

'I won't need an actual piano – I can get an electric one. They don't take up as much space. We can fit it in the dining room. Or in here.' She waved a hand. 'Although maybe not, because they don't like rooms that get too hot. If I do get an electric piano, I can wear headphones to practise. To save driving you mad, Kenny.' She glanced at him. Her face had gone pink. Was she still hot or embarrassed?

Kenny tugged his beard. 'If that's what you'd like to do, love. It's fine by me.'

Of course it was. Lovely Kenny worshipped the ground she walked on. Poppy had always known that.

Kenny's wife, Patsy, had died after a short but devastating illness, a couple of years before Poppy's father had died, but as far as Poppy knew he had never dated anyone else. He'd focused on helping Alice get through her GCSEs and then uni. A few years later his friendship with her mother had deepened before it drifted naturally into romance.

'Well, on the plus side, that'll save all our present-buying conundrums for a while,' Rose said. 'We can buy you music books and metronomes and stuff. And once you've mastered a few tunes, you can entertain us on curry nights.'

Their mother shook her head, but she looked pleased.

Holy guacamole, Poppy thought, *the things you don't know about your parents.*

'Did you realise you'd sent me a weird text, by the way?' Rose asked. 'Happy frying day? Was that supposed to be Happy Friday?'

'Of course it was, darling. I must have pressed a wrong button.'

Their conversation drifted away from their mother and the spotlight of their interest focused on Poppy, which didn't surprise her because her entire family was really excited about *Date for a Day.* How much did she still have to organise? When would the filming start? Had she chosen all of the contestants yet?

Rose said she knew a guy who was a funeral director, who really fancied an audition if there was room.

'Jack met him in the pub on a stag night and said he's really nice and he's tall. He was on *Family Fortunes* once, apparently. Is it OK to give him your number? I don't think he's on any of those agency websites.'

'Can he ride a horse?' Poppy asked.

'A horse? I don't know. Does that matter?'

'Yes, it does. If he can, get him to leave a message on my voice-mail. If he's suitable, he can come along to the live auditions. We're auditioning properly the week after next.'

Poppy didn't mention Phil Grimshaw, who had, without even trying, bagged himself a place as one of her contestants. He had shot straight to the top of her shortlist. Which begged the question, was her interest in him really on behalf of Alice or did it maybe lie closer to home?

5

In order to make sure Alice was free for lunch, Poppy had arranged it a fortnight ago. That was another standing joke in their family. You had to book an appointment well in advance to see Alice because every minute of her time was scheduled.

Poppy had a full life, but Alice took workaholism to a whole new level. She worked all round the country. She ran her own company, Alice Bennett's Prestigious Productions, so she could pick her own hours, which, as far as Poppy could see, meant most of them. Also, when Alice wasn't working, her idea of relaxing was to cram useful activities (she called them hobbies) into her spare time. She had once learned French in her sleep, or so the story went, with the aid of an audio recording that you played as you were dropping off. No one was sure whether this was as successful as Alice claimed, but she could certainly hold a conversation with the owner of the French restaurant where they sometimes went to eat. Currently she was rereading the classics, albeit by listening to audiobooks, but this time in her car. She spent hours travelling around the country and time was too precious to be wasted. This was a maxim that Alice lived by.

For as long as Poppy could remember, she had put Alice on a very high pedestal. The Allen family had lived next door to the Bennett family from the year dot. It had been much more fun having an honorary elder sister than it had been having two older brothers who were forever fighting.

One of her earliest memories of Alice was of them playing in the back garden of her home – she'd been about six and Alice about ten. Rose would have been tiny and she hadn't been outside. It had been a hot, sunny day and Poppy had been eating an apple when she'd accidentally dropped it on the grass. Up until that point she'd only taken a couple of bites and she burst into tears. She'd been enjoying that apple.

Alice had bent down and picked it up. 'Don't cry. You can still eat it.'

'But it's dirty.'

'My mum says a bit of dirt's good for your moon system. It's fine.' Alice brushed some crumbs of earth off the apple with her fingers and Poppy looked at her suspiciously. She had no idea what a moon system was. But Alice sounded very sure of herself. 'Honest. It won't hurt you.' Alice took a bite of the apple herself to prove it and handed it back to Poppy.

She'd been right. Poppy had finished it and nothing bad had happened, despite the dirt. From that point on, Poppy had trusted Alice implicitly. Much more so than her own brothers. Lennox was six years older than her and liked to tease, and Micky, who was five years older, was more interested in his precious Lego constructions than his little sisters.

When the two girls were more grown-up, they'd laughed about the 'moon system'. 'I much prefer that to immune system,' Poppy had told Alice. She still referred to having a moon system sometimes when she wasn't thinking and actually she still thought that Alice's mother had been right. A bit of dirt probably was good for you.

When the twelve-year-old Alice had lost her mother, Poppy had given her honorary elder sister Big Bo, her favourite, most-loved, mustard-yellow teddy bear.

'He's a bit of a scruff, but there's a lot of cuddles in him,' Poppy had told her, giving Big Bo a kiss before she handed him over.

When Poppy had lost her father two years later when she was ten and Alice fourteen, Alice had given Big Bo back with the words, 'He helped me when I lost my mum. Now it's his turn to help you again.'

When Poppy's mum had married Alice's dad and joined the two families legally into one, Poppy had been thirteen, Alice had been eighteen and Rose just ten. It was the girls who had been the most thrilled. The boys had taken it all in their stride. It barely affected them anyway as they were both getting ready to move out, eighteen-year-old Micky to go to uni to study law and nineteen-year-old Lennox to go travelling.

Poppy was close to Rose too, of course, but it was a different kind of closeness. With Rose, she felt protective and was always in her corner. Not that Rose needed her protection – she could fight her own corner perfectly well. But Alice was her mentor, the person she'd always trust.

As they'd grown up, Poppy and Alice had stayed close, despite the fact that Alice had already been on an unstoppable trajectory to workaholism.

It had been Alice who'd encouraged Poppy to set up her own production company. 'Why earn money for someone else when you can do it for yourself?' she had said. 'Go for it. You're one of the most talented people I know.'

Poppy had doubted that – Alice mixed in some pretty illustrious circles – but she'd taken her advice and gone for it and her older stepsister had been right. Things had worked out very well.

It had also been Alice who'd encouraged Poppy to buy her own apartment rather than rent after she'd split up with Stephen. It had been tough, cobbling enough money together for a deposit, even though Poppy's mother had helped her out – thanks to a life insurance left by their father to be handed over when Eleanor had decreed they were mature enough not to waste it.

For the first year, Poppy had let out her box-room bedroom to students, for whom she cooked. Then she'd moved on to Airbnb, which was easier. The box room was empty at the moment. Poppy wasn't as desperate for the money as she'd once been and the truth was she preferred living alone.

Alice lived alone too. She also had an apartment on Poole Quay. Hers was bigger and posher than Poppy's. It was a penthouse, which meant it had fabulous views over the harbour and a flash kitchen that Poppy would have adored and that Alice barely used because cookery wasn't one of her talents and she thought it a waste of time. 'Why cook when you can buy in delicious home-made food?' she'd once told Poppy. 'If that's not a complete contradiction in terms.'

They'd both giggled and Poppy had agreed, even though she liked the soothing repetitive focus of cooking and found it relaxing to be holed up in her kitchen cooking meals for friends.

The one thing that did surprise Poppy was that Alice hadn't yet found her Mr Right. Particularly as she'd always professed she wanted a large family and was now thirty-seven, with no sign of a steady relationship on the horizon.

Alice rarely had relationships that lasted more than a couple of months. This certainly wasn't because of what she looked like. She was stunning: blonde, glamorous and five foot eleven in her stockinged feet. She put Poppy in mind of Katherine Heigl and there'd been a time when they were younger when she'd thought Alice might become a model or an actress. She had the looks and the height, not that this had ever stopped her wearing heels, which meant she towered above most women and a fair few men.

It had also been Alice who'd sown the seed for *Date for a Day*, after she and Poppy had been watching YouTube clips one drunken Christmas of *Take Me Out* outtakes, followed by clips of *It's a Knockout*.

'Someone should make a programme that combines the two,' Alice had said, laughing as she topped up their wine.

'What a great idea,' Poppy had replied and they'd clinked glasses. 'If I ever do it, you can be my star.'

And, true to her word, Alice was about to become the star of Poppy's show.

* * *

Today, Poppy was meeting Alice at Swanage Railway, where her stepsister had a pre-lunch meeting with the chairman of the volunteers' committee about a promotional event they were planning later in the summer.

Poppy drew into the car park, just before one.

Swanage Railway was run by a charity staffed by volunteers who were all massive rail enthusiasts. Keeping it going was a labour of love. There was only a six-mile stretch of track, but it wound its way through fabulous countryside scenery and included a stunning view of Corfe Castle from an angle you'd never normally see.

Groups of people poured through the exit. A train must have disembarked.

There was no sign of Alice. Poppy was early as usual, but she could hear the hiss of steam in the distance as she strolled through to the platform.

The train was still in situ. A smattering of people were admiring it. It had a dark green engine with a blue nameplate on the side that said:

257 Squadron

above an emblem with a picture of a lion and a crown. There were clouds of steam running along its black roof and dissipating into the chilly air.

Poppy couldn't stop smiling as she breathed in hot oil and smoke. On old interviews, she'd heard people describe steam trains as messy, dirty and smelly, yet there was something incredibly romantic about them. Perhaps it was simply because they were an endangered species.

'Pop-eeee.'

She heard her name called. Pulling her gaze away from the steam train, she glanced back along the platform. Alice was striding towards her.

Power-dressed in a beautifully cut suit, her blonde hair was piled on her head, making her even taller than usual, and the sun shining through it gave her the impression of having a halo. She was waving. She was also turning heads and Poppy was put in mind of some beautiful Amazonian woman striding through a jungle. It was a pity Alice hadn't gone into the acting profession – she could have made a killing.

Poppy went to meet her and the two women halted halfway along the platform. They hugged and kissed. No air kisses here. Then Alice stood back again and appraised her.

'You're looking extra gorgeous, angel. Have you lost weight?'

'No such luck.'

'Me neither. Annoyingly, I think I've put some on. I need to diet before I have any cameras pointing in my direction. Don't they add on half a stone? Where did I read that?'

'You look amazing,' Poppy said. 'No dieting required. Shall we chat in my car or have you got time for lunch?'

'I have. Let's go into Corfe and chat. Not just about the show.' She patted her briefcase. 'Although I do have a few things to ask. But it's been ages since we've caught up. I need gossip.'

* * *

They got one of the last tables in the pub and were seated by the window which backed on to a garden overlooking the railway line. They could hear the whistle and hiss of steam through the glass as the train set off on its next journey.

As soon as they'd both ordered – ham ploughman's, which arrived swiftly, along with a chunk of warm crusty bread and a pat of butter in a white dish – they caught up on gossip. They talked about Rose's forthcoming party. 'We've hired a hall at the Fisherman's Haunt,' Poppy said. 'Jack and I have invited all her friends. Nearly everyone has said yes. One girl's flying over from Switzerland.'

Alice clapped her hands in glee. 'She'll love that. I can't wait. I've got the date circled three times in my diary. I'm buying her a new iPad. Jack said her old one's on its last legs.' She caught Poppy's look of surprise. 'What? Is that too much, do you think? I thought as it was a special birthday.'

'Er, no, it's fine.' Poppy wondered whether she should revise her plan to get her younger sister a bottle of her favourite scent plus a charm bracelet. It suddenly seemed insufficient, but Alice had always been extraordinarily generous and she also earned megabucks. Financially, Poppy knew she couldn't compete. Not that Rose would mind, of course. She would be equally happy with both presents.

'Rose and I had coffee with the parents on Saturday,' Poppy said. 'Did you hear that Mum's planning on learning the piano?'

'No. But that sounds like an excellent idea. I always thought that string-art thing wasn't really her.' Alice broke off a piece of bread and buttered it. 'She must be wondering what to do with herself since the library. That was her life, wasn't it? Apart from us lot and my father, I mean.' Her eyes sparkled. 'I want to talk to her, actually. I've been listening to *Lady Chatterley's Lover*.'

'Oh yes. Are you getting in the mood for lurve?' Poppy asked, pleased.

'I might be!' Alice teased.

'Mum hasn't read much lately, I don't think. Although I'm sure she'd be up for chatting about books. She knows all the classics inside out.'

They touched on the ongoing saga of Lennox, their eldest brother, who wanted to start a family but couldn't persuade his career-orientated wife, Dana, to give up her teaching job at the local school.

'I'd have thought teaching would have fitted in well with having a family,' Alice said, puzzled.

'It would, but apparently she's in line for a headship. Lennox thinks they're leaving it too late.'

'She's not that old, is she?'

'Thirty-nine, same as Lennox.'

'Two years older than me. She's got loads of time.' Alice tore off another chunk of bread. 'This bread is delicious. Mind you, I suppose it depends on how many she wants. At least she has a husband, so time isn't pressing.'

As she spoke, something flashed in her eyes. The tiniest spark of – what? Regret? It was gone so quickly that Poppy thought she may have imagined it.

'Lennox doesn't want to be an old father. And talking of old, did Micky tell you that he's worried about going bald?'

Alice exclaimed, 'He's not losing his hair, is he? I hadn't noticed.'

'He's got a receding hairline, same as our father had, and he's worried he's getting a bald patch. Lennox already has a bald patch, but he doesn't care.'

'Men,' Alice said, with a rueful shake of her head. 'And, on that note, let's get on to dating.' She clicked her tongue. 'Bit of a tenuous link, I know, but...'

'Not at all. It's why we're here.' Poppy got out her file. 'You have all the dates. But I'll send you a detailed schedule nearer the time. And you're staying over for the three days' filming, aren't you? Is that still OK?'

'Perfect. It's in my diary. I'm actually getting quite excited.'

'So you should be – it will be excellent fun.'

'Can you tell me about the contenders yet? Or does that have to stay secret until we start filming?' She put her elbows on the table and leaned forward, her eyes gleaming with fun. 'Is there anyone hot?'

'They are all hot. That's one of the criteria. I put it on the advert. "Hot men required for date with sexy blonde on Dorset beach. Must be prepared to get all their kit off and be up for action."'

A passing waiter did a double take and nearly dropped his tray of drinks. She must have spoken louder than she'd planned and Alice's eyes widened.

'You did NOT say that!'

Poppy giggled. 'No, of course I didn't. I'd have the Advertising

Standards Authority after me. Actually, that's not true, is it – look at *Naked Attraction!*'

What she'd actually put was, 'Single guys and girls wanted for brand-new dating show for major online streaming network.'

'I'm very glad we're keeping our kit on,' Alice said with feeling.

Poppy giggled. 'Me too, actually. But, trust me, you don't need to worry. I've had a look at their profiles and all of my shortlist are hot. I wanted to check with you about height. Do you have a preference?'

'Do I mind if they're a foot shorter than me, you mean?' Alice bit her lip. 'No, although maybe not a foot. A couple of inches is fine. I'm quite a fan of brooding men – like – ooh, I don't know, Aidan Turner – especially when he was in *Poldark*. Is he tall? It's hard to tell in movies.'

'I think he's about five foot ten.'

'Sounds all right.'

'You're five foot eleven. And you always wear heels.' Poppy made a note on her file. 'Five eleven minimum. I'll look out for a taller Aidan Turner.'

An image of Phil Grimshaw flashed into her head. He was tall. She was pretty sure he topped six feet. Dave was six foot one, but she seemed to remember that Phil had the edge. Phil definitely had that slightly brooding look too. Very *Poldark*, although he was perhaps slightly stockier and had those black, bad-boy eyes. He'd agreed to come for an audition. She hoped it would live up to the promise of the video clips that she'd asked him for, which had been fab.

A commotion by the bar caused both women to look up. There was some kind of altercation going on between a barmaid and a guy with his back to them.

'I'm sorry, sir, we don't have a table for twenty minutes – it is best to make a reservation.'

'Do you know who I am?' The customer raised his voice imperiously and the barmaid, who clearly didn't know or possibly didn't care, looked harassed.

But Poppy felt suddenly cold. She knew who he was. It was Stephen Knight and next to him, holding the hand of a grizzling child whose voice rose to compete with her dad's, was her erstwhile best friend, Serena. Although she was only just recognisable as Serena. She was in profile and had put on a fair bit of weight since Poppy had last seen her. She was obviously having a bad hair day too. Her once-glossy dark hair looked uncared for and greasy.

As well as the grizzling child, there was another one in a buggy. He or she had also just started to yell.

'Will you shut up?' snapped Serena to the child in the buggy.

'Great idea,' called a customer from a nearby table.

'Is that who I think it is?' Alice said, catching on.

'Yep.' Poppy couldn't drag her gaze away.

'Blimey,' Alice said. 'They don't look like they're living the dream, do they?'

'No,' Poppy agreed, watching as the manager appeared and shook her head. The noise levels had gone up again.

'I won't forget this,' Stephen shouted – he had to shout to be heard. 'I'll be on Tripadvisor. I'll be leaving a one-star review.'

'We could do them a couple of five-star reviews to make up for it,' Alice said with a glint of mischief in her eyes. 'This pub clearly has very good taste when it comes to who they let in.'

Poppy nodded. 'I can't believe how different they look. He's gone grey. And he used to be a much snappier dresser.'

'Karma,' Alice said. 'Nice to know it really does exist! Now then, let's get back to hot men.'

Poppy nodded. Her heart was racing madly, but in that moment she realised that, karma or no karma, she didn't bear the couple any ill will. The old pain had finally gone. They might have been any other harassed parents having a bad day. She also had a strong sense that she'd had a lucky escape.

She turned her attention to Alice once more.

'I'm not that picky about what my date looks like,' Alice was saying. 'I'd really just like it if they were nice – and not the kind of person who shouts at barmaids.'

Poppy smiled in acknowledgement.

'And a bit outdoorsy would be good too. I'm not sure I'd get on too well with a couch potato.'

'No, I can't see you hitting it off with a couch potato. They'd have to be a football player rather than a football watcher, wouldn't they?'

'I think so.' Alice blinked and her clear blue eyes were suddenly vulnerable. 'I haven't exactly got a very good track record with men, have I?'

'Neither have I.' Poppy glanced back at the bar, but Stephen and Serena had gone.

'You had a narrow escape, angel. But what happened certainly wasn't your fault. At least it lasted a while. I've never had a relationship last more than six months.' She counted on her fingers. 'In fact, make that five. It just never happens.'

Poppy looked at the sadness in her stepsister's eyes. 'I don't understand it. You're so lovely and you have so much to give.'

'I think men are a bit scared of me. I'm tall, I'm loud and I have a high-powered job. I think all of those things can scare men off. Twice I've gone out with a guy who's gone off the boil when he's found out how much I earn. One of them actually came out straight and told me he could never go out with someone who earned twice what he did.'

'Unbelievable,' Poppy said, making a mental note to find out what all of the *Date for a Day* contenders did for a living. No sexists with massive egos required.

Alice sighed. 'Lately I've thought quite a bit about settling down. I know I'd need to work less, but I could do that now I'm in a position to pick and choose my projects. I thought maybe if I invested more time in having a relationship...' She hesitated. 'I know I'm only doing it because it's your baby. But do you really think I'm likely to find someone I like? I mean, honestly truly? In your heart?'

Poppy sipped her drink. She had never knowingly lied to Alice and she wasn't planning to start now, but that was a tough one. 'What I do know is that there have been couples who've met on dating shows and then gone on to get married. I did a research piece when I was working for City Productions and I spoke to a woman who was on one of the original dating shows, Cilla Black's *Blind Date*. She got married and it lasted twenty-five years.'

'What happened after that?'

'I'm not sure, but that was certainly a success story.'

There had been other dating shows where couples had got married too. *Take Me Out* boasted a few. There were incidences where they'd gone on to have a family, but Poppy knew the chances weren't that high. Dating shows tended to be about fun, viewing figures and audience entertainment – they weren't about matchmaking and longevity. For the first time, she wondered if involving someone she cared so deeply about had been a wise move.

She met Alice's eyes. 'In my heart, the truth is I don't know. I'm going to do my very, very best to make sure you have a choice of some eminently suitable guys. But what happens after the show is in the lap of the gods.' She took a deep breath. 'Are you sure you want to go ahead? It's not too late to drop out.'

'Of course I'm sure. I wouldn't let you down at the eleventh hour.'

They smiled at each other and linked fingers and Poppy felt a mix of emotions. Relief, anxiety and a certain amount of fear. One thing she was sure about was that the stakes were higher than they'd been a few moments ago. For Alice's sake, she had to do her very best to get this right.

6

'No pressure then,' said Dave when Poppy was driving them both to a job at a studio in Southampton the following week. The rest of her crew were meeting them there to make a three-minute commercial for a ball bearings company that would take all day to film.

'I've always worked best under pressure,' Poppy told him. This was true, but she knew this wasn't what Dave meant and he confirmed it with his next words.

'Is your Alice the kind of girl who takes things seriously? Or will she treat all this as a bit of a laugh?'

'She has a pretty good sense of humour,' Poppy said. But she could still remember that flash in Alice's eyes when they'd been talking about Lennox wanting children. 'But I also think she may have high hopes that she'll meet someone nice on *Date for a Day*.'

'You can't let that affect your choice of contestant,' Dave said, and she could hear his concern. 'When it comes down to it, Poppy, it's a show. It has to be entertaining. It's not supposed to be serious.'

'I know.' The old adage you shouldn't mix business with

friends or family flashed into Poppy's head and she bit her lip. Had it been such a wise plan to involve Alice? This could all still blow up in her face.

'Who's on the shortlist anyway?' Dave asked.

'I'm down to nine, plus Phil Grimshaw, the maître d' from the Bluebell. I've fast-tracked him on to the shortlist. But, as for the rest of them, I have a funeral director, an accountant, a builder, a couple of city boys, a doctor, a human rights lawyer and a concert pianist.'

'Did you say a builder? I thought you said Alice was a high-flyer.'

'Yes, she is, but this one's a self-employed builder who owns his own company – high end – he earns a fortune.' She had thought quite a bit about what Alice had said on the salary front. It had helped her to make the final shortlist. She and the rest of the crew were seeing all of the applicants this coming Thursday so they could firm up on the final choice of seven. 'There's also a lifeguard. He's a bit of a wild card too. But Alice is a big fan of the sea, so I thought it would be worth throwing him in.'

'Not literally, I hope. Lifeguard rescue yourself, as opposed to physician heal thyself.' She could hear the smirk in Dave's voice from his position in the passenger seat. She glanced at him. 'Are you even taking this seriously? It's your future career as well, Dave Blackwell.'

'I am just a humble cameraman. There will always be work for cameramen.'

'Thanks very much,' she said, as they drew into the industrial estate where Dockside Studios was housed. 'I thought you were on my side.'

He huffed, but a few moments later when they had both got out of the Jeep, he came round to where she stood. When they were face to face, he put his hands on her arms and said, 'Poppy, honey, I will always be on your side. But I'm worried about you. You've been looking very stressed the last couple of days. This should be fun. It's your dream job, remember. Your dream project. You told me to remind you of that at the beginning of all of this. Should you ever get overstressed.'

It was true. She had told him that and standing there in the car park in the chilly dockside air, alongside the rather nondescript television studio, which she knew was state of the art inside, she was grateful for their friendship. He was better at grounding her than anyone else she knew.

'You're right,' she said. 'I'm overthinking this. It will be fun. Alice is a grown-up. She knows exactly what she's letting herself in for.'

'And you're not on your own. Your excellent team, including yours truly, will be there on Thursday to help you pick the final selection.'

'I know.' She felt slightly choked. She hadn't been worried about the casting up until this point. She'd asked for video auditions and she'd gone through them with a fine-tooth comb. Diversity and personality were the key to choosing reality TV contestants and they had plenty of both in her selection. Not to mention the fact that they were all also tall, good-looking and in a reasonable income bracket, some more than others, and able to ride a horse (or so they said).

She'd also hired a brilliant presenter. Taylor Stanton was an up-and-coming host who'd wowed the whole industry after rising to fame on a CBBC show. She would get the best from all the contenders. She was funny, witty and enormously quick off the mark without ever being cruel or poking fun at anyone but herself. She had a knack of putting people at their ease and getting the best from everyone. Poppy knew they'd been lucky to get her now while she was still young – she was only twenty-two and (only just) affordable. Taylor Stanton was on a trajectory to presenter stardom.

Poppy hoped that *Date for a Day* would follow the same path.

* * *

On Wednesday evening, Poppy got an odd text from her mother which said:

Did you see the headlice about doubting reality check getting best ratings ever?

She had got in early from work for once so she phoned her mother straight back to ask for a translation. 'Mum, are you by any chance using the predictive text on your new phone?'

'I'm not sure. Micky set it up for me. Why?'

'Because you just sent me a text that's completely nonsensical.'

'Did I? Oh! Hang on a minute.' There was a little pause and the sound of things being shifted around. 'I can't find my phone. Bear with.'

'You're on it, Mum. I just phoned you on it.'

'Ah. Yes, of course you did. I knew that.' She laughed self-consciously. 'Sorry, darling. I'm not losing the plot, I promise you. I don't think I know how to look at this phone and talk at the same time. What did the nonsensical text say?'

Poppy put her on hands-free and flicked to the text. 'It starts off, did you see the headlice? I figure that's actually headlines?'

'Of course it is. Headlice! Why on earth would it put that? I'm sure I typed it right.'

'You may have done, but sometimes the phone changes

random words because it thinks it knows better. Predictive text can be a pain in the neck.'

Her mother laughed. 'New technology is a double-edged sword, isn't it? A nuisance as well as a blessing.'

'Agreed. I can't make head nor tail of the rest of the text. It says something about a doubting reality check.'

'I typed dating reality show. I don't know where it's getting reality check from. That doesn't even make sense, although I suppose it does really, doesn't it? In that you might quite often use the term reality check. If you think about it, that predictive text option is quite clever in linguistic terms. I think I might leave it on.'

'I suppose it is.' Trust her mother to be thinking in linguistic terms. Poppy glanced back at the text. 'So what you actually meant to say was, did I see the headlines about a dating reality show getting the best rankings ever?'

'Yes. That's exactly what I typed. That bodes well for your show, doesn't it?'

'Or maybe it means the market's already flooded,' Poppy said, feeling a flicker of doubt.

'Of course it isn't. Romance is eternally popular. Mills and Boon is one of the bestselling publishers in the world. You can't have too much romance. It makes the world go round.'

'Yes, I suppose that's true,' Poppy said, feeling better. 'How are the piano lessons going?'

'It's harder than I thought, but I am enjoying myself. The piano teacher is very good. He's done recitals all across the country. You can hear him playing on YouTube. Look him up if you've got five minutes. His name's Gord Granger.'

'I might do that.' It was lovely to hear her mother sounding so enthusiastic. 'When I get a spare five minutes.'

'Your grandmother had piano lessons when she was a little

girl. Did she ever tell you the story of how her piano teacher used to rap her over the knuckles with a ruler if she played a wrong note?'

'No way. I'm surprised she didn't hit him back!' Poppy was very fond of her feisty grandmother, who was currently on a cruise with her grandfather. They were always off on some jaunt or another. She couldn't imagine her taking treatment like that from anyone.

'Things were different in those days. No wonder she gave it up as soon as she could. Anyway, as I was saying, Gord is excellent. When your grandmother comes back from her travels, I might introduce them. He can probably restore her faith in piano tutors. I think she got as far as grade three before she gave it up.'

'So you're glad you didn't pursue the bell-ringing then?' Poppy went on, pleased that her mother was in such a good mood.

'Definitely. I'd need more than a bit of bell-ringing to get me back into a church. Piano lessons are just what I need to keep me out of mischief.'

'Good. And, Mum, regarding predictive text. If you do decide to leave it on, maybe have a quick read of your messages before you send them. Just to make sure you've typed what you think you have. If you're messaging anyone important, I mean. It obviously doesn't matter to me.'

'Yes, I'll do that. Good idea. See you on Friday for curry night.'

'It can't come quick enough.'

'Good luck with the auditions tomorrow. Kenny and I are looking forward to hearing all about them.'

'I won't be able to tell you too much because Alice will be there. We want her surprise when she finds out who they all are to be as authentic as possible.'

'Of course, yes. I understand. I love you, darling.'

'I love you too, Mum.'

* * *

By the following morning, Poppy's nerves had arrived back with a vengeance. Like most independent production companies, she didn't own premises; she hired a studio when she needed one.

They were doing the final auditions in a rehearsal room in Poole. Rehearsal rooms were cheaper than studios and Poole was central and not a million miles from where they'd be filming. She had decided it would be more time efficient to bring the prospective contestants to one place than to go out to their homes, as was often done to film reality TV contenders. She wanted to see them all personally before she made a final decision. Then she would instruct the due-diligence company she used to do background checks before contracts were signed. She wanted to oversee as much as possible herself. She had too much invested in this series on a personal level to use even a trusted casting director.

She also wanted her own crew to be there, which meant Dave, Mike the Mic and Corinna Dawes, who was her assistant producer and a mature twenty-four-year-old, who'd originally joined Beauty Spot as an intern. Lenny the Light had also said he'd pop by as a favour, even though technically they wouldn't need him today.

They were starting at ten and all of the would-be contestants had been asked to prepare a twenty-second summary about themselves and their professions that they thought would best sum up their appeal as a hot date. Poppy was looking forward to seeing what they came up with and she hoped that their résumés could also later be refined into a sentence that could be used for the first challenge, Picture Me.

Corinna was acting as the presenter. The auditions would be filmed, but Poppy knew she would make most of her decisions there and then. Hence, she, Corinna, Dave and Mike the Mic, who'd been in the business for longer than anyone, were all in situ by nine. As was Si the boom operator, who had sticky-up hair and high eyebrows which made him look as though he was in a perpetual state of surprise. They were all drinking vast quantities of coffee. There was a lot of banter going on. Mike had brought a box of Pringles with him and was noisily munching his way through them.

'What?' he said when Corinna threw him a look of disapproval. 'I missed my breakfast.'

'Pringles for breakfast! You should get up earlier.'

'I was out jogging.'

'Were you really?' Si looked even more surprised than usual as he eyed Mike's protruding stomach and Corinna shook her head in disbelief.

'Of course he wasn't,' Dave said. 'Although getting fit might not be a bad idea actually, Mike. Did the boss tell you we've got to traipse up and down a sheer cliff when we film the location part of this job?'

'I thought we were doing waterskiing and horse riding,' Mike said. 'Is it abseiling as well?'

'It's just a picnic at Durdle Door,' Poppy told him. 'There's no abseiling involved.'

'Phew!' Mike popped another Pringle in his mouth and crunched loudly, before handing round the tube. 'Cheese and onion. Anyone else want one?'

Everyone except Si declined.

'The auditionees are going to start arriving soon,' Poppy looked at her clipboard. 'Are we all ready?'

'Bring it on,' Dave said, just as there was a buzzing from the main door. The rehearsal room had a kitchen and utility area attached.

'They're keen,' Corinna said as Poppy went to answer it and

discovered Lenny the Light, swinging a plastic bag which looked like it contained a lunch box.

'I wasn't expecting you this early. Thank you.'

'No problem. I must admit I'm curious to see who's going to be on the programme.' He ran a hand through his mop of unruly hair and grinned at her. Now forty-two, he'd always reminded her of Bradley Cooper with his slightly dishevelled look and shrewd blue eyes.

She let him in and showed him where the coffee was.

Lenny was a people-person and she'd worked with him several times across the years before she'd invited him to join her regular crew. He'd started his career working in a lighting-hire company. One of his jobs had been loading lights for film companies. This had happened a lot and Lenny had ended up getting to know one particular company so well that they'd offered him a job helping out on a shoot. The rest, as Lenny often said, was history. He'd loved it so much that he'd been in the industry ever since.

Apart from Corinna and Si, her whole crew were older than her, Poppy reflected. It was good having experienced people around her. And they were all nice too, which mattered to her. The industry was exacting enough without having to cope with difficult personalities too.

Armed with a coffee, Lenny disappeared into the rehearsal room and Poppy saw a car drawing into the car park. It turned out to be a dark-gold Volvo and a man in a pinstriped suit climbed out.

It had to be Guy, the funeral director who'd been on *Family Fortunes*, that Rose had mentioned. Poppy had half-expected him to turn up in a hearse. He straightened his tie as he walked across the car park, then realised she was holding the door for him and quickened his pace.

Like Phil, he was a late entrant and Poppy didn't know as much about him as the rest of her contenders. He was a fair-haired six-foot-three Adonis and wore a white shirt that showed off his deep tan; he'd clearly been on a sunbed to get a tan like that at the beginning of March.

Poppy handed him over to Corinna to get his instructions and went back to her seat in the rehearsal room.

Mike the Mic winked at her and Dave gave her the thumbs up as she sat down. She felt warmed. The room was buzzing with positivity. They all wanted this to be a success as much as she did.

7

The room hushed as Guy paused as instructed and looked into the camera.

'Tell us about yourself,' Corinna said. 'Just a sentence or two if you can.'

'I spend my days among very cool people,' Guy began. 'In fact, you could say they're positively cold. But if you decide to chill out with me, I promise that the temperatures will soon be rising off the scale.'

Everyone groaned. Poppy wondered if he'd been watching outtakes of Cilla Black's *Blind Date*. It was exactly the kind of corny line that Cilla's voice-over man would have used. But, overall, Guy proved to be charming and came over better in person than he had on his video.

The doctor, whose name was Nigel, was up next and he was a disappointment. He fluffed his lines the first two times and apologised repeatedly. He was also sweating profusely. He finally got it right on take three, by which time he'd managed to make Poppy feel pretty nervous too. It was a shame because he was nice-looking and he seemed a decent guy. Maybe she would put him on the reserve list.

The city guys were slick. They came at different times, but they both wore very smooth suits and ties, as if they were in transit to work. Maybe they were. It was clear they were also both born performers and revelled in the pressure.

The first, Matthew, was quieter and, in comparison to his contemporary, a bit bland. The second, whose name was Jack, was perhaps a little too cocky, but he was a dream on camera. Poppy put a tick by his name.

The builder was a surprise. Despite the fact she knew he owned his own multimillion-pound company, Brick by Brick, Poppy had expected to see someone a bit more rough and ready, the kind of guy who'd be used to shouting at brickies and stroppy contractors. She already knew Rob Smith had a Somerset accent and rolled his Rs, but he was eloquent and funny and incredibly good at thinking on his feet. He made them all laugh with his very smooth intro, 'I could offer you a castle in the airrr, but a red-brick one's more practical. I build rrrred-brick castles. Solid as I am.' He patted his taut torso and flexed a shapely bicep. 'I'd love the chance to offer you a proper viewing.'

She marked him down as a definite.

The human rights lawyer, Alistair Long, was impressive. He was on just after lunch when everyone was feeling jaded and a bit sleepy. Not that they'd had all that much of a break and Poppy was so keyed up she barely ate. On the video he'd sent he had looked like a young Barack Obama. He was even more like him in the flesh. He had the same open smile and intense eyes and he had the same sense of passion about him too.

'I care about freedom,' he said. 'Mine and yours.' He extended a hand towards the camera as he said the word 'yours'. 'I believe that all human beings have a right to be with another person, but

I will never tie you down. If you choose a date with me, it will be on an equal footing.'

It wasn't so much the words he used, Poppy observed, but the way he said them. He spoke with a quiet and confident authority so that she instantly knew he was the kind of guy you could trust. She imagined he was awesome at his job. Confidence-inspiring, authentic and utterly dependable. You'd want him in your corner in a courtroom. Another definite tick.

The lifeguard, Liam McTaggart, was sexy as hell, with eyes bluer than the Caribbean Sea. He was also a part-time lifeboat-man, he told Poppy just before he took his turn. Oh wow, Alice would love that. All the family would love that. He couldn't possibly know, but it gave him a golden ticket.

'My job is to watch you when you're wearing next to nothing without ever making you feel uncomfortable.' He gave the slightest raise of an eyebrow. 'It's to make you feel protected, but never threatened. If you shout for my help, I'll be by your side in an instant.'

Holy guacamole, thought Poppy. He had a good tan as well as those gorgeous blue eyes. Not to mention that lovely voice. Woodsmoke-smooth and confident, but with a spark of vulnera-bility. Voices had always been a bit of a thing for her, which was probably why she'd fallen for Stephen. She was half-tempted to cross Liam McTaggart off the list and ask him out for a drink herself and she and Corinna, who clearly felt something similar, exchanged approving glances.

Charles, the concert pianist, was hilarious.

'See these.' He held up his fingers. 'They're insured for a million pounds. They're sensitive, gentle, firm, and extremely well-trained. But don't take my word for it... Let me take you on a date...'

Coming from some men, it could have sounded a bit creepy,

but Charles clearly didn't take himself too seriously. He wore geeky glasses and a very high-end suit and at the end of his sentence, his lips twitched with laughter and he gave a deep bow.

'God, I fancy him myself,' Corinna whispered to Poppy. 'He is FIT.'

Poppy nodded. She couldn't imagine Charles on a horse, though, however hard she tried. She couldn't imagine him water-skiing either. Wouldn't he be worried about damaging his hands?

The accountant didn't arrive, which blew all of Poppy's stereotypical preconceptions about accountants being boring and reliable out of the window. Well, she supposed he might have been boring, but they weren't going to find out now. They got a message saying he'd got a flat on the M27 on his way in and was waiting for the RAC.

At least it gave them the chance to have a breather and get some air. The room was hot and it didn't smell as fresh as it had earlier in the day, what with all that testosterone and nervous sweating.

Poppy and Corinna sat on the low wall that ran around the car park and talked about how lucky they were to have ended up with a job that allowed them to interview attractive men all day and actually get paid for doing it.

They would get paid eventually anyway. Poppy tried not to think about the bills she was running up. Commissions weren't paid in lump sums; everything was monitored by money men and the funds had to be cleared at each stage of the budget before coming through in dribs and drabs.

'We're really lucky,' she agreed with Corinna, caught up in the younger woman's enthusiasm.

'Go us,' Corinna said, and they high-fived before going back into the studio to wait for the next contender.

'The accountant's a no-show,' Dave told Poppy. 'He's decided to go home. He didn't have a spare tyre.'

'That's a shame.' Poppy pouted. 'He was a Kevin Jonas lookalike.'

'And there's me thinking this show was to find Alice a man,' Dave teased. 'Not you.'

'Oh, it is,' she said, hoping she wasn't blushing. 'My interest is strictly professional.'

Corinna laughed. 'Who says a girl can't window-shop,' she told Dave and Mike, who was eavesdropping.

Then, finally, just after five, Phil Grimshaw came in to audition on his way to the Bluebell Cliff to do a shift. He too was wearing a suit. Or at least he was wearing black trousers and a white shirt with a bow tie. There was nothing particularly impressive about his clothes, Poppy thought, trying to analyse what it was about him that was so jaw-dropping. In repose, there was a moody broodiness about him. His mouth was slightly sulky, and when he came into the room, people looked. Even the men's eyes were drawn to him. She was aware of a sudden alertness in her team. Lenny, who'd ended up staying all day, fussed around with the lighting, although Poppy knew it didn't need adjusting. Mike the Mic looked interested. Even Dave's shoulders seemed a little straighter.

Phil Grimshaw could have just come on set and said nothing and Poppy thought the room would have stilled and then gathered itself to take a second look. But, of course, he wasn't there to say nothing.

He began to speak in his beautiful, resonant voice. 'I live more than one life. By night, I work in a hotel designed to make people's dreams come true. By day, I follow my own dreams.' He was speaking into the camera, which meant he was looking directly at Poppy, and it was as though he was talking to her.

'Maybe we can spend a day together,' he continued, 'and you can tell me yours?'

'OK,' said Poppy's heart before she remembered he wasn't talking to her. He did have an amazing voice. She found herself wondering if he sang. Most actors could sing. Just as most actors could ride horses. The more skills you could put on your résumé, the more work options you got.

She wasn't the only one who was holding on to his every word. The room was silent as he inclined his head very slightly and stepped back.

Poppy could hear Corinna's breathing beside her. 'Oh my God. I've died and gone to heaven. Where on earth did you find him?'

'He's a waiter,' Dave hissed in an uncharacteristic snipe as Phil left the room.

Poppy glanced at him. 'He's a *maître d'*. Not quite the same thing.'

Dave didn't reply. He was busy doing something to his camera.

Poppy and Corinna exchanged glances.

'I don't care what he does,' Corinna said, her face all lit up. 'He'd be in my final two. Never mind the top ten. I'd say it's between him and the concert pianist.'

'Or the lawyer,' Poppy said, still slightly unnerved by Dave's remark. 'He was impressive.'

'We definitely need the lifeguard. And the builder and the doctor – do you think?' Corinna consulted her notes. 'I know he tripped over his words, but he was quite endearing, wasn't he, and women like doctors. What kind of doctor is he?'

'A paediatrician,' Poppy told her. 'That would go down well with viewers.'

'The undertaker was pretty cool,' Lenny called. 'Did you notice his name was Guy Bury? That can't be real?'

'Guy Bury from the Burns Crematorium,' Poppy said. 'Apparently it is real. The Burns Crematorium is in Salisbury. I looked it up. Amusing that he's called Bury, though. What comes first, the profession or the name?'

Everyone looked at Mike.

'Microphones weren't invented when you were born, were they?' Corinna quipped.

'I'm not that old, you cheeky mare. I'll have you know that microphones were invented in 1877.'

'Yeah, but I did once hear that people's names can define them long before they get a job,' Lenny said, 'Names are important. You should be very careful what you call your kids. A chap in my class was called Cliff Sharp and he ended up working as a music teacher.'

Dave gave him a blank look.

'C. Sharp, mate. Keep up.'

'I knew a Becky Graves at college who was studying to become an architect,' Corinna said.

There were even more blank looks this time.

'I mean an archaeologist,' Corinna added quickly. 'Blimey, all that testosterone must have addled my brain.'

'And there's a BBC newsreader called Mathew Correspondent,' Poppy added.

The banter went backwards and forwards and she was pleased to see that Dave's good humour had returned.

'Anyway,' she said at last. 'I've got to let our contenders know which of them have made the final cut within twenty-four hours, so if anyone's got any more thoughts?

Mike coughed. 'In my experience, the female of the species goes for snappy dressers with big wallets, so I'd go for at least one of the stockbrokers. And the pianist. Did you clock that hand-made suit? That was four grand right there.'

'You'd have to be nuts to pay that much for a suit,' Dave said.

'I'm guessing concert pianists earn a few pounds,' Lenny replied. 'Ones of his calibre, I mean.'

'Shall we head to the pub and discuss this further?' Poppy's smile encompassed the room. 'Drinks on me, guys.'

There was a murmur of approval and she felt a thrill of pleasure. This was happening. It was really happening. *Date for a Day*, her baby, was taking shape.

Her mind flicked back to what Phil Grimshaw had said. She couldn't remember his exact words – she'd been too mesmerised – but it had been something about dreams. Then he'd finished with, 'Maybe we can spend a day together and you can tell me yours?' Although he'd been talking into the camera, he'd been looking straight at her. And she had felt herself respond. Or, more to the point, she had felt her body respond in a way that she didn't remember happening since the early days of falling for Stephen.

That was something she hadn't expected to come out of making this pilot. The urge to dip her own toes back into the dangerous waters of the dating game. It was such a long time since she'd wanted to let anyone close.

She became aware that she and Dave were the last two left in the building and he was waiting for her to turn off the lights.

'Sorry, I was miles away,' she said. 'I think Corinna was right. All that testosterone has addled my brain too.'

'Is that in a general sense or was it one particular set of testosterone?' Dave asked in that ultra-casual way he had when he wanted you to think the answer wasn't important but actually it was.

It was on the tip of her tongue to say Phil Grimshaw, but at the last moment some instinct stopped her. 'No one in particular. They were all attractive guys. I think Alice is going to have a hard job choosing between them.'

'Which should make for excellent viewing, wouldn't you say, boss?'

'Indeed, I would,' Poppy said, reminding herself sternly that this was about Alice, not her.

8

It was finally Friday Curry Night. Poppy was really looking forward to the chance to chill and catch up with her family. It felt as though it had been a long week, even though logic told her they were all long – she rarely worked less than a twelve-hour day, and often it was much more. No wonder producers retired young.

It was hard work doing your dream job. She remembered a conversation she'd had with Alice once, when Alice had been encouraging her to set up on her own. 'People think working for yourself is easy. Don't expect it to be easy. Expect it to be gruelling, frustrating, disappointing and heartbreaking. That's why so many give up after the first year.'

'You're really selling it to me,' Poppy had said, with her best mock frown. 'So what exactly are the plus points?'

'The plus points,' Alice had said with a flash of her lovely smile, 'are that it's also brilliant, freeing and the most wonderful thing on earth. I don't necessarily mean working for yourself, not everyone is cut out for it. I mean working for yourself in your dream job. Knowing that you're spending every waking hour doing what you know you were put on this earth to do.'

'Is that how you feel about events organising?' Poppy had asked curiously.

'Yes, it is.' Alice hadn't hesitated for a microsecond. 'It satisfies all of my criteria for the perfect job. I'm working with people. I'm serving them, if you like. I'm helping them to create events they're proud of – in some cases events they didn't even dream were possible. I get to boss people around. And I get to earn shedloads of money in the process. What's not to like!'

Poppy hadn't known until that moment that her stepsister felt so strongly about her career. Although she had known she loved it. 'Wouldn't you have rather done something outside, though? Like, I don't know, teaching scuba diving or maybe being a waterskiing instructor like your friend, Matt.'

It was Matt whom Poppy had hired, via Alice, to help out on the *Date for a Day* shoot.

Alice had shaken her head. 'No. There are too many elements outside your control if you teach water sports. The weather, for one. Matt's at the mercy of the sea. If it's stormy, he has to cancel bookings.'

Poppy had argued that events organising was similar, lots of things relied on the weather, but Alice had said there was always a backup plan. There was no backup plan for a sea that was too bumpy to waterski on, unless of course you knew a handy sheltered lake, but even that wasn't foolproof.

Poppy was getting a little bit worried about the waterskiing aspect of *Date for a Day*. They only had one day scheduled to film the date itself and they didn't have that many options to reschedule it. Rescheduling was expensive.

Horse riding was easier. You could ride in the rain if necessary. Maybe it had been overambitious of her to think they could do both. She had got caught up in Alice's punch-drunk enthusiasm. 'It's such a brilliant opportunity to showcase Dorset,' she had said, when they'd first talked about what you might do on an activity date. 'Cantering along a gorgeous beach, skimming across the waves on a speedboat. Your dad would have loved it, wouldn't he?'

Alice's eyes had shone with enthusiasm and Poppy had known she was right. She owed it to her father to show off the Dorset coastline at its most beautiful. She hadn't known how strongly she felt about that until recently either. But as the date for shooting grew closer, she was aware of a slowly increasing pressure to get everything right.

She was still thinking about this when she arrived at her parents' house just before eight. She bumped into Lennox and Dana outside, who'd clearly just arrived too. Dana was getting a plate of something covered in cling film from the back of the car. *Oh good*, thought Poppy, *it must be her turn to provide dessert*. She usually did something home-made. Cooking was her hobby – she said it gave her the opportunity to wind down from teaching truculent kids.

'Hey, Popsicle, how's it going?' Lennox called. Her eldest brother was the only person in the world who got away with calling her Popsicle. It was a nickname that secretly irritated the hell out of her, but she knew if she told him that he'd just do it more. That was Lennox all over. Wind-ups were what kept him going. Lennox bounded through life with a cheeky smile on his face and a happy-go-lucky attitude. He never stayed at a job for very long – his record was eighteen months. He was a bar manager and he got bored of being in the same place, but he always seemed to find another job without too many problems. People liked him.

It was only recently that Poppy had started seeing a different side of him. It was as though he'd suddenly realised his biological clock was ticking. Or that Dana's was – Poppy wasn't quite sure which. But he'd started stressing out about wanting a family just after last Christmas. It was a shame that Dana was resisting, Poppy thought, not that she'd ever have pressurised anyone into having kids before they were ready, but the pair of them would make great parents.

Poppy waved at Lennox and he blew her a kiss as he went to help his wife with another couple of bags. Poppy tried the front door and discovered it was on the latch. Micky had to be already here – whoever arrived first for a family gathering left the door on the latch for the others.

Micky was like her, in that he was usually early for arrangements. It was one of the things they had in common, as well as both being single, she mused, out of choice, not necessity. Micky was the quiet one of the family. He took things much more seriously than the rest of them. He worried about minutiae and he could get quite obsessive over tiny details, which came in handy at his job – he was a legal clerk in a family law firm. He would occasionally tip into bouts of depression, though, and he was prone to getting stress-related illnesses like eczema and migraines. He was the dark to Lennox's light, the shadow to Rose's sunshine.

He was also as reliable as the dawn and he had an amazing memory and an astounding capacity for general knowledge. If you wanted anything important done or remembered, you could rely on Micky to do it, and if you wanted a quiz partner, you wouldn't find a better one than Micky.

Micky met her in the hall. 'Hiya, Pops.' She much preferred Pops to Popsicle. 'I thought I heard car doors. I was just coming to see if anyone needed help to carry things in.' Micky was also the most thoughtful person you could ever hope to meet.

'You can take these if you like. Thanks.' She handed him the carrier of two bottles of wine and a bottle of pink lemonade she'd brought with her. 'How's it going?'

'All right.' He looked as if he was about to say something else, but then Lennox appeared and he clearly thought better of it.

A few minutes later, the brothers and Dana were installed in the conservatory, lounging on the comfy sofas and chatting to Kenny, while Poppy helped her mother in the kitchen, getting glasses and plates out.

There was a brochure on the worktop with an electric piano on the front. She swooped on it. 'Hey, this looks good. Are you going to get one?'

'I'm not sure yet. Digital pianos are expensive. I think I'll have a few more lessons before I commit myself. But I am going to need something to practise on.'

'Of course you will.' Poppy put the brochure back. 'Are you reading any good books at the moment, Mum?'

'Not at the moment, no. Unless you count music books, although they're going to take me a while to master.' Eleanor brushed her hair back off her forehead and squinted at the dishwasher, which was on its drying cycle. 'We were out of plates,' she explained. 'That should be finished in a minute.'

The dishwasher pinged obligingly as she spoke.

'It seems odd not seeing you with your head stuck in a book. You haven't run out of book tokens, have you?' Poppy enquired.

'No. I've got enough book tokens in my bedside drawer to keep me going until 2030. Now stop asking me senseless questions and get four more plates out of the dishwasher for me, could you, please?'

Poppy did as she was bid. She had told Rose about the odd text and her sister had been reassured to hear that it had been down to predictive text all along. Rose had also decided that she'd probably overreacted about their mother's sudden interest in unusual new hobbies. Why shouldn't she try something new? Retirement was a strange time for anyone. Especially if you hadn't planned to retire. It wasn't surprising that Eleanor was keen on finding ways to fill up her time. Poppy decided to put it out of her mind for now. There was no sense in looking for problems that weren't there.

* * *

Rose and Jack arrived in a flurry of chatter and bags. Rose was wearing her heart-shaped red glasses again, which set Lennox off on a mickey-taking diatribe.

'Couldn't you afford proper ones, sis? I'd have lent you the money.'

'They're Chloe. They're not cheap.'

'I'd give them back to her if I were you. They probably suit her better.' Lennox chuckled.

'You're not funny and you're not clever.'

'Oh, so true,' Dana said, laughing, but Rose wasn't finished.

'I'll have you know they're funky and they're right on trend. Not that you'd know what that meant.'

Lennox smirked and had just opened his mouth to say something else when Dana thumped him none too gently on the arm. 'Stop it. I think those glasses are fabulous.'

Kenny, the peacemaker, offered Lennox a bowl of olives to divert him.

'Thank you.' Rose gave him a thumbs up. 'How's the truck going?'

'I could show you my big ends if you like...?'

There was a chorus of no thanks and maybe next times from

everyone in the room. Then, before anyone else could say anything, Alice rushed in, looking harassed.

'Sorry, everybody, it's been one of those days. Awkward client. I thought I was never going to get away.'

'Don't worry, darling,' their mother reassured her. 'You're here now. Right then. Is everybody having their usual? Kenny, have you got the notepad?'

There was quite a bit of toing and froing and shouting out and changing of minds and tutting as Kenny wrote things down and crossed them out again until finally they were happy with the curry order. Then, in time-honoured tradition, Kenny phoned it through to Spice Nights and read out his debit card details and they all rummaged in wallets and bags to give him their share of the cash.

After that, it was just a question of organising drinks and putting condiments and cutlery on the low glass conservatory table and the little bowls of peanuts and olives that Eleanor always insisted on putting out in case anyone was too hungry to last, which one or more of them usually were, until the food was delivered.

The chat moved from Dana's job at Park Heights to Rose's coming birthday celebrations. Everyone in the family apart from Rose knew about the surprise party, but no one let anything slip. They were all ostensibly going along with Rose's plan that she would make the celebrations last for at least six weeks by organising different activities with various friends and family. They would have a big extravagant family meal on the Saturday of the party, just to put her off the scent.

'Do you know what you want, present-wise?' Lennox asked her, emptying a peanut bowl with one tip into his mouth.

'Not really – maybe some nice perfume?'

He wrinkled his nose. 'Yeah – you could use some. What is that stuff you're wearing? It smells like furniture polish.'

'It does not smell like furniture polish.' She threw a peacock-blue cushion at him and narrowly missed Dana's wine. 'It's orange blossom and vanilla.'

'I rest my case.'

'Ignore him,' Dana said, rescuing her wine. 'He's never had any taste. Except in women.' She smirked at her husband, who pulled a face at her.

'He certainly hasn't got any taste in socks,' Rose said, gesturing towards her brother's socks. He'd taken off his shoes and his feet were tucked up on his chair and now everyone in the family followed Rose's gaze.

'What do you mean? What colour are they?' Lennox glanced in alarm at his socks. He was colour-blind so he genuinely didn't know what colour they were.

'They're chartreuse,' Rose said.

'What colour's that?'

'A kind of garish lime green,' his sister told him gleefully.

'Are they?' Lennox looked at Dana. 'Why am I wearing lime-green socks?'

'Because you'd run out of black ones,' she said peaceably. 'Chartreuse is a nice colour.'

'Well, I don't want to wear garish colours. I want to wear sensible black ones, or navy at a push.'

'Then I suggest you let me know when you're running out of socks,' she said. 'Or you could try operating the washing machine yourself. It's not hard.'

'Have I been wearing lime-green socks to work?'

'No, of course not.' Dana smirked.

'You had those lovely scarlet ones on last time we saw you,'

Rose goaded. 'Or was it the sunflower-yellow ones – actually, it might have been those.'

'Is that true?' Lennox accused Dana, who rolled her eyes and said she couldn't remember.

Lennox huffed and Poppy wondered if she was imagining the slight edge of tension between them.

The chat moved on to *Date for a Day* and the part that Alice was going to play in it. Micky wanted to know if she was getting nervous.

'No,' Alice said breezily. 'Well, maybe a little.' She glanced at Poppy. 'I've never done anything like this before.'

'She was brilliant on the screen test,' Poppy reassured.

'None of us have been on television,' their mother said. 'Apart from Poppy. It's a big thing.'

'It's definitely a thing,' Lennox said.

'I'm mainly behind the cameras, not in front of them,' Poppy put in quickly.

'I know you're choosing a guy to go on a date with, but do you actually get filmed going on the date as well?' Micky asked.

'Yes, we'll be filming the date – that's part of it.' Everyone had gone quiet for a moment and Poppy looked around at their expectant faces.

'A romantic night out with a film crew videoing your every move.' Lennox screwed up his nose. 'It doesn't sound very romantic to me.'

Alice laughed self-consciously and Poppy intervened. 'We'll be filming more of the daytime stuff than the evening. It's *Date for a Day*, after all. Alice and her... beau will be filmed doing various activities around our gorgeous coastline.' She held up her hands and counted them off on her fingers. 'Waterskiing, weather permitting, a lunchtime picnic at Durdle Door and then a romantic horse ride along Studland Beach.'

'That sounds romantic,' Micky said. 'And right up your street, Alice.' She'd ridden since she was little.

'Did you choose the waterskiing?' Kenny asked, glancing at his daughter. 'Because you're a dab hand?'

'I may have had some influence,' Alice told him, looking at Poppy.

'Basically, it's an activity date,' Poppy said, looking round at them all. 'The whole concept of the programme is that the couple get to see each other under pressure, which makes for more exciting viewing than doing something very passive, like, say, going for a trip on a steam train. It also has to be something that can be done at the coast, because another objective of the series is to show people how beautiful the UK coast is. I want to get people back to the UK beaches. Revitalise our tourist trade.' She knew she was off on one. She could hear the passion in her own voice. She had probably told them far more than they wanted to hear. But they were all nodding.

'Good for you,' Micky said loyally.

'Hear hear,' Dana said.

'It's a good idea about the activity date.' Their mother spoke for the first time. 'It's always good to see a prospective partner under pressure. You can see what they're made of then, can't you?'

'You can tell a lot about a man by how he acts under pressure,' Rose agreed. 'Like when he's lost, for example, and the satnav's broken. And also by how he treats waiters.' She glanced tenderly at Jack. He had clearly passed both tests.

'There won't be many waiters on a picnic at Durdle Door, though,' Lennox said silkily, and then backtracked when Dana glared at him. 'Although a picnic can be romantic, I suppose.'

'There'll be a very romantic slap-up meal at the Bluebell Cliff

Hotel in the evening,' Poppy explained. 'I imagine there will be a waiter or two there.'

'I'd like to try that place sometime.' Eleanor blinked. 'Hasn't it got a Michelin star? Actually, I'd love a go on a steam train too.'

'There's nothing to stop us going on a steam train, love,' Kenny said with surprise. 'Why didn't you say? There's one at Swanage still, isn't there?'

'Very much so,' Alice told them. 'Poppy and I were there just the other day.'

'Not on the steam train,' Poppy added. 'We met there after a meeting Alice had.' She paused. 'Actually, we saw my ex, didn't we, Alice?' She knew Alice would never have mentioned it if she hadn't. No one ever mentioned Stephen Knight in her hearing.

'We did.' Alice's face sobered. 'He didn't look happy.' She filled them in on the details and everyone agreed that karma clearly was a thing. Then Alice diplomatically changed the subject to classic books – she'd just asked Eleanor about *Lady Chatterley's Lover* when the doorbell rang. Eleanor looked relieved that they'd been diverted.

'Curry delivery.' Micky jumped up. 'I'll go.'

'I'll help you,' Poppy said, and they left the others still chatting animatedly while they went to collect the curries.

In the hall, Micky touched Poppy's arm. 'Do you think my bald patch has got smaller?' He dipped his head by the hall light so she could see. 'Only, I've just started on this new herbal remedy.'

Micky had tried various herbal remedies lately, some definitely odder than others.

'It might be a little smaller,' Poppy said, diplomatically. 'Maybe you could take photos – you know, like before and after. That would be a more scientific way of keeping track.'

'True. Anyway, I guess it's early days. Thanks for looking.' His dark eyes were vulnerable and she had an urge to hug him.

'You look great, Micky. You always do. Let's get this takeaway to the troops, shall we?'

Very soon, the conservatory was full of the fragrant scents of madras, tikka masala, rice, cardamom, spices and naan bread. Rose and Dana poured more drinks. Jack opened another bottle of wine and some soft drinks for the drivers. Then for a brief while there was almost silence as they ate in the companionable warmth of the conservatory. Poppy noticed that the windows had steamed up and the dark night beyond pressed against them, making everything seem ultra-cosy and safe. All you could see were their reflections on the glass, a harmonious picture of happy families. At least for as long as Lennox had his mouth full!

Poppy knew there was nowhere else she'd rather have been than eating a curry with her family safely ensconced in the familiar warmth and banter of a Friday night. It was an oasis of peace in her hectic life. At that moment, she wouldn't have swapped places with anyone in the world.

9

Over the next fortnight, Poppy wished she could have bottled that feeling of peace and got it out at intervals to dab on her wrists like a soothing balm. She had never been so busy. The preparations for *Date for a Day* were now taking up much of her time and even more of her headspace.

The contestants, plus their standbys, had been informed. The necessary extensive background checks had been done and they had all signed their contracts. She had her own team organised and she'd hired a crew of five studio-camera ops for the main filming. She and Dave had finished the external location risk assessments without too much dissent. Risk assessments had a habit of creating divisions, because around 50 per cent of people who worked in her industry looked upon them as a massive paper-chasing exercise and a waste of time, and the other 50 per cent took them ultra-seriously and kicked off if every i wasn't dotted and every t wasn't crossed. Poppy fell somewhere between the two, although she had definitely moved closer into the t-crossing brigade since the buck stopped with her. Litigation was no joke. Not that it could be entirely avoided by having proper risk assessments in place, but they certainly helped. It was the old-timers who had always relied on their common sense who didn't tend to like the minutiae of risk assessments. People who'd come in more recently had never known anything else. Fortunately, Dave, despite all of his cynicism, was supportive and helpful and not obstructive as she'd occasionally found photographers to be in the past. He was hugely experienced both in a studio and on location.

Over the last few years, there had been a shift in dating shows that were filmed in front of a studio audience to shows that were filmed on location. Poppy had decided when she'd come up with the original concept that *Date for a Day* would be filmed on what was, despite the makeshift studio, effectively location, as part of the show's ethos was to showcase the UK's beauty spots.

Another reason she had chosen the Bluebell Cliff Hotel, apart from its gorgeous position overlooking Old Harry Rocks, was because it had more than one purpose-built room that had been designed for the sole function of enabling guests to live out their dreams.

The original owner, who had both refurbished and been responsible for the concept of the Bluebell Cliff, had been an eccentric multimillionaire who had made her money as a world-famous concert pianist. The hotel had been her swansong and she'd lavished both money and love on her creation. There was a recording studio for musicians, a yoga studio that converted to a creative writing space, and a ballroom with a stage at one end that doubled as a music room big enough to hold a Steinway grand piano and a brass band, not to mention a few dozen wedding guests.

The ballroom would become their makeshift studio and it was here that most of the show would be filmed. Poppy had hired an outside broadcasting truck, or OB truck as everyone called them, for the filming itself. This would be situated in the grounds adjacent to the ballroom, which had French windows so they could run out cables. The OB truck would house the gallery, which was the nerve centre of operations. The gallery was where the studio director, in this case Poppy and also Dave, would be directing the action. They'd be sitting in front of several monitors that showed exactly what was taking place in the studio from the angle of each camera and also how the whole thing came together on screen. The adjoining rooms would be used for make-up and wardrobe and there would be a green room for contestants to wait.

It had made sense to use the Bluebell Cliff's kitchens, which were modern and beautiful, not to mention big enough, to film the signature-dish part of the show. The hotel would be closed to the public while filming took place. The Beauty Spot Productions team were all staying for the duration of filming anyway and so were most of the camera ops. Fortunately, a couple of camera ops lived locally or they'd have run out of room. Poppy and her team were taking every bedroom and Alice would be staying too.

It was essential that Alice stay at the hotel because she'd be on camera every day, but Poppy was also really looking forward to spending some time with her stepsister. There wouldn't be much spare time, but they would be able to snatch some in the evenings.

* * *

On the Tuesday before filming began, Poppy and Dave went to the Bluebell so that Dave could risk assess the kitchens.

'Have I warned you about the chef?' Poppy said as she and Dave got out of his Mercedes into the fresh air of the Bluebell's clifftop car park.

'Er, no. Do you need to?' Dave paused from gathering equipment from the back of his car.

'I'm not sure. I may just have caught him on a bad day last time I was here. But he's definitely a bit odd.' Aware that Dave was waiting for her to continue, she said, 'It's hard to put my finger on it exactly. But for a start everyone calls him Mr B. Even Clara. No one seems to know his real name.'

'Chefs have a reputation for being eccentric, though, don't they?'

'I suppose that's true. But he struck me as a little paranoid. He insisted that he be here today while we did the risk assessments.'

'Fair enough. It's his kitchen.'

Dave didn't look too put out and Poppy decided she'd said enough. It was hard to sum up Mr B. Maybe it was best to just let Dave meet him and judge for himself. They didn't have long to wait. As they approached the front entrance, the door opened and Clara shot out, with a dog that looked very much like a small red fox trotting on a lead by her side.

'Good morning,' she said cheerfully. 'I've just got to nip out, but reception is expecting you and I've left instructions for Mr B to show you everything you need to see.' She glanced at her dog and added, 'I'd have stayed to help, but I'm off to the vet with Foxy.'

'Oh no, is she OK?' Poppy looked at the dog, who pricked her ears at the sound of her name and wagged her tail enthusiastically when Dave bent to stroke her shiny head.

'Yes, it's nothing major.' Clara's face had gone bright pink for some reason. How odd. 'I won't be long,' she added, flicking a swift glance back over her shoulder as though she was worried someone might have followed her out. 'Better dash. Don't want to be late.'

'That dog looked the picture of health to me,' Dave remarked as they went into the hotel. 'Apart from the fact that she only had three legs, that is.'

'I don't suppose the vet can do much about that.' Poppy hesitated. 'But Clara did seem in a hurry to get away, didn't she? Do you think she's avoiding us?'

'I can't imagine why she would be. Maybe she's escaping from an awkward customer.'

'That's probably it.'

They walked into reception at exactly the same moment as a very tall, very thin man emerged through the restaurant door and came hurrying to greet them.

'Ah. Good morning, Miss Allen. I believe you're here to see me.' He spoke to Poppy and then held out his hand towards Dave. 'I don't believe we've met. I'm Mr B.'

'Dave Blackwell,' Dave said, and Poppy resisted the urge to say, 'Two Mr Bs,' and took a step back as Dave shook the chef's hand.

Poppy decided that the chef probably wasn't much older than her, but he looked a lot older, partly because there was an intensity about him that had creased his face into frown lines that never quite went, even when he wasn't frowning.

Dave didn't seem to notice. She heard them exchanging pleasantries as they nodded at the cheerful young receptionist and went through the restaurant and into the kitchen beyond. Feeling suddenly surplus to requirements, Poppy followed.

They were still clearing up after breakfast. A youngster was wiping down a stainless-steel work surface and a wiry older guy was emptying a huge commercial dishwasher. The kitchen smelled of steam and bleach with an underlay of bacon.

Poppy heard Dave say, 'I suppose we've missed breakfast then?' and Mr B's terse reply, 'You certainly have.'

'Just kidding,' Dave said, and the chef looked startled, but then seemed to relax a bit.

'Forgive me,' Mr B said. 'Very tight deadlines in kitchens. Schedules. Health and safety. I can't give you much of my time.'

'We won't take much.' Dave glanced towards Poppy. 'We just plan to go through one or two risk ass... er, risk assessments, don't we, boss?'

'Risk assessments are my speciality.' Mr B rubbed his hands together and for a moment he looked positively gleeful. 'I have some questions.'

'Ask away,' Poppy said, undoing the buckle on her briefcase and getting out a clipboard and a notepad.

'First of all, I need to know what kind of cameras you are planning to bring into my kitchen.'

'Nothing too big, but maybe Dave could expand...'

Dave launched into an explanation about the fact that they'd be treating the kitchen as another location and therefore would be using handheld cameras and not the kind they'd be using in the studio which had to be rolled around on pedestals. 'They shouldn't get in the way...'

'I don't mean the size,' Mr B interrupted impatiently. 'I mean the make.'

'The make?' Dave sounded puzzled and Poppy noticed that the two kitchen staff who'd been clearing up were now making exaggerated raised eyebrows and exchanging looks of mock horror behind the chef's back. Clearly, they were aware of something she and Dave weren't.

'I'll cut to the chase,' Mr B said. 'Are they Chinese?'

'Chinese? I, er...' Dave broke off. Like Poppy, he'd been distracted by the two kitchen staff behind Mr B, both of whom were now jumping up and down and miming cut-throat motions with their hands across their necks.

Poppy had no idea why, but they'd definitely got more animated at the word 'Chinese'. 'I don't think they are Chinese, Dave, are they?' she interrupted smoothly. 'Why do you ask?'

'Because the Chinese government have been spying on us for decades,' Mr B said. 'And I won't have anything that's a security risk in my kitchen.'

'I think our equipment's Japanese,' Dave said, cottoning on. 'Or American. We can check.'

'Even the lenses?' Mr B pressed.

'I'm certain they are. Maybe even British.'

'Almost certainly assembled in Britain,' Poppy added.

'How about the sound equipment?' Mr B waved a hand. 'Booms and suchlike.'

'I'll check that out for you.' One of the prerequisites of being a successful producer was being able to get along with people and Poppy had often joked that she had a first in diplomacy, as well as her first in media and journalism. Filming was 90 per cent being polite to people and 10 per cent making the programme.

'I'd be grateful if you could check the lights too, please. And anything that's on Bluetooth.'

Dave looked slightly startled at the mention of Bluetooth, but he agreed. 'On the subject of lights,' he added, clearly keen to divert the conversation, 'we'll bring in sandbags to weigh them down properly and your staff and ours will need to be aware of cables and trip hazards.'

Mr B's eyes widened in horror. 'I'm afraid sandbags are out of the question. I can't have great, cumbersome, unhygienic sandbags in my kitchen. It's a health and safety disaster waiting to happen.'

'They're not your average sandbags. They're purpose-built ones in small black pouches. They can be sterilised.' Dave was beginning to sound strained.

Poppy touched Mr B's arm. 'We're all totally aware of kitchen health and safety,' she said. 'My crew will be instructed not to touch anything unless shown how to by a member of your staff. You won't need to be here on the day. Everything can be set up with our home economist in advance. I'm sure you have far more important things to do.' Having him around on the day would be a major hindrance, she knew that!

'Nothing is more important than what goes on in my kitchen. I will be here.' He folded his arms as if daring them to try to talk him out of it. 'I don't know if you've been made aware, but I have had experience of being behind the scenes of a television production before. So I do actually have some insight and experience of what you're trying to achieve here.'

Poppy hadn't been expecting that. 'You've been involved in a reality television show?'

'No, no, no. Not a reality show. It was a crime drama. The screenwriters asked me if I'd be a story consultant on the project – they wanted my catering industry background, you see. It was set in a hotel and it starred a conspiracy theorist chef. The man was completely bonkers – I'm telling you, you couldn't make it up. He had all sorts of weird theories about governments and mind control and Big Brother. Very George Orwell, but set today. Nothing to do with reality at all. Very much fiction.'

Poppy suppressed a smile. The irony of what he'd just said had clearly escaped him.

'I was very proud to be involved,' he went on. 'They said that my input helped them to add authenticity.'

'That's fabulous,' Poppy replied, aware of a snort from Dave, who had been writing things down for the last few minutes and was pretending not to listen.

Mr B looked at him suspiciously and Dave covered a second snort with a sudden coughing fit. Thankfully, the two kitchen assistants had now disappeared, and it was just the three of them in the kitchen.

They moved on to more regular risk assessment items – the handling of knives, which Poppy assured him would be done only by those with appropriate training, the use of ovens and hot pans, the possibility of spills and other hazardous materials.

Poppy was just beginning to wrap up the discussion – there was only so much you could say about risk assessments, even if you were a paranoid conspiracy theorist – when Mr B said, 'I have another concern. It regards the accidental exposure of confidential documents.'

'What confidential documents?' Even Dave sounded brusque now, which wasn't surprising as they had been in the kitchen for nearly two hours.

'I am concerned that your cameras may pick up things in the background of shots that they shouldn't.'

'I can assure you that nothing will be in shot that shouldn't,' Poppy told him, closing her file with an air of finality. 'It's the job of my crew to make sure there isn't.'

'It might well be, but I have confidential procedures. Secret ingredients. I can't risk them being leaked to competitors. They're everywhere. Last year, a would-be competitor stole my Dorset apple cake recipe, the pediculous scumbag.' His eyes flashed with annoyance. 'Flagitious villain very nearly got away with it too.'

To Poppy's intense relief, Clara chose that moment to come into the kitchens. 'Is everything OK? I thought you'd all be finished by now.' Her eyes contradicted her words.

No wonder she'd escaped to the vet. Poppy couldn't entirely blame her.

'You and me both,' Dave muttered as Mr B repeated his concerns.

His manager put an appeasing hand on his arm. 'Anything

confidential can be put out of sight. In fact, it should be. Think of our kitchens as an entirely neutral space, a backdrop for *Date for a Day*. There will be nothing of the Bluebell here. At least there will be nothing of the Bluebell's kitchen on display. We obviously do want viewers to know that the show is filmed here. That's the whole point.'

'Any confidential items will need to be under lock and key,' Mr B insisted, looking mutinous.

'You can make sure that's done,' Clara said. 'Buy a padlock if necessary next time you're at the wholesalers.' He had just opened his mouth to speak again when Clara added, 'I think we've taken up enough of Poppy and Dave's time. I'm sure that any other concerns or questions can go into a follow-up email, can't they?'

She steered them out of the kitchen before he had the chance to reply.

'Thank you,' Poppy said when they were out of earshot. 'Is he always like that?'

'Only when he gets a bee in his bonnet about something. Don't worry, I'll make sure he stays out of your way when you're filming.'

'That might be easier said than done,' Dave said quietly when Clara had gone again. 'She'd probably have to lock him in a cupboard and put a pediculous padlock on the door.'

10

After the kitchen risk assessment marathon, the rest of the morning was a breeze, and when Clara asked if they would like to stop for lunch, on the house of course, Poppy looked at Dave, who nodded. They thanked her and walked back through to reception.

'It's probably warm enough to sit on the terrace,' Clara said as she took them into the restaurant and then through to an outside table. She shot an anxious glance towards the door that led to the kitchens as they passed, and then found them a table that was tucked away so that, even if Mr B did decide to pop outside, he wouldn't catch sight of them.

'I'll be back to take your order shortly,' Clara promised and disappeared.

She was right. It was warm for March. Even on the coast. It was one of those beautiful spring days where the sky is a powder blue and the sea looks as unruffled as a silken scarf with just the odd ripple to prove it's real. Seagulls soared high above their heads, a couple hanging almost motionless as they hovered on the thermals. The air smelled vibrant and fresh and new.

'This really is idyllic,' Poppy said, looking out past the terrace across the lush green lawns which stretched down to a low wall that separated the Bluebell Cliff gardens from the South West Coast Path beyond. 'Apparently, you can see dolphins out there on a good day.'

Dave followed her gaze. 'Fingers crossed they'll make an appearance when I've got a camera in my hands. Is that the bluebell woods?' He shielded his eyes with one hand and shifted round in his chair, the legs scraping on the concrete terrace. 'It's a big plot this, isn't it?'

'Bigger than it looks. The grounds run all the way round to the lighthouse, and yes, that little copse is the bluebell woods. Clara said calling it a bluebell wood is rather grandiose, but there are silver birches and there are bluebells. Or there will be in another month. You can't see it from here, but there's an amphitheatre too.'

'It's a shame we can't use more of the outside area for filming.'

'Maybe we can in the future. If we get the go-ahead for a full series.' She hardly dared to put it into words, as if by doing so she would somehow jinx it, but Dave was nodding, his eyes unusually serious for once.

'"To achieve great things, we must not only act, but also dream, not only plan, but also believe."' He dropped his gaze and picked up the menu. 'That's not my quote. It's by Anatole France. He was a French novelist. He died in 1924. But it still holds just as true today as it ever did.'

Poppy looked at him, surprised, and he tapped his nose.

'Not just a pretty face, you know.'

Usually, she would have made some quip about him not being that either, but there was something so peaceful and beautiful about the moment that she didn't want to spoil it. 'Thanks, Dave.'

He nodded again and she wondered if he knew that she was trying to thank him for so much more than just being her director of photography. She wanted to thank him for always being there in her corner, for not getting uppity with people like Mr B, for being kind when she got stressed. 'Thanks, Dave' didn't seem enough for all this.

Movement distracted her and Clara King arrived back at their table with a notepad. 'What can I get you? Are you ready to order? If you'd like a recommendation I can personally vouch for the kedgeree.'

They both ordered the kedgeree which, when it came, surpassed their expectations. Light and delicate, the flaked haddock and golden soft-boiled eggs were perfectly cooked. The dish was accompanied with a selection of home-made bread, some slices dotted with olives and some with sundried tomato, and butter that was at just the right temperature to spread.

'Mr B might create a fair bit of fuss, but he cooks like an angel,' Dave proclaimed when they finished eating.

Poppy dabbed her mouth with a serviette. 'Agreed. I'm tempted to order that again for dessert.'

'Or we could just order dessert.'

'I can't. One lingering look at a chocolate brownie and I put on weight. Why don't we go and check out the bluebell wood instead? Just in case we can use it.'

'I'm up for that.'

They strolled in peaceful silence along the path that skirted the gardens and led towards the copse. The path narrowed to little more than a cinder track as it meandered into the bluebell wood and became immediately dappled as the foliage of the silver birches closed over their heads. It smelled earthy and damp beneath the trees and, as their eyes adjusted, Poppy saw a few green shoots sprouting up amidst the mouldering ground coverage. The musty wood smell reminded Poppy of climbing trees as a kid and going home with her hands covered in tree moss.

Dave bent to finger a green stalk at their feet. 'It's too early,' he said. 'It'll be another few weeks before we have a carpet of bluebells. They're very weather-dependent.'

'You're an expert on bluebells, are you?' Poppy asked.

'I am actually. There was a woodland at the back of our house when we were kids. Me and my brother were always in there. Making dens, climbing trees. Dad helped us build a tree house one summer.'

'That sounds fantastic.' She felt her eyes mist at the nostalgia in his voice.

'It was until Jonathan pushed me out of it one day and I broke my arm.'

'No way.'

'Yes way. Reality versus fiction, huh?' He grinned. 'Don't look so worried. We were fighting and I think I started it. I was a stroppy little beggar when I was young. I had small-kid syndrome. I was always trying to prove something. Usually I was trying to prove that I was tougher and meaner than Jonathan. Which I clearly wasn't on that day because I ended up on the ground bawling and he ended up peering down through the trees and laughing his head off.'

Poppy shook her head in disbelief.

'What?' Dave asked. 'Didn't you fight with your sisters?'

'I don't think I ever got physical with them. Although I had brothers too and Micky and Lennox fought.'

'All part of growing up, I guess. Jonathan changed his tune when he realised I was hurt. He went and got our mother and she drove us to the emergency department. After that, I had a ball. I got first dibs on sweets and I ended up with a blue plaster cast on my arm, which back then seemed the height of cool. Jonathan was the first to write on it.'

'Do you remember what he wrote?' she asked, laughing.

'No, the bugger wrote it right near the elbow so I couldn't read it.'

'Brothers,' Poppy said, amused, as they came out of the woods, blinking into the early-afternoon sun. She looked up at Dave. 'When did you stop being the small kid?'

'Never, as far as Jonathan was concerned. He was six foot four by the time he was fifteen. I never did quite catch up.' He squared his shoulders. He had several inches on her. 'I stopped minding, though. I guess that's part of growing up.'

'That's what happened with me and Alice. She kept growing and I stopped. I'm exactly the same height as my biological sister Rose, though, so we didn't have the same problem.'

They crossed to the amphitheatre, which was set off to one side between the lighthouse and the hotel. It was a tiny affair with seating for about forty people at a push, but the gardeners clearly looked after it. The grassy aisles were neatly mowed and the stone-slab seats that swept up from the lowered stage had also recently seen a broom. It reminded Poppy of the Minack Theatre in Cornwall, albeit a scaled-down version.

Dave took a few shots. 'We could come out here for the party piece part of the show, presuming the guys don't need a grand piano. It would be pretty cool to film someone spouting an oratory from here or singing a song.'

'It had crossed my mind. But I was trying not to complicate things too much.'

'If needs be, we can do an on-the-spot risk ass at the time,' he suggested.

'That's a very fine plan.'

'Like I said. Not just a pretty face!'

* * *

They'd wrapped up for the day and were on their way across the car park to Dave's car, ready to leave, when they bumped into Phil Grimshaw. He must have just arrived for work. He was in jeans and a pale cotton shirt and looked more casual than Poppy had ever seen him, but he still had that same powerful presence that she remembered. He came across to speak to them and somewhere in the region of her chest her heart jumped in response.

Down, girl, she told it. She was not in the market for a man, especially not one who she had high hopes would be her star contender and a match for her stepsister.

'How's it all going?' he asked, pausing and giving Dave a brief nod, which he returned, before excusing himself.

'We're getting there.' Poppy hesitated, a little surprised by Dave's abrupt disappearance and feeling the need to say something. This was the first time she'd seen Phil since the audition, but when she had called to confirm he was on the show they had chatted and he'd told her he was in between acting jobs so the timing of *Date for a Day* was perfect. 'Have you worked with Mr B long?' she asked.

'I've worked with him for far too long,' His eyes glinted with amusement. 'The man is a fruit loop, as I suspect you've discovered. But he's also a very good chef, so we all make allowances. Don't worry, once you get past the conspiracy theories, he's OK.' He leaned a shade closer. 'Top tip, if you want to sidetrack him from whatever obsession he's on, ask him about his kunekunes. They're his favourite subject.'

'Right,' Poppy said. 'Er, thanks.'

He smiled properly now. He had very good teeth. Nice without being too perfect. It was commonplace for actors to have them whitened these days, but many of them seemed to take it a step too far and their teeth were more luminous than white, like glowsticks at a music festival.

'Is there anything else I can help you with?' he asked, and Poppy became aware that she'd been staring at his mouth. Oops, wasn't that supposed to be code for: I want to kiss you? She most definitely did not want to kiss him.

'Yes, just one more thing. Um – what exactly are kunekunes?'

'Pet pigs. Mr B has two.'

'I see. Right.'

With that, Phil walked towards the staff entrance of the Bluebell Cliff and she tore her gaze away. He did have a disturbing effect on her. She knew that already and it didn't help that spring was well and truly in the air. Spring was a time for romance. It would be Easter in less than three weeks, new beginnings, rebirth and fertility. Also, it was hardly surprising that her thoughts were on romance when it was the focus of her show. Phil was an attractive man, that was certainly true. He had awoken something in her long dormant. Maybe it wasn't Phil himself she fancied but simply the idea of romance.

Dave was on his phone when she got back to the car. It sounded as though he was talking to someone about a job. 'If I possibly can, I will,' he said just before he hung up and turned to her. 'You ready to go now?'

'Yes, please.'

Was she imagining the slight atmosphere in the car? She wasn't sure, but Dave was quiet on the drive back home. Even the mention of the kunekunes didn't raise much of a response and she wondered if he was regretting telling her about his childhood exploits.

Dave wasn't the touchy-feely type. While he was always happy to listen, he didn't often open up about his own personal life. She knew he had never been married, although he dated occasionally.

She'd heard him exchange online-dating horror stories with Mike and Lenny, both of whom were also currently single. It was hard to maintain a relationship in their profession. Maybe after they had a wrap and she wasn't so busy, she would try online dating again. There were dating websites for actors. There ought to be dating websites for her profession. A normal life was impossible if you were part of the film and TV industry. You had to work incredibly long hours, often away on location. It was very hard to fit in a social life. She made a mental note that she would do it and sent out a silent thank you to Phil Grimshaw for putting the idea in her head – even though he didn't know he had.

11

Before the beginning of shooting, there was Rose's surprise birthday party, which was the last Saturday in March. The arrangements for that were a breeze compared to the arrangements for shooting her pilot. Or at least they would have been if people didn't keep trying to complicate them at the last minute.

Poppy had expected the guest list to be tricky. After all, she and Jack had invited people that Rose hadn't seen since she was small and they were coming from all corners of the globe. One of Rose's old school friends, who now lived in Switzerland, was catching a flight to Heathrow and one of her bridesmaids who lived in France was catching a ferry to Dover. Both of them wanted Poppy's help with onward travel. Another of Rose's friends, Dorinda Mannings-Jones, had moved to Nottingham and she was booking an Airbnb, but she wanted to bring Sinbad.

'I'm sure that's fine,' Poppy told her a few days before the party. 'The more the merrier.'

'No, you don't understand, Sinbad's my Siamese cat. He's no trouble, but the last two venues I've tried have said he can't be left unattended. I can hardly bring him to the party. He'd be terrified.'

'Ah,' Poppy said. 'Leave it with me.' She wanted to suggest that they could both stay with her, but she was allergic to cats and even the thought of Sinbad wandering around her tiny apartment was making her nose itch.

She phoned Alice.

'Tell her she can stay with me,' Alice said promptly. 'You don't want to be sneezing all the way through the party. Let alone for the entire night. I'm quite happy for him to mooch around here for the weekend, as long as she's happy to pay for any damage. I think Siamese cats can be quite destructive.'

'Sinbad has never so much as raised a claw to a curtain,' Dorinda Mannings-Jones said, a mite sniffily Poppy thought, considering she wasn't going to have to fork out for Airbnb now because, in typical Alice fashion, she was more than happy to put her up – no charge.

'If it helps, someone else can stay in my other spare bedroom,' Alice had said when they confirmed it.

It was now 9.30 p.m. on Thursday night and Poppy had only just got in from work, but she'd been trying to catch up with Alice for a while about the party and so when she saw her name flash up on the mobile, she picked up straight away.

'Is everything still OK for the weekend?' she asked.

'It's fine, angel, don't stress. I now have Sinbad, Dorinda Mannings-Jones and some bloke called Terry stopping at mine.'

'Are you sure that's OK? My spare room's still available.' She may have to move some boxes. It had become a dumping ground lately for Beauty Spot Productions paperwork.

'It's fine. I've got more space than you. I only wanted to touch base. Is Jack still doing the whole "We're all going out for a meal" thing and then driving her to the party?'

'That's the plan,' Poppy said. 'She'll be suspicious the second we drive into the back car park of the Fisherman's Haunt. She'll know we're not going there to eat.'

'She'll be suspicious, but she won't know for sure until she opens the door and we all leap out banging party poppers and shouting happy birthday... Have you decided what you're going to wear yet?'

'I actually haven't given it much thought,' Poppy said truthfully. 'I've been spinning too many plates lately and they're all circling madly in my head. Party outfits haven't had a look-in.'

'Hmm, I know that feeling. I don't suppose you've got time to go shopping either.' Alice didn't wait for an answer. 'If you want to borrow any tops, be my guest. Go along and help yourself when you get a spare moment. You've got a key.'

Alice was three inches taller than Poppy, but all her height was in her legs – they were identical in size from the waist up.

'Thanks,' Poppy said. 'That would be great. If I don't have time to go shopping before Saturday.' They both knew she wouldn't. Alice had the best taste in clothes anyway – she had a selection of very expensive designer numbers – and they were both blonde, so they tended to favour the same colours.

'Are you taking anyone?' Alice asked.

'I hadn't planned to. Why?'

'I know you say that being single suits you. But don't you ever think it would be nice to find someone you like?'

'I like lots of people,' Poppy said, taken aback because Alice rarely asked her about her love life.

'You know perfectly well what I mean, Poppy Allen. Now this is your big sister talking, so pay attention.' She put on her sternest voice. 'Seriously, angel, I worry about you sometimes. You spend so much time working and then, in your spare time, running around doing things to make other people happy, that I think you forget about yourself.'

'That really is the pot calling the kettle black,' Poppy said, feeling defensive.

'Yes, but I'm doing something about it, aren't I? At least, I am on the romantic side. I'm doing your show.'

'I'm doing something about it too. I've joined an online dating agency.' The words came out of her mouth before she'd had time to edit them. What she'd meant to say was that she was *planning* to join an online dating agency. Hell, she must be more tired than she thought. Which wasn't surprising, considering she'd only got in from work half an hour ago.

'That's brilliant news,' Alice was saying. 'Is it one of the big ones? Or one of those little boutique ones? I think they're better – the little ones.'

'Um, boutique.' Why didn't she just fess up? She wasn't in the habit of lying – especially not to Alice, but she had sounded so delighted that Poppy didn't have the heart to backtrack and disappoint her. To divert her from asking any more tricky questions, she said quickly, 'I've seen a couple of nice-sounding possibles already, actually.'

'That's brilliant. In that case, will you do something for me?'

'Of course. If I can,' Poppy said, wondering what on earth she was letting herself in for.

'Will you ask one of them to the party as your plus-one? Parties are great places for first dates. And we'll all be there, so we can suss him out for you.'

Poppy was almost certain that parties were not great places for first dates, but she was too tired to argue. 'I'll think about it,' she said. 'When I've had a good night's sleep.'

'Excellent. You've made my day.'

Poppy suppressed a sigh, knowing she'd just dug herself into a very deep hole. And the chances of her signing up to a dating agency – didn't you need a profile and pictures and things for that? – and actually getting in conversation with someone enough to ask them to go to a party by Saturday were remote.

It was as she was dropping off to sleep that the solution hit her. She had been Dave's plus-one for a wedding once, she could just ask him.

* * *

Her chance came sooner than she'd anticipated because Dave phoned her the following morning. He wasn't working for Beauty Spot – he was on another job – so she hadn't been expecting to hear from him. He sounded stressed.

'Poppy, sorry to bother you, but I've just broken down in Poole and I'm on my way to the Mill Studio to do an advert. I don't suppose you're local, are you? They've got a full crew over there and I don't want to let them down – that studio costs a fortune.'

'You're in luck. I was just going through some rushes. I can stop. Where exactly are you?'

He told her. 'I'm in the RAC, but they said two hours minimum and—'

'It's fine. I'm on my way. I can be there in fifteen minutes.' She heard his sigh of relief just before she disconnected.

Twenty minutes later, she had picked him up and they'd loaded all his kit into her car and were on their way to the Mill.

'What are you going to do about your car?' she asked.

'I'll get the RAC to meet me here after the job. No worries. I really, really appreciate this.' He glanced at her. 'I owe you one.'

'It just so happens that I was going to ask you a favour,' she said as they pulled into the studio car park.

'Consider it done.'

'It depends on whether you're free this coming Saturday. I need a plus-one to take to Rose's party.'

Dave did a double take. 'I wasn't expecting that. Have you got cold feet about going on your own?' He knew how much she hated parties.

'It's a long story. I'll tell you when we've got more time.'

'I'll look forward to hearing it,' he said, as they unloaded. 'But yes, that's fine. I'm not doing anything on Saturday that I can't cancel.'

'I don't want to put you out.'

'You're not. Honestly. I had a date with a pint and a box set.'

'Ah. Thanks.' She met his gaze. He actually seemed quite pleased to be asked, although it was sometimes hard to tell with Dave. He gave her a thumbs up and then disappeared towards the entrance of the Mill and she watched the solid figure of his departing back.

Alice would soon discover she hadn't met Dave online. And even if she didn't, she would recognise him the minute they started filming, but Poppy decided she would cross that bridge when she came to it. For now, her problems were solved and actually it would be quite fun to take Dave to Rose's party. At least they could talk shop and discuss the shoot the week after. That sounded a lot more appealing than making polite conversation with a whole bunch of people she barely knew.

* * *

On the afternoon of the party, Poppy had said she would pick up the food from the catering company and take it over to the Fisherman's Haunt. Jack didn't want to arouse suspicion by going out on the day of his wife's party. Then Alice and Micky and hopefully Lennox and Dana were meeting her at the venue in order to decorate it with party streamers, helium balloons and a lot of embarrassing old photos of Rose which they had blown up to A4 size and were going to put on the walls.

Poppy and Jack had recced the hall already and it was perfect. It was a long oblong room attached to the back of the pub, with windows down both sides and a wooden floor, a nod to the fact it had once been a skittle alley. There was a bar in one of the corners, which would be manned later by staff from the pub, and a mobile DJ was coming to do the music. It was the perfect size for a party of about sixty, which she hoped there would be. Not so big that it would feel half-empty and not too cramped they'd be tripping over each other.

Poppy got there at three and found Micky already in situ. 'Hey, Pops,' he called across the room to her. 'Alice has gone to get the cake, but she just texted to say the traffic was bad.'

'There's no rush,' she said, going to him. He was standing at one of the long trestle tables that ran along one wall with a cardboard box at his feet. The table was already dotted with photographs.

'I thought I'd lay them out first so we could decide where to put them,' he said. 'What do you think? Maybe have them in increasing age, starting at the door where people come in?'

Typical Micky, Poppy thought, needing everything organised and structured.

'I'm happy with that. Shall we get the food in first? I thought Lennox and Dana were coming too.'

Micky shrugged. 'I expect they'll be along soon.'

For the next half an hour, they worked. First, they laid out the cellophane-wrapped platters of food. They hadn't gone too overboard. Jack had found a family-run business called Party Without The Perspiration, which specialised in doing the kind of party food you'd do yourself at home if you had the time and energy. They had sandwiches, sausage on sticks, mini quiches, crisps, olives, chicken drumsticks and various cheeses, all of them on silver tinfoil platters.

'By the way, I heard from a colleague at work that your ex is suing his record label. Apparently, they dropped him,' Micky said.

'Really?' Poppy nearly dropped a plate. 'Why?'

'He said they were duplicitous bastards. But my colleague seemed to think he was the duplicitous one. He'd broken several conditions of his contract.'

'Gosh,' Poppy said.

'I hope you don't feel sorry for him.' Micky glanced at her. 'Serves him right, if you want my opinion.'

Neither of them said anything else. It wasn't in either of their natures to gloat.

Micky started on the photos and Poppy started filling up balloons with the helium. While she was doing that, Alice arrived.

'I'm so sorry I'm late.' Alice looked anxious. 'Is no one else helping? I thought Lennox and Dana were coming too...'

'They probably got held up,' Poppy said – although, actually, neither of them had texted.

'I'll bring the cake in. It's gorgeous.' She didn't, though. Instead, she loitered by Poppy. 'Any news you want to tell me? Did you – er – ask anyone along to be your date tonight?'

'I may have done,' Poppy said, ultra-casually.

'Oooh, how exciting.' Alice clapped her hands. 'Tell me more.'

Micky chose that moment to come over and say hi. 'What's all this? Did I hear something about a date? You kept that quiet, Pops.'

Crap, she was going to have to tell them before it got out of hand. She took a deep breath and was about to say, 'It's just someone I work with', when the door flew open and Lennox appeared.

'Hi, everyone. We're not too late, are we? We were just in town. Appalling traffic. Dana's just getting some more party stuff.'

'I'll go and help her.' Poppy made her escape. No way was she going to say anything in front of Lennox. She'd never hear the end of it. He'd tease her mercilessly when she showed up with Dave later as it was – she didn't want to give him a head start.

* * *

By four thirty, they were done. The ex-skittle alley had been turned from a dull, oblong, magnolia-painted room into a party venue extraordinaire. The cake was still boxed up in its heavy-duty white packaging so there could be a big reveal later, but they'd all had a sneak peek. It was half vanilla sponge and half chocolate – Rose loved both – and it was covered in buttercream icing and had Happy 30th piped in pink alongside a tiny edible-icing model of a girl with blonde hair in a gym outfit and trainers, which the cake artist had managed to make look a bit like Rose. She'd been working from a photo Poppy had found. A huge banner with:

Happy 30th Birthday

was strung over the door.

'I was going to get Happy 40th for a laugh,' Lennox said, 'but Dana stopped me.'

'Good,' Alice said. 'That's just mean. We're supposed to be celebrating with our little sister. Not taking the mickey.'

Lennox pouted. 'Rose wouldn't have minded. No sense of humour, that's your trouble.'

'Whereas yours is clearly overdeveloped.' Alice glanced in the direction of his shoes. 'Pink socks. Nice.'

'They are not pink.' He stared at his feet. 'Are they?'

'They're black,' Dana told him, grinning.

'You'd say that anyway. You women always stick together.' He appealed to Micky. 'What colour are they, mate? You're the only one I can trust round here.'

'They're definitely not pink,' Micky told him, and then added idly, 'possibly orange – is that the colour that you would call terracotta? I'm not sure.'

'No way.' Lennox started to unlace his trainer. He tugged it off, closely followed by his sock.

'What are you doing?' Alice asked.

'I'm getting an unbiased opinion. Someone in the pub will tell me. I'll have a poll. I'll stand on the table and get people to vote on the exact colour of my socks.'

'He'll get us barred before the party's even started,' Micky said in alarm as Lennox hopped out of the door on one leg, clutching a sock.

'No, he won't,' Dana said, as the door closed behind him. 'He'll be back any second.' They all looked at each other expectantly. 'Three, two, one,' Dana said confidently. Then she said it again for good measure. On the third time, just as Micky was beginning to look a bit fidgety, the door swung open again.

'Got you,' Lennox said. 'Got you worried. Admit it.'

'Juvenile,' Dana said.

'They're black,' Poppy told him. 'Really. I promise. Put them back on before we need to fumigate the entire room.'

'I knew that.' Lennox made a big thing of putting his sock back on.

Poppy felt a surge of relief. This was what she loved – the good-natured banter of being in her family. And it meant the pressure was off her too. They'd forgotten all about her date. The date who was actually Dave. Those two words really didn't fit comfortably in the same sentence.

Just for a second, the image of Phil Grimshaw's face flickered in her mind. Now, if he had been her date tonight... She blinked it swiftly away. The very last thing she needed was to fall for the man she hoped would be the perfect match for Alice.

She put him firmly out of her mind and cleared her throat. 'Right, you lot. Enough of all this jollity. If this is going to be the party of the decade, isn't it about time we all got home and put on our glad rags? We'll need to be back here in a couple of hours.'

* * *

Dave had offered to drive round and pick her up, even though that meant he'd be passing the venue on the way and would have to double back. 'That way you can let your hair down,' he'd said. 'I don't drink much anyway.'

'We both know that's not true.'

'All right, I don't drink much at parties where I'm trying to make a good impression,' he'd amended.

'You don't need to make a good impression.'

'I do,' he had said. 'They're your family. And I like working with you. What's the dress code?'

'Smart casual. The kind of stuff you usually wear will be fine.'

She had to admit she'd felt quite touched and relieved. Asking Dave to go with her had been the right thing to do. It would shut Alice up, even when she did find out that Dave wasn't an online suitor. Her mother and Kenny had given up asking her if she was ever planning to start dating again. They'd seemed to accept that she and Alice were the career women – not that Alice didn't regularly dip a toe into the dating scene. But they'd be pleased to meet Dave even if he was only Poppy's colleague.

Besides, Dave was good company. He'd surprised her at the wedding he'd taken her to, which had been hosted at a country mansion in Norfolk and had been much posher than she'd expected. She'd known he was a personable kind of guy who mixed well with most people. Yet somehow she'd never expected this to include the kind of people who had parents who were lords and had chauffeur-driven Bentleys and country estates. People who, when they mentioned shoots, meant the kind with guns and Labradors, not cameras.

He'd been the same with them as he was with everyone – straightforward and pleasant, making sure he included her in every conversation and shielding her from too many prying comments about their relationship, saying frequently, 'Poppy and I are good friends.' Because of the distance from home, they had stayed in a Travelodge nearby. He'd booked two separate rooms and hadn't let her pay.

'It was my idea to bring you, after all,' he'd said when she offered. 'And I'm glad I did.'

Even when they'd arrived back at the Travelodge, there had been not a single moment of awkwardness, which she had thought there might be when they'd parted at their separate doors around midnight. She had wondered if he'd had any ulterior motive – if he had been going to make some kind of move on her, but it seemed he hadn't. He'd been the perfect gentleman. It was one of the reasons she'd felt safe enough to invite him as her plus-one tonight.

As she drove home, she realised with surprise that she was actually looking forward to tonight.

12

Poppy had decided in an impulsive moment to wear a dress to Rose's party. She only had three in her wardrobe – a very flattering summer floral sundress that Rose had persuaded her to buy for a barbecue once, a little black dress she wore for functions (she'd worn that to the posh wedding) and a gorgeous maroon Vivienne Westwood off-the-shoulder dress that had been marked down in a sale. The LBD didn't seem right for Rose's party, so she'd decided on the maroon dress and had borrowed one of Alice's designer jackets to go with it. She added a simple gold choker necklace that Mum and Kenny had given her on her twenty-first birthday and stood back from the mirror. Not bad, if she did say so herself.

The doorbell rang at just before six. Dave was early then. Not that he was ever late, but she'd impressed upon him the need to be on time because they all had to be at the venue, ready to surprise Rose by seven.

'Hi,' she said, whisking back the door of her apartment to let him in.

'Hi.' He gave a low whistle. 'You look stunning.'

'Thanks.' Alice had taught her never to argue with people who complimented you but to accept their praise graciously. 'You look pretty good yourself.'

It was true. He did. He was wearing dark trousers and a crisp pale shirt, open at the neck. He was clean-shaven and she caught a whiff of some expensive scent. Not his usual one. He was also carrying a little party bag with a gift-wrapped present.

'It's just a small thing,' he said, as she glanced at it. 'I seem to remember you said Rose likes perfume. I was out shopping for something for my mother – it was her birthday yesterday – and the woman on the make-up counter recommended it.'

'That's very thoughtful,' she said, grabbing her own gift-wrapped parcel from the hall table by the door, along with her keys. She'd gone for Rose's favourite perfume and a gorgeous charm bracelet in the end. 'Let's get going, shall we?'

As he opened the passenger door for her, she asked about his car trouble.

'New starter motor. Don't panic. We'll get there OK. Did you say the Fisherman's Haunt?'

'I did. Thanks for agreeing to be my plus-one, Dave, and for driving. I hope it's not too much of an ordeal, you know what family dos can be like sometimes.'

'I'm happy to help. In fact, I'm quite an old hand. This is the third time someone's asked me to be their plus-one lately. The last one was a twenty-fifth wedding anniversary and the one before that was an engagement do.'

'Wow.' She looked at him in surprise. 'Was it the same person who asked you?' She caught herself. 'Not that it's any of my business. Sorry, don't feel you have to answer that.'

'It's fine. Yes it was, as it happens. It was an old friend of mine. Angie. Someone I used to work with.' He didn't elaborate and she didn't like to pry any further. After a couple of moments of silence while he negotiated the traffic up to the main road, he added, 'Maybe I should set up in business as a plus-one. What do you reckon?'

'Aren't businesses like that called escort agencies?' she quipped, and he smiled and she felt as though they were back on safe ground.

It was only a short drive to the Fisherman's Haunt and they spent the rest of it chatting about his mother's birthday meal that he and his brother had gone to the previous evening. It had been a quiet event, apparently. Family-only, at his mother's favourite Italian. Poppy wondered what he would make of tonight. Quiet was not the first adjective that sprang to mind when she thought of her own family.

* * *

The car park was already filling up, Poppy saw as they arrived. A few people dressed in party clothes and carrying presents were milling about, clearly unsure where to go. She recognised one of them as Rose's old school friend and went across to direct them to the entrance of the hall, which was off the overflow car park at the back of the pub.

Not that it was hard to spot once you were in the vicinity. Lennox had had the brainwave of putting fairy lights up over the door – and it looked great, all lit up. Her happy-go-lucky brother might be a pain in the butt sometimes, but when it came to all things family, he could come up with the goods.

Inside the venue, she did a swift headcount. There were about forty-five people here already, including her mum and Kenny, who were chatting to a couple of Rose's friends by the food table. Lennox and Dana were directing people to put birthday presents on another table. The DJ was setting up equipment. They'd arranged that he would play 'Happy Birthday' at the appointed time. The volume levels were already high and the oblong room smelled of party scents and excitement. Despite her dislike of large gatherings, Poppy felt a buzz of anticipation.

Alice was already here too. She waved when she spotted Poppy and began to head over.

'I need to introduce you to someone,' Poppy told Dave. 'Alice, my stepsister.'

'The star of our show?' Dave said, glancing at her.

'Yes.' She realised suddenly that she hadn't warned him about the online dating scenario. Oh crap, how had she forgotten that? 'Er, this may sound odd, Dave, but would you mind not mentioning the show to anyone for now? Or, um, that you're our director of photography. I'll fill you in later.'

'O... K.' He strung the word into two quizzical syllables, but he didn't ask her anything else. There wasn't really time because someone else was tapping Poppy's arm. It was Auntie Sheila, one of Mum's sisters. There were four and three of them were coming tonight. Auntie Sheila was the one who talked a lot but didn't listen.

'Poppy, darling, how are you? Eleanor tells me you're going to be on Netflix. With your own programme, you clever girl.'

Oh God. Yes, of course her mother would have done that. Even though Poppy had told her to keep it hush-hush – you couldn't guarantee any programme you made actually making it on to the screen. Nothing was definite about being aired until you saw the credits roll.

'I'm hoping to be, Auntie Sheila. No guarantees.'

'And who is this lovely young man?' Auntie Sheila turned her laser-beam gaze towards Dave. 'I don't think we've met before.'

She held out her hand and Dave took it politely and introduced himself.

'What do you do then, Dave? Are you in the entertainments business too?'

'No. I'm... er... I'm an undertaker. I spend my days around very cool people. Dead people, I mean. In freezers. Mostly.' He broke off, looking stricken. He'd gone pink, in contrast to Auntie Sheila, who'd gone a little pale.

'Are you? Good gracious... And is that something you've always wanted to do? Work with the dead?'

'It's very peaceful,' he told her, 'because, um, they don't say a lot. I mean, anything. They don't say anything. They're very quiet.'

'That must be a huge relief.'

'Oh, it is. It definitely is. Although we have the radio on – you know, for company... For me, not them. Radio 4. *The Archers*.'

'I see, er...' Auntie Sheila's mouth opened and shut a few more times, goldfish-style.

Poppy had never seen her aunt speechless, and she didn't remember ever seeing Dave look so flustered. Not surprisingly, considering she'd given him approximately ten seconds' warning to come up with a whole new career for himself. He'd clearly just said the first thing that had come into his head and Guy Bury, contender number one on the list for *Date for a Day*, must have been fresh in his mind. Before she could say anything to help him, she became aware that Alice was by their side too and she was looking at Dave with interest.

'An undertaker – I don't think I've ever met one of those before. How fascinating. It's good to meet you, Dave. I'm Alice.'

'It's good to meet you too.' He inclined his head.

Poppy was surprised he hadn't run for the door. Good grief, it was true what they said about lying. It didn't help anything. It just got you deeper and deeper into deceit. She needed to stop it now before it got any more out of hand. 'Alice,' she began. 'Dave and I didn't actually meet—'

The sound of someone bashing a glass and calling for quiet cut across her.

It was Kenny, she saw, spotting him standing by the door with a fork and a pint glass held aloft. 'Ladies and gentlemen, can I have your attention please?'

He had to do it another couple of times and there was a great deal of collective shushing from others before the noise slowly hushed enough for him to speak.

'First of all, thank you for coming. As you're aware, this is a surprise party for Rose. And I've just had a text from Jack. They're about to pull into the road. So quiet please, everyone. Get your party poppers ready. I'm putting the lights off now, but as soon as this door opens, I'll turn them back on and that's your signal to shout "Surprise". At which point, the DJ will also play "Happy Birthday".'

The lights went off. It was amazing how quiet a room of sixty people could be, Poppy thought, her stomach crunching with anticipation. There were a couple of quite young children present, one of Rose's friends had seven-year-old twin girls and even they hushed obediently.

She didn't dare look at either Dave or Alice. Everyone's eyes were focused on the door. Then it opened to reveal Rose and Jack and everyone was shouting 'SURPRISE' as loudly as they could. 'Happy Birthday' was belting out of the speakers to compete and the streamers from the party poppers were flying everywhere.

Rose, dressed in a gorgeous Karen Millen number, was doing her very best impression of a hugely surprised person with her mouth in a perfect O. But Poppy knew it was an impression. Her eyebrows were too raised and her eyes too wide. She must have guessed, but she was far too gracious to let on. Not that it mattered. She looked delighted to be the centre of attention.

As soon as the final notes of 'Happy Birthday' had faded, there were cries of 'Speech! Speech!' from all corners of the room, and Kenny had to bash the pint glass again until it was quiet enough for Rose to actually say anything.

'I am incredibly touched and delighted that you've all made so much effort on my behalf.' She glanced around the room, before removing several streamers from her hair and tossing them dramatically into the air. 'It's wonderful to see you all. Thank you all for coming.' She punched the air with her other arm. 'Enough of speeches. Let's get this party started.'

A few people were filming or taking pictures on their phones. But at Rose's words, there was another rousing cheer.

Dave leaned a little closer to Poppy. 'Wowee. Your family certainly know how to party.'

Did he look slightly shell-shocked? Or was that her imagination? She supposed her family was a bit loud, but she was used to them. Dave only had the one elder brother, whom he wasn't close to, and she didn't remember him ever mentioning aunts or uncles or cousins. There were several cousins in Poppy's family too – a lot of them were here tonight. In fact, she was probably directly related to about half the people in the room. No wonder poor Dave looked a bit overwhelmed.

Poppy glanced at Alice, who was still standing beside her and clearly wanted to say something. Auntie Sheila had moved away, thank goodness.

'How about I go and get us a drink from the bar,' Dave offered, 'while you catch up with your sister?'

'Thanks.' She turned towards Alice as he escaped.

'You did not meet *him* online,' Alice said, 'and I'd bet my best

Ted Baker bag that he's not an undertaker either. So come on, spill. Who is he?'

'You're right. On both counts. Dave's my director of photography.' She dropped her gaze, shamefaced.

'Why did you pretend he was someone else?'

'A moment of madness.' Poppy met Alice's eyes again. 'When I told you the other night that I'd started online dating, I meant to say I was planning to start after the shoot, but I got my words tangled and I said I'd already done it and you sounded so pleased that I didn't correct myself. I'm really sorry. I didn't mean to lie.'

'It's fine.' Alice touched her arm and her eyes were utterly non-judgemental. 'I'm sorry too. I was nagging you, wasn't I, about dating. You're under enough pressure at the moment without me diving in with my size nines.'

'You didn't nag me.'

'Yeah, I did.'

'I'm sorry I lied.'

'It's cool. No one died.' Alice laughed at her own joke. 'Although, on that note, I'm relieved he isn't an undertaker. I'm not sure I like the idea of my sister dating someone who's around dead bodies all day.'

'We're not really dating,' Poppy said hastily. 'I asked him to be my plus-one. Just for tonight.'

'I see you two have caught up.' Dave arrived back with a tray on which was a bottle of wine, two glasses and what looked like a pint of orange juice and lemonade. 'I brought Alice a glass just in case.' He turned to Alice with his most charming smile and she lit up in the warmth of his attention. 'So now you know we're not dating. What else has she told you about me?'

Poppy felt warmed. Telling Alice the truth had been a huge relief. She was not cut out for deceit. It was a relief too that Alice and Dave clearly liked each other. That would be handy. Being around a film crew when you weren't used to it was a nerve-wracking process. At least Alice would have a friendly face on set now.

* * *

By eight thirty, the party was in full swing. Micky was the only one who'd inherited the shyness gene in her family, Poppy decided, wondering how on earth she had thought there would be a quiet enough corner or enough time to sit and chat to Dave about the next week's shooting. Most people were dancing. The food had been unwrapped at eight, but that hadn't slowed anyone up for long.

It helped that the DJ was playing really good music. There was enough of a mix to please the older guests as well as the young ones and it was practically all music that made you want to leap up and dance. It also helped that she'd had a few glasses of wine, Poppy thought, although she had decided not to drink any more. She was at that nice level between everything being rosy and relaxed and not having any inhibitions at all.

She became aware that Dave was saying something. She leaned closer to him so she could hear.

'Do you fancy a dance?' he shouted into her ear and gestured towards the throng.

'Why not?' She took his outstretched hand, pleased that he was getting into the spirit of things. They had danced at the posh wedding, she seemed to remember, but that had been to a big band and she didn't remember feeling as relaxed as this.

Dave was a good mover, even though he didn't exactly play it straight. His approach to dancing was a little like Lennox's – a mix of larking about in exaggerated moves and blatant micky-taking of himself, by way of a series of pulled faces. But Poppy was aware as she mirrored his gestures, giggling a little – she had to be tipsier than she thought – that he was also in tune with the rhythm. Never once did he miss a beat.

When they finally came off the dance floor, she was hot and breathless and the dress was sticking to her back. She'd had to abandon Alice's posh jacket on the back of a chair ages ago.

Rose, who'd been dancing alongside them, came across to speak to her. 'Your Dave's hot. It's a pity you're just friends. You know what they say about men who can move on the dance floor like that, don't you?' Rose had flushed cheeks and sparkling eyes and she leaned in closer to Poppy's ear, which was a relief because Poppy was pretty sure Dave hadn't heard what she said.

Although Dana clearly had. She was standing on Poppy's other side. 'It's nice to see you letting your hair down for once. Have you known him long?'

'We're just friends.' Poppy felt as though she was repeating that line for the umpteenth time.

'Ah,' Dana said. 'Shame.'

When Poppy next looked round, Dave had disappeared. A few moments later, she realised he was back on the dance floor again. This time he was dancing with Alice. He had just leaned forward to say something to her which had made her laugh.

'They're getting on well,' Dana observed a few seconds later. 'She's another one who doesn't let her hair down enough.'

'Yes,' Poppy said, but a shadow had just fallen over her heart. For a moment she felt blindsided and she wasn't sure why. Then she realised what was bothering her.

The last thing she needed was Alice pairing up with Dave before they'd even started shooting *Date for a Day*. That would throw a very big spanner in the works.

13

The following morning, Poppy woke up with a splitting headache. She couldn't remember the last time she'd had a hangover. But then she hadn't let her hair down quite so completely for ages either.

She stumbled bleary-eyed into the bathroom. She hadn't taken her make-up off either judging by how much of it was still smeared over her face. Morning-After Make-Up was not a good look.

As she splashed water over her forehead, grateful for its soothing coolness, memories of the previous evening came back to her in bits. Dancing with Dave in a throng of sweaty people – he'd been a good dancer; she could remember that. He'd been a good sport too. He'd come and picked her up, driven her to the party and they'd barely been there five minutes when she'd asked him to lie to Auntie Sheila about what he did for a living. That hadn't been one of her finest moments. In fact, suddenly she felt quite bad about it. She probably owed him an apology for that.

Also, she had a vague memory of going outside into the car park part way through the evening because she was so hot and of the fresh air hitting her and making her head spin. She'd felt sick. Oh God, she hadn't actually been sick, had she? Surely she hadn't thrown up in a car park at her sister's thirtieth birthday party.

Another flicker of a memory pierced through the fog of the hangover. Dave had been there in the car park too. He must have come out looking for her. Or had that been at the end of the evening? It was all a bit hazy.

She turned the shower on to full and stood under the hot jets, hoping the blast of steaming water would help restore her memory to its usual working order. It helped a bit.

No, she didn't think she'd been sick in the car park. She remembered being very giggly – having too much wine always had that effect on her. Hang on a second, she had a feeling Alice had been there too. Yes, she had. She would phone Alice and ask her.

First, though, she needed paracetamol and water and coffee. Lots and lots of coffee.

Feeling marginally more human after the shower, she got dressed and went into her tiny kitchen. Armed with a steaming mug of coffee, she called Alice.

Frustratingly, she didn't answer and Poppy realised it was only just gone nine. Maybe she was having a lie-in. No. Alice didn't do lie-ins.

She was on her second mug of coffee when Alice phoned back. She sounded irritatingly bright and breezy. 'Hello, angel. Sorry I missed your call. I'm just on my way to see a client in Swanage. I'm on my Bluetooth in the car and the signal's a bit up and down. But it should be OK now. How's your head?'

'It hurts,' Poppy told her, plugging her wired earbuds into the mobile so she didn't have to hold it against her throbbing head. 'Alice, I won't keep you, but I just wanted to ask if I did anything stupid last night. Or, um... out of character?'

'Out of character. Oooh, where do I start? You brought a man. You did actual dancing with him on the dance floor – I had no idea you knew moves like that – and then you whisked him out into the car park for a snog.'

'Oh, please tell me that's not true.' Good grief, that was ten times worse than being sick in a dark corner. Pawing a stone-cold sober Dave when she was three sheets to the wind – it didn't bear thinking about. Especially as she was going to have to work with him for the next four days.

Alice chuckled. 'You didn't snog him. Although I think that had more to do with him than you. Do you really not remember?'

'No,' Poppy said, feeling her face get hotter and hotter.

'Don't worry, he didn't seem to mind. But what actually happened was that you disappeared and Dave asked me if I'd seen you, which I hadn't, but then some guy who'd just come in from having a vape said you'd gone outside, so we both went out to look. Dave and I, not the vape guy. So...'

There was a silence and Poppy realised that Alice must have lost the signal again. She could have screamed with frustration.

Her phone beeped with a WhatsApp message, which turned out to be from Rose.

Thanks for helping organise my awesome party. I had a ball. Looked like you were enjoying yourself too. Dave's nice.

There was a winking emoji, followed by a row of hearts.

Poppy groaned. Did everyone in her family think there was something going on between her and Dave?

Alice rang back and she stopped typing a WhatsApp denial to Rose and pressed the answer button immediately.

'What did I do? Tell me.'

'All that happened,' Alice was clearly choosing her words

carefully, Poppy knew that tone, 'was that you grabbed hold of Dave's arm and you said something like, "Are you as good at kissing as you are at dancing?"'

Shit, it was worse than she'd thought.

'And then you, er, puckered up.'

'Puckered up?'

'Yes, you know – like you do when you're going to blow someone a kiss but don't. That was it. Nothing too bad.'

'What did Dave do?'

'He just laughed and said he thought you would probably regret that in the morning. In fact, he knew from actual experience that you definitely would.'

'Right,' Poppy said bleakly. 'Thanks.'

'I was just about to ring you anyway. So did anything else happen when he took you home?'

'I don't know,' Poppy said truthfully. 'I don't think so.' She stood up and walked around her flat with the earbuds still in place. There was no sign of Dave having been in her kitchen. No giveaway clues, like an extra mug on the drainer. Would he have washed it up? She checked for dirty mugs everywhere else and didn't find any. She had another flitter of memory. 'I think I may have invited him in for a coffee and he said no,' she told Alice. 'Thank goodness.'

Alice laughed. 'He did strike me as the perfect gentleman. I thought he was a really nice guy. In fact, I was thinking it's a shame he's going to be behind the camera on Tuesday instead of in front of it, because I really liked him. Do you really not fancy him?'

'He's not my type,' Poppy said, even though right now she wasn't sure how she felt about anything. Thanks to the hangover, it hurt to think. All she really wanted was to lie down in a darkened room.

'I've got to go,' Alice said. 'I'll be at my clients in two minutes. I'll see you on Tuesday morning. We'll be on set before we know it. Good luck with the rigging day tomorrow.'

'Thanks,' Poppy said, amused, despite the hangover, that Alice had already picked up quite a few bits of filming terminology. 'Are you excited?'

'Very excited. See you Tuesday, angel.'

Poppy disconnected, wondering whether it would be less embarrassing to call Dave now or wait until tomorrow when she could speak to him face to face. They were travelling to the Bluebell Cliff Hotel together. It made sense as they lived so close. She picked up the phone. She needed to speak to him now. At the very least she owed him an apology.

To her relief, he answered on the fourth ring. 'Morning, boss.'

'Morning, Dave. I want to apologise. About last night.'

'What for? I had a great time.' To her relief, he sounded his usual easy-going self.

'Good, I'm glad, but I put you on the spot with, um... Auntie Sheila.' Easier to get that one out of the way first.

'Not at all. I'm sorry I didn't come up with a more convincing job. It was the first thing that popped into my head. Then I tried to turn it into a joke and made it all worse. Bad move. Sorry. I'm rubbish at improvising.'

Was he deliberately talking a lot so she couldn't?

She waited for a gap and then said, 'Also, I'm sorry about the bit later on in the car park.'

'Ah. That.'

Poppy wished they were face to face so she could see his expression. 'I think I had too many glasses of wine,' she added quickly.

'We've all been there.'

'I know, but I couldn't regret it more. The whole night must have been hideously embarrassing. I'm so sorry, Dave.'

'Really, it's fine. You don't need to apologise. But thank you. I have to go. I'm supposed to be somewhere.'

'Oh, of course. Sorry again.' Now she felt wrong-footed.

He disconnected and for a few seconds she sat holding the mobile and wishing she could try that conversation again from the beginning. She wasn't sure if she'd made things more awkward or less. He'd sounded as though he couldn't wait to get off the phone and she really couldn't blame him.

* * *

Thankfully, an early night and a surprisingly good night's sleep put things back in perspective and on Monday morning, when she met Dave outside her flat in the communal car park just before 6 a.m. clutching her small travel case and her laptop and all the other paraphernalia she needed for the four days ahead, she felt a million times better.

Poppy was glad it was still dark because she couldn't see Dave's expression clearly. She hoped he wasn't still feeling awkward about Saturday night. He didn't mention it and she decided it would be best if she didn't either. She was glad they'd drawn a line under it and moved on.

He helped her load her things into his car without speaking and they didn't talk about the party as he drove them out towards Wareham and on to the road to Swanage. They were going the road way round because the first ferry didn't leave Sandbanks until seven.

They talked about work and the day ahead. A subject they were both comfortable with, Poppy thought as the dawn broke and the sky slowly lightened. The closest they got to anything that wasn't work was when he said, 'I know this job means we burn the candle at both ends, but I like this end best. I like getting up before daybreak and watching the sky slowly lighten.'

'Me too,' she said. 'Sunsets are for softies.'

'Yeah, I couldn't agree more.'

It was a relief to know they were both on the same wavelength.

* * *

Despite the early hour, the Bluebell Cliff was already buzzing with people by the time they got there.

Rigging day was always hard work. It was when all of the preparation and behind-the-scenes work came together. It was the day when Poppy would discover if all of her careful plans and meticulous arrangements would actually make sense in reality.

Most of her team would rock up at some point today. Mike the mic and Si, the boom operator, would be setting up the sound, Lenny was overseeing lighting, Corinna was helping out, Kate, the floor assistant, would be there, and various other people would be in and out, although possibly not staying for the whole day. The hired camera ops would be in today too, getting the cameras set up ready for filming the next day.

The art department were already on site, busy converting the ballroom into the makeshift studio where they would be filming much of the show. It was a fairly simple set-up in that Alice and Taylor Stanton would be standing up facing a semicircle of the would-be dates. Each of the seven contenders would stand on a large, red, numbered heart, which would be lit from beneath. It would glow a vibrant Valentine's Day shade of red when the contender was speaking and dim to darker red when he had finished. If he got through a round, the light would flash on and off in quick succession. When he was eliminated from a round, it would go out completely.

This had given the lighting department a challenge. There had been so many technical problems and blown fuses when they had built the props that Poppy had been tempted to abandon the idea, but under Lenny's guidance, the sparks had persevered and they had finally cracked it. It looked fantastic in action.

Most of the show would be filmed by way of five or six cameras set on pedestals, which meant they could be shifting about easily, gliding like soundless daleks across the floor, in order to get the best shots. They would also be using a camera on a jib. A camera assistant was fiddling with the jib, which looked like a small crane and was brilliant for covering as much movement as possible and getting lots of nice swooping shots.

The ballroom had also been big enough for them to create a second, smaller set, screened off from the main studio. This would feature a romantic table, which would be set up for one with gleaming silver cutlery. It was here that the signature dish would be served up so that Alice could make her choice of both dish and man.

Poppy had agreed that the Steinway grand piano, a great gleaming beast of an instrument, could be left in its usual position near the stage. Clara had been relieved about that when they'd discussed it, as they weren't the easiest objects to manoeuvre.

It had transpired that at least three of Poppy's contestants were keen to perform their party piece on a Steinway anyway. Another two were 'would-be thespians' and Poppy was hoping one of them would make it to the party-piece round so the amphitheatre could be used, as it made such a lovely backdrop up on the cliffs with the sea in the distance. But, of course, it would all be down to Alice, and Poppy hoped she'd chosen the right contestants.

* * *

By eleven, Poppy was feeling quietly confident. She checked her call sheet. Everyone who'd promised to turn up had turned up and things were going smoothly, aided by several gallons of coffee, supplied partly by Clara and now by a catering truck that was parked outside.

The OB truck had just arrived too, and Dave was chatting to the guys who'd come with it, to help them set up the gallery. People were milling about with cables and equipment ready to connect up to the cameras that were dotted around the studio.

Corinna was on her knees, her head close to a light, winding gaffer tape around a cable to secure it to the floor. Her tongue poked out of the side of her mouth, as it always did when she was concentrating. 'This is my favourite bit... not,' she said, straightening up when she saw Poppy. 'Taping down endless cables. When is someone going to invent sticky tape that is easier to use than this stuff but that still actually works?'

'I'll give you a hand in a sec,' Poppy promised, diverted by a call for her to check out the 'romantic table' set.

'You want this laid up for one, yah?' said the intern who had just covered the table in a snowy linen tablecloth and produced a small vase of freesias which smelled gorgeous.

'For now. Yes. Thank you. But put the freesias out later,' Poppy said, whisking the vase off the table. 'They'll wilt if they're out too long.' At some later stage, the freesias would be swapped for a red rose in a stem vase and there would be linen serviettes and leather-backed menus and a silver wine cooler and lead crystal wine glasses. It was here, too, that Alice and her winning date would sit for their evening meal, which would be served up to them by a member of the Bluebell Cliff waiting staff, but not the maître d'.

Poppy's thoughts flicked briefly towards Phil Grimshaw. If he won *Date for a Day*, he would be sitting here opposite Alice. He could end up as her brother-in-law. That was a discomforting thought. But she was getting ahead of herself. He might not even make the final.

An annoyed shout from beyond the open French doors distracted her. It sounded like Mike, she thought, as she hurried to see what had happened. It took a lot to get Mike to raise his voice. What on earth was going on?

She heard a further tirade of muttered curses as she emerged into the sun. Mike was shielding his eyes and pointing at something beyond them on the far side of the pristine lawns.

'Did anyone see that? A flaming three-legged fox just nicked my bacon butty. The bloody cheek of it. It was moving pretty sharpish for a three-legged fox too. Unbelievable. I hadn't even had a bite.' He stamped a foot in irritation and glared around at everyone.

A camera op sniggered.

Mike grumbled on, 'Not a single bloody bite. I was looking forward to that.'

Someone else guffawed.

'It had just the right amount of bloody ketchup on.'

The crosser and more outraged Mike got, the more everyone else laughed.

'I don't think that's a fox, mate.' Dave was bent double with mirth. 'That's the hotel manager's dog.'

'Well, I want it back. Get after it, someone.' Mike looked around him for a likely candidate, but everyone was laughing too much to pursue Foxy, who had paused at what she clearly considered was a safe enough distance away to eat her prize.

Poppy caught Dave's eyes and looked away before she started laughing too. 'I'll get you another butty,' she told Mike, heading towards the catering van.

A few minutes later, she brought it back and presented it to him.

'Don't leave it anywhere she can get it, this time.'

He thanked her and shoved it straight in his mouth. He obviously wasn't taking any more chances.

Noticing that Si and Lenny were now helping Corinna with the taping down of the cables that snaked everywhere, Poppy went to check the state of play in the room they'd commandeered to be the green room. It wouldn't be needed until tomorrow. Neither would the make-up room, where everyone would be made to look television-ready. All was in order.

The Bluebell Cliff was pretty much the perfect venue. It was a pity they couldn't use it for every show in the series. But she was getting ahead of herself again. There may not be a series – if Netflix didn't like the pilot, that would be it. Game over and this show would never get as far as the screen.

She put that thought out of her head. Today was all about being positive. She was standing right on the threshold of her dream.

She went back out into reception and found Clara.

'Is everything OK?' the manager asked. 'Do you need anything?'

'Only an endless supply of coffee, which we seem to have, thank you.' Poppy decided to keep quiet about Foxy stealing the bacon butty.

'I guess this is all routine to you,' Clara said, waving her hand as a couple of guys shot by with their arms full of cables. 'Another day at the office. But it's really exciting, isn't it? All the technology: microphones; lights; all those cameras. I had no idea how much was involved – it's amazing.'

'It's amazing that we need so much equipment to film what is technically "reality".' Poppy mimed the inverted commas around the word. 'It's not as bad when we're outside. You can get away with a couple of cameramen and a sound guy, but studio work is more intensive.' Poppy thought she'd just caught a glimpse of Mr B. What was he doing here? She had thought the kitchens were closed most of today and tomorrow for filming. 'I was just on my way to the kitchen,' she said to Clara, who didn't appear to have noticed Mr B.

'Fab. Don't let me hold you up. I've told my staff – the ones who are here this week – to stay out of the way and do what they're told.'

'Thanks.' From the few dealings she'd had with him, Poppy was pretty sure Mr B was not the type of person to either stay out of the way or do as he was told. She was still trying to think of a diplomatic way of banning him from his own kitchen, although she had a feeling this was going to be tricky.

She walked through the restaurant and through the door marked 'Staff Only', hoping it had been someone else she'd glimpsed just now.

It wasn't.

Mr B was standing by the big commercial oven, his tall frame slightly bent as he peered at a gas ring intently. He straightened as he became aware of her presence and turned. 'Good morning, Poppy. Is it OK to call you Poppy or does one need to address television producers as ma'am?'

Was he being serious? His face was deadpan.

'Poppy is fine,' she said, giving him her most disarming smile. 'May I call you something a little less formal than Mr B?'

'Mr B is what I prefer.' Round one to him then. 'I don't wish to be rude,' he added. 'It's what everyone calls me.'

'OK. Mr B it is.' She stayed where she was, feeling like an antelope who'd found herself caught squarely in a lion's territory. 'We won't be in your kitchen today. We won't be shooting that part of the show until tomorrow.'

'I'm aware of the schedule. But I just wanted to check something with you. An urgent matter.'

'Of course,' she said, hoping he wasn't going to start off on the security implications of using Chinese cameras again.

But it seemed this wasn't his concern today. He coughed self-importantly. 'Do your food-prep operatives have up-to-date certificates in food prep and hygiene?' His eyes gleamed in anticipation of her answer, which he had to know was no.

'I'm not sure if they do. I'll check with our home economist. I will, of course, take full responsibility should there be any consequences of them not having the certification.'

'It would be easier to use my highly trained staff.'

How highly trained did you have to be to chop a few peppers and onions and weigh out flour exactly? She suppressed the urge to scream. She knew there was no point in arguing with him.

'Thank you,' she said. 'That would be marvellous. I'll get you a copy of the list of things we need.'

'I've already seen the list.'

'Right.' She wondered who had shown him. One of her production team had already procured all the ingredients. They weren't relying on the Bluebell Cliff to provide them.

'Not much happens in my kitchen without me knowing about it,' he said silkily. He drew himself up to his full height. He was very tall.

'Right. Good. And will you be here tomorrow yourself, Mr B?' *Please don't let the answer be yes*, Poppy thought.

'I will indeed. I'll be overseeing my staff. I'll be making sure their work is up to standard. And ensuring that they obey all the protocol of filming.' He folded his arms across his chest and Poppy decided not to argue. One of the things she had learned in her profession was that you picked your battles. She had no doubt that she would end up having some kind of conflict with Mr B before she got a wrap on this pilot, but it would be better for both of them if that battle was not today.

14

It was a long day. But there were no more major teething problems and by 6 p.m. the only people left at the Bluebell were Poppy's team and the four camera operatives who were staying over for the two days of studio filming.

To Poppy's surprise, Clara had offered them all dinner in the Bluebell's restaurant. 'It was Mr B's idea,' she said. 'After all, the kitchens will be closed tomorrow for filming, so he's had to come in today to prepare tomorrow's evening meal. He said it was no problem to cater for you and your crew tonight as well.'

'In that case, thank you,' Poppy said. 'That's very good of him.' Why was there a part of her that had immediately jumped to the conclusion that Mr B must have an ulterior motive for being nice?

'He's probably planning phase two of his interrogation,' Dave said, clearly of the same opinion, as soon as Clara was out of earshot. 'He'll be laying down the law about his last-minute requirements and you won't be able to argue with him because you'll have your mouth full of soup.'

'He's already done a bit of that.' Poppy told him about Mr B's insistence on doing the food preparation. 'It saves us some time anyway,' she said. 'And we do have the ingredients. All his staff have to do is prepare them.'

'Well, that's probably a good thing too. The more jurisdiction he has over his kitchen, the less he can blame us for anything that goes wrong.'

'Yes, that's what I thought.'

'Not that anything is going to go wrong.' He met her gaze. 'Thanks to your brilliant planning and your superb team.' A beat. 'I think we're all set, aren't we?'

'I think we are.'

* * *

To Poppy's relief, Dave's dark prophecies about Mr B continuing his interrogation came to nothing. There was no sign of him over dinner. There was no sign of Phil either. They were served by a teenage waitress. Poppy assumed Phil must have been relieved of hotel duties for the next few days so he could take part in the filming.

They sat on two tables of six. Herself, Dave, Corinna, Kate the floor manager, Mike and Lenny were on one table; Si and the camera ops on another.

Tomorrow, when they were joined by Alice, the male contenders, Taylor Stanton, the make-up ladies, and the rest of the crew, the restaurant would be practically full.

While they were drinking coffee, Poppy looked at the schedule for the following day, one more time.

8.00 a.m.: Crew arrive and set up. Call time for talent –
into make-up.
9.00 a.m.: Walk-throughs/rehearsals with talent
contributors.

10.00 a.m.: Contenders introduce themselves and Alice chooses four.

12.00 p.m.: Lunch – reset in the kitchen for dish prep. While this is happening, reset the area for serving.

1.00–2.00 p.m.: Dish 1.

2.00 p.m.: Reset.

2.30–3.30 p.m.: Dish 2.

3.30 p.m.: Reset.

4.00–5.00 p.m.: Dish 3.

5.00 p.m.: Reset.

5.30–6.30 p.m.: Dish 4.

7.00 p.m.: Dishes are served.

8.00 p.m.: Wrap.

'It's quite tight,' Poppy remarked, aware that Dave was looking over her shoulder.

'But eminently doable,' he said, stirring sugar into his coffee.

Lenny leaned across the table. 'Did you realise it was April Fool's Day tomorrow? That could disrupt things.'

'I should think everyone's sensible enough to know that if they play any tricks that disrupt my schedule, they'll regret it.' Poppy didn't smile.

'Hear hear,' Mike said.

Lenny widened his eyes in an expression of mock abject fear and withdrew.

'Am I being too uptight?' Poppy asked Kate, who was on her left and was known for her no-nonsense attitude.

'Nah,' Kate said, helping herself to a coffee top-up. 'I think you're being fair.' She tucked a strand of shiny hair behind her ear and blinked a few times. Kate's angelic looks covered a shrewd brain and quick wit that often took people by surprise. It was a formidable combination.

'No fooling about till we've wrapped,' Corinna said. 'Talking of fooling about, though, I was chatting to a couple of guys who work in the kitchen earlier. There's a history of April Fool's in the Bluebell's kitchen. But then I think there's quite a bit of messing about that goes on in kitchens generally.'

'It's nothing major,' Kate put in. 'I heard that story too. Most of the pranks seem to be between Mr B and the maître d'. One year someone put a red scarf in with the chef's whites and turned everything pink. Mr B blamed Phil.'

'I wouldn't have liked to be in Phil's shoes when Mr B caught up with him,' Poppy said, looking at day two of their schedule, which included the reveal of the final two contestants who'd perform their party piece, plus reactions, as well as the party pieces themselves and then, at 3 p.m. if all went to plan, the final reveal of the winner. She'd left some time on day two for pickups, which meant they could reshoot any extra shots from day one if needed. 'I don't suppose Clara was too impressed with pink whites either,' Poppy added. 'It sounds expensive.'

'You can sort it out with half a capful of bleach,' Kate said. 'I heard that Mr B got his own back by drawing a picture of a massive spider on the kitchen roll so that Phil got the shock of his life when he pulled the next sheet out of the dispenser. Apparently he's scared of spiders. Then Phil retaliated by dusting all the chef's hats with itching powder. Mr B had an evening of scratching his head before he fathomed it out.'

There were several guffaws. Mr B's reputation had gone before him.

'Does Mr B know that Phil's a contestant?' Corinna said to the table in general and a couple of people shrugged.

'I would have thought so,' Poppy replied, chewing the inside of her mouth and hoping she didn't look as nervous as she felt. 'He's got time off to do the filming.'

Mike drained his coffee. 'Much as I'd like to sit here and listen to the fascinating exploits that go on in hotel kitchens, I think I'll get an early night.'

There were murmurs of agreement from everyone else and the table slowly emptied. Dave and Poppy were the last to get up.

'We've got this,' he said, as they climbed up the Bluebell's ornate staircase to their bedrooms on the first floor. 'Don't let anyone put you off. Tomorrow is going to run like clockwork.'

'Are you sure that's not you tempting fate?' she said.

'No, boss. It's me being positive.'

* * *

To Poppy's surprise, she slept well in the strange bed, although as her eyes snapped open as usual just before six, she had a vague memory of a dream in which all of the male contestants turned up in chef's whites that weren't pristine white but streaked with pale pink stripes.

Over breakfast, she had several texts wishing her good luck. One from Rose, who must have got up early to send it, bless her. One from Micky and one from her mother which, to her relief, just said:

Kenny and I are sending you all the luck in the world darling. We are very proud of you.

No more predictive text mistakes then, or maybe she was now checking them as she'd promised.

Poppy texted back a thank you and a smiley face emoji to each of them and then turned her phone on to vibrate and slipped it into her pocket.

Alice arrived half an hour earlier than she needed to, complete with her outfits in suit carriers.

'The most important thing about today,' Poppy told her, 'is to have fun.'

'I intend to,' Alice said, her voice perfectly calm so even Poppy couldn't tell for sure if she was nervous behind her poised exterior.

There was just time for a hug before she was whisked away by wardrobe and make-up.

Taylor Stanton arrived and caused a buzz in reception. Apparently, Keith the nightwatchman had seen her on CBBC and had asked her for a selfie, to which she'd gracefully acquiesced.

To Poppy's relief, all seven of their male contenders turned up on time. Now they had all been through make-up amidst a lot of good-natured bantering and were in the green room. They were Guy the funeral director, Liam the lifeguard, Alistair the human rights lawyer, Rob the builder, Jack the stockbroker, who'd already earned himself the nickname of 'I'm-all-right-Jack' because of an incident with a spilt coffee, Charles the concert pianist and, of course, Phil the maître d'.

The three backup contestants had turned up too and had been asked to wait in case they were needed. The backups had been told that while there was no guarantee they'd be on the pilot they would be top of the list for future episodes of the series. Also, the backups were paid for their time, unlike the actual contenders, who were all here for their five minutes of fame and the chance of a date with Alice.

Taylor Stanton and Alice were now television-ready. Taylor was in one of her trademark beautifully cut navy suits and Alice was wearing a gorgeous pastel-blue dress that skimmed every curve of her figure and lent her a feminine softness. Her shoulder-length blonde hair framed her beautiful face. She'd been a little alarmed by the heaviness of the make-up, but Poppy had reassured her the lights made everyone look like a ghost. Studio make-up was a whole art form in itself.

Alice and Taylor were waiting in a different room to the guys. Poppy didn't want her to see her prospective dates until she actually walked on to set and faced them. Alice wore her heart on her sleeve when it came to romance and she had such an open, expressive face. Poppy wanted to catch her emotions and reactions on camera.

She was looking forward to seeing which three guys Alice would eliminate first. The members of her crew who'd seen the auditions had already laid bets on it.

'I reckon she'll get rid of the builder, the undertaker and the stockbroker,' Dave had said earlier when they'd been setting up, and most of the crew had agreed with him.

'She'll get rid of that lifeguard if her head isn't turned,' Mike the Mic had said. 'Too cocky by half, that one.'

There were murmurs of assent.

'Jack the lad's definitely out,' said Corinna, who'd been chasing about since the crack of dawn. 'But I don't think she'll be getting rid of that lifeguard in a hurry and I'm not so sure she'll get rid of Rrrrrob the builder either. I love his Somerset accent, and did you see those biceps?'

Lenny had adjusted one of the lights on the set and frowned. 'It's not all about looks, though, is it? Do you know how much stockbrokers earn? I watched this YouTube video the other day and it's obscene. Most of them retire at thirty-five.'

'Or burn out,' Corinna had replied. 'It's not all about money either. Didn't you hear what she said about wanting someone who's kind?'

'If it's about money, the maître d' would have to go,' Lenny had said thoughtfully. 'He's hardly earning a fortune, is he?'

Everyone in hearing range had stared at him.

'He's too good-looking to go,' Corinna had said, 'although he is a bit long in the tooth, isn't he?'

Mike had spluttered into his coffee. 'He's not old! He's just a nipper. Bloody hell! How do you lot manage to work with a dinosaur like me?'

'I didn't mean you were old, Mike, honey. I simply meant that Alice is very young and beautiful.' Corinna had shot a sweet smile at their sound guy and he shook his head, clearly only partly mollified.

'Alice is thirty-seven,' Poppy had said, aware that Dave was smirking. He hadn't taken to Phil and she had no idea why. 'And Phil is just forty. So that makes him the perfect age for her.'

Poppy was pretty sure that Alice would get rid of the funeral director, after what she'd said about them at Rose's party. She was also 99 per cent sure she would choose the lifeguard because boats and all things water sports were her thing, but she kept this to herself as it was inside information. Dave and her crew knew that Alice was a relative, but it wasn't common knowledge.

'It will be very interesting to see what she does,' she had said, wrapping up the speculation with a clap of her hands. 'Come on, you lot. It's time we got cracking.'

* * *

From their seats in the gallery in the OB truck, Poppy and Dave were facing a panel of monitors. Yellow Post-it notes were stuck on the screens, marking up camera one, camera two, camera three and camera four so they could see what each camera angle saw, while another monitor showed what was being recorded.

Poppy adjusted her headset. The words 'action' and 'cut' had become so clichéd across the years that she always felt vaguely self-conscious saying them. But experience had taught her that if you didn't use them then no one in the studio knew when to start and stop and the whole thing could easily descend into chaos.

She glanced at Dave to check he was ready and he nodded.

She spoke into her mic, 'Three, two, one... and action.'

'Welcome to *Date for a Day*, where one lucky lady gets to choose her date from our seven hand-picked contestants.' Taylor Stanton's gorgeously confident voice sounded as enthusiastic and expectant as it had the first time she'd said those words. This was take five. 'It's my pleasure to introduce Alice Bennett, our delightful Dorset lady who has the enviable task of making that choice.'

Alice had been fine in the rehearsals but now she was more nervous than Poppy had ever seen her. Bless her. Not that she was surprised. What was it about being surrounded by cameras all of which were pointing at you that turned the most self-confident and poised of people into gibbering wrecks?

'Tell me, Alice,' Taylor continued brightly, 'if you had to sum up your date in one sentence, what would it be?'

'He'd be a kind person and he'd also be the mind of can... I mean the kind of man...' She broke off. 'Bollocks! Argh. Sorry. Why can't I get this right?'

'Cut,' Poppy called unnecessarily. She glanced at Dave. 'Hang fire a sec. I'm just going to have a quick word with her.' She left the gallery and went into the studio, where she walked across and touched Alice's arm. 'Don't worry. This is totally normal. Why don't we simplify it a bit?'

'Can it get any simpler than one sentence?' Alice asked, sighing heavily. 'I'm so sorry.'

'Why don't we try one word?' Poppy glanced at Taylor, who was nodding.

'Good idea.' She also gave Alice a genuine look of warmth and

Poppy could see exactly how she'd got so far in her profession at such a young age. She was lovely. And while it was easy to be lovely in front of a lens, not as many people in the industry managed it when the cameras weren't running.

Poppy walked back outside and leapt up into the OB truck, trying not to think about her tight schedule, and sat down once more. Dave crossed his fingers in front of him.

They began again with Taylor introducing the show and then turning towards Alice. 'Tell me, Alice. If you had to sum up your date in one word, what would it be?'

In the split second before Alice answered, the whole room held its breath.

'Kind,' Alice said. 'He'd be kind and he'd be nice. And maybe a little bit old-fashioned. If I'm being honest, I'd quite like to meet a Dorset gentleman.' Her beautiful face lit up as she got into her stride.

'A Dorset gentleman. Well, you're certainly in the right place for that,' Taylor went on smoothly. All of the contestants had to have been born in Dorset, even if they didn't live there currently. 'I'm guessing you'd like him to be tall too. Being such a gorgeous tall lady yourself?' Taylor wasn't lacking in the height department, but Alice was taller and the figure-skimming dress she wore only enhanced it. 'Are you actually six feet, Alice?'

'I'm five eleven, but I do like to wear heels.' Alice bent her leg and tilted her heel and the jib camera moved in to focus on her three-inch stiletto. 'Tall would be good,' she added.

'And did you have any particular profession in mind for your ideal partner? What would your soulmate do?'

'I hope he'd do whatever made him happy,' Alice said with a slowly rising warmth in her voice. 'I'd really love it if he had a job he was passionate about.'

'Oh, yes. We'd all like a man who was passionate, wouldn't we, ladies?' Taylor winked at the camera and gave her trademark laugh that managed to be sexy without being girlish. Apparently, in a recent magazine survey she'd won the top spot in 'Sexiest Laugh On The Planet'.

Now everyone in the studio laughed with her.

'And cut,' Poppy called with a little sigh of relief.

15

Once they'd got through the tricky introductory part, the filming continued very smoothly.

Kate, the floor manager, had just directed the seven contenders to their red heart-shaped numbered spot on the floor.

'If I don't win, are you up for a coffee, sweetheart?' Guy, the undertaker, shouted to Kate as she ushered him into position.

'I'm gay, darling,' she shouted back at him and his face fell in disappointment.

So did the stockbroker's, Poppy noticed with amusement. There was so much testosterone in the studio, you could taste it.

In time-honoured tradition of dating shows the world over, the order in which the men summed themselves up in a sentence had been left up to Alice.

She had regained her usual poise and confidence. As she stood next to Taylor, very straight-backed and her face serious once more, she put Poppy in mind of some royal princess who was about to address her subjects. An image of Daenerys Targaryen from *Game of Thrones* sprung into her head. Alice was almost a foot taller than the Dragon Queen, but she was every bit as icily beautiful.

Suddenly Poppy realised what Alice had meant about scaring off men. She looked every inch the imperious princess and that serious face she had when she was nervous could easily be misconstrued as haughtiness.

Alice picked on the funeral director to introduce himself first and he launched into his spiel about being around very cool people all day and Poppy was reminded of Dave's improvising at Rose's party. She glanced at his face, but he was issuing instructions to camera one, which moved slightly in response.

Alice turned towards the lifeguard next. Both the funeral director and the lifeguard were fair-haired, Poppy noted, which was curious when she recalled the conversation they'd had about Aidan Turner. Alice had said she liked the darkly handsome, brooding type and Phil fitted the profile perfectly.

Poppy was torn between wanting Alice to put Phil through to the next round because he was so gorgeous on camera and not wanting her to pick him because she found him so attractive herself. That man did something strange to her insides. There was no doubt about it. Even when he was in a different room and she was only viewing his image on a monitor. No matter which way it went, Poppy told herself, Phil had reminded her, without having to say a single word, that it was time to get back into the dating game. It was high time her love life had a bit more action than the occasional bout of 'going nowhere' flirting with her director of photography. As soon as she'd put this show to bed, she was going to honour the promise she'd made to Alice and join an online dating site for real.

Phil was the third person that Alice asked to sum himself up in a sentence. 'Number seven,' she said, turning her beautiful gaze towards him. 'Tell me about yourself.'

There was the slightest of pauses before Phil launched into his sentence. It was masterful timing and it added to the electricity in the studio. Poppy was surprised he was still a maître d' and hadn't been able to go into the acting profession full time. But then the acting profession was a capricious mistress. Sometimes the most outstanding people just didn't get their lucky break.

Phil began to speak. 'By day, I work in a hotel designed to make people's dreams come true and, by night, I follow my own dreams, but if I'm lucky enough to go on a date with you, we'll discuss your dreams, not mine.'

The words were corny, but his voice was rich and authentic. The whole studio stilled, just as the rehearsal room had done when they'd auditioned him.

For a second, Alice and Phil were locked into a bubble of chemistry that was obvious even from where Dave and Poppy sat in the gallery. It fizzed. Poppy felt a tingle of excitement running through the faint thread of disappointment of knowing her stepsister couldn't fail to be impressed. No way was Phil being kicked out of this round.

Alice was flying now. It was obvious that she was enjoying herself immensely and the guys were very entertaining, all of them entering into the spirit of friendly competitiveness. The atmosphere in the studio was upbeat and the air buzzed with the energy and tension of filming with real people as opposed to practised actors.

One by one, the other four guys introduced themselves. Charles, the concert pianist, got some raised eyebrows from his fellow contestants and the ladies when he said his fingers were insured for a million pounds. Jack, the stockbroker, was smooth charm. Rob, the builder, provoked a flattering compliment from Taylor when he flexed his 'builder's bicep'. Alistair, the lawyer, wowed them with his quiet confidence and Barack Obama passion.

Dave was pleased too, with how things were going. 'She's great, your Alice,' he said when they paused for a break after the round. 'The camera loves her. A classic English rose. She looks stunning and she's got just the right amount of vulnerability to poise. Men will want her – and women will want to be her.'

Poppy could hear his admiration. 'Yes, she's beautiful. Inside and out. I hope she finds her perfect date. I know it's all a bit unreal and the chances of that happening are really quite remote, but it would be lovely, wouldn't it?'

'It would make a great pilot.'

'I don't just mean for that reason,' she said, irked that he was assuming she had an ulterior motive.

'Have I hit a nerve?' He gave her a sharp look. 'After all, it was you who said sunsets were for softies, wasn't it?' It was hard to tell whether he was joking or not. Now he was smiling again, but she knew she hadn't imagined that slight edge.

'We'd better get on and see who she picks,' Poppy said, turning back to the screen, where everyone was in place once more to find out who had got through to the next round. 'Three, two, one and... action,' she said, and Taylor launched smoothly into her spiel.

'So then, Alice my darling. It's *Date for a Day* Decision Time. Which three of our contestants are you sending home and which of them are you asking to stay for round two?' Taylor glanced at the autocue camera. 'It's a very difficult decision, as I'm sure all of you ladies at home will agree.'

At this point in the show, there would be an on-screen reminder of the seven guys' names and professions, on the remote chance that the audience might have forgotten during the last five minutes.

Alice paused. 'It's so difficult. They're all so lovely.'

'Indeed they are, but you can't date them all. Not on *Date for a Day* anyway.' That sexy laugh again. 'You have to choose, my darling. I need the numbers and names of the three men you will not be dating tomorrow.'

'OK.' Alice took a deep breath. 'This is absolutely nothing personal, guys. You are all lovely, but I have to make a decision.' A beat. 'In no particular order then, the men I will not be dating tomorrow are: number one, Jack.'

No surprises there, Poppy thought as the red heart below Jack's feet dimmed down to nothing.

'Number three, Rob.'

That was more of a surprise. Poppy had thought Alice was quite a fan of Rob. Rob looked disappointed too as his red heart dimmed and went out.

'And number six, Guy.'

Poppy had expected that all along. Clearly, so had Guy because he was smiling good-naturedly as his light died too.

Taylor listened to Poppy's voice in the mic in her ear. 'So, just to clarify that for our audience at home, you have chosen to send away: number one, Jack the stockbroker; number three, Rob the builder; and number six, Guy the funeral director.'

'Yes,' Alice said, sombre-faced.

'Which means that the lucky four gentlemen who get to go forward into round two are – in no particular order – number two, Charles, the concert pianist; number four, Alistair, the lawyer; number five, Liam, the lifeguard; and number seven, Phil, the maître d'.'

Not only did their lights remain on, but the hearts beneath their feet began to glow a deeper, more vibrant valentine-heart red before flashing on and off. It was all very tacky, but it would look wonderfully visual on television and no viewer could be in any doubt about who had won the round.

Alice nodded. 'Absolutely. They are my choices for round two.' Poppy could see on camera two that her cheeks had gone a fetching pink, although they couldn't compete with the hearts.

'Well, we are very much looking forward to round two where your chosen gentlemen will get the chance to impress you by cooking their signature dish. Are you a cook yourself, Alice?'

'I don't cook much,' Alice said. 'But I am a fan of fine dining. So I'll be expecting more than a boiled egg.'

'No pressure then, boys.' Taylor looked around at the remaining contestants and the cameras swooped along the line to get all the reactions on their faces. They were all smiling – even Phil. Poppy's heart gave a little twinge.

Get over yourself, she said inwardly.

'Cut,' she said out loud before turning to Dave by her side. 'Do you know, I think the Bluebell's maître d' might make it into the final.'

Dave didn't answer. He was talking to one of the camera ops on his microphone, she realised belatedly, and probably hadn't heard her.

* * *

At lunchtime, which was a swift sandwich from the catering truck for most of the crew, Poppy grabbed a moment to catch up with Alice.

'How are you feeling? You're doing brilliantly.'

'Really? I can't believe how many times I fluffed my lines.'

'It's not easy being in such an artificial environment and having an audience of cameramen. You'll be fine now we've got going. The first day is always the hardest. Everything's new and a little bit frightening. Even the most experienced actors mess it up.'

'Not as much as I did, surely?'

'Yeah, they do. Seriously. Why do you think there are so many outtakes shows? They always have plenty of material.'

'Yes, I seem to remember a statistic I've heard bandied about. Isn't it about ten minutes footage for a whole day of filming?'

'I wish,' Poppy said. 'If you're making a drama, it's actually one to three minutes' worth of show for every whole day of filming. But if it's daytime TV, you sometimes have to make a whole half-hour show in a day.' She gave her stepsister a hug. 'You're doing great, trust me.'

She looked around for Dave but couldn't see him anywhere. For a moment in the gallery earlier there had been a sense of real awkwardness. Or perhaps they were just both tense. First-day filming nerves. This project was a big deal for him as well as for her. She decided to give him the benefit of the doubt, picked up her briefcase and went to find Corinna.

* * *

The whole of the cooking sequence would be filmed in the kitchen this afternoon, which technically meant it would be shot on location with just two camera operators, one of whom was Dave, with Mike doing sound. Then it would be fitted into the final programme as a video tape insert, or VT. They were starting the kitchen filming after lunch to allow time for food preparation. Poppy didn't foresee any major problems with it, although she did still have niggling doubts about the presence of Mr B. Not that she'd seen him anywhere today. Maybe that meant he had taken some notice of Clara's instructions to stay out of the way, after all. She could only hope.

Unlike *MasterChef*, Poppy had decided that the four guys wouldn't be filmed cooking simultaneously – that would have required a lot more equipment to be set up in the kitchens. They would film each cook separately and then edit the footage later. This way, she could keep things as simple as possible.

The signature dishes had to be cooked in ten minutes, but all of the preparation, things like the chopping of vegetables and the whisking of eggs and the weighing of ingredients, would be done in advance. Ovens would be heated and pans would be warmed and all the ingredients laid out ready for the would-be chefs. All they had to do was the actual mixing and cooking bit.

The finished signature dish would be plated up and served to Alice, by its creator, at the romantic table in the studio, but this would be filmed later on in the day. Their home economist, Peter, was responsible for reheating the dishes so they looked as pristine as they had when they'd first been cooked.

The rules stated that the dish could be savoury or sweet. Poppy glanced at the list to remind herself what the four guys had chosen to cook.

Liam the lifeguard planned to cook salsa-simmered salmon. He was continuing on a seafaring theme then. That would go down well with Alice.

Alistair was cooking spaghetti with pan-fried cherry tomatoes, garlic and basil. Poppy knew Alice would appreciate the simplicity of that if it was done well. She was a fan of Italian food.

Charles had bucked the trend for savoury and had chosen to do sweet pancakes. Poppy pictured those clever pianist fingers of his clasped around a pan tossing pancakes. That would be a great visual and a lot of fun to film. There was the added element of danger too – what if he dropped a pancake on the floor? There'd be no second chances.

Phil had also chosen to create a sweet dish. It was a chocolate mug cake. Poppy felt her eyebrows go up. What on earth was that? She hoped he knew what he was doing. He probably did. He worked in a kitchen – well, not quite in the actual kitchen, but he was in the catering business, which was a very good start. Chocolate cake was one of her stepsister's big weaknesses. If Phil got that right, he'd be sailing through to the final.

16

Liam, the lifeguard, was up first after lunch. He had the 1 p.m. to 2 p.m. slot. To Poppy's relief, Mr B had been as good as his word and the ingredients had been prepared and laid out as she'd asked without a flicker of resistance from him.

'Perhaps he just needed to feel in control,' Peter said when Poppy asked him if there had been any problems. 'It must be a bit strange, having a bunch of strangers rock up in your kitchen, wanting to take over.'

Poppy wasn't convinced that Mr B had been feeling insecure, he'd given the impression of someone who was a total control freak, but she was happy to give him the benefit of the doubt, for now. Although, it would be interesting to see how the afternoon progressed. She had once worked on a cookery programme where a chef had insisted on getting in the way of every shot, washing pots that didn't need washing and spoiling the continuity of the sequence. Would Mr B manage to restrain himself? She guessed they would soon find out.

Because they were effectively shooting the cookery part of the show 'on location', there were only six of them in the kitchen: her,

Dave, Mike, another camera op, and of course Taylor and the contestant. Fortunately, the Bluebell had large kitchens or it would have been a bit of a squeeze.

Liam had clearly cooked his salsa-simmered salmon signature dish many times before and he completed it with clockwork perfection and ladled it on to a serving platter, before stepping back triumphantly just before the timer buzzer went. It smelled very Mexican, a combination of cumin and garlic filled the air and brought to mind images of sombreros and tequila and far-off, hot places.

Poppy had a brief, cosy image of Alice and Liam going scuba diving on a Caribbean reef somewhere and then Liam cooking her a meal while she hunched over her laptop scheduling work for the week ahead. That could work well. On the other hand, how would the laid-back Liam get on in a relationship with a workaholic? Would their shared love of the sea be enough?

Poppy decided she was definitely overthinking things as Dave panned the camera across the dish to get a mouth-watering close up of the salsa-simmered salmon. This was what they called the 'hero shot' and was the close-up of the dish that the audience at home would see, just before it was presented to Alice.

Charles, the concert pianist, was up next with his pancakes. He broke the eggs, forked them lightly into the milk and then whisked the mix expertly into the flour. Then he heated the fat until it was smoking blue and poured the first lot of batter into the pan so that it sizzled loudly.

Poppy sneaked a glance at the smoke detector – she'd been tempted to turn it off but had decided against it. It might get into a stray camera shot and if it looked like it was switched off, there were bound to be some health and safety repercussions. Fortunately, the detector remained mute as the pancakes slowly turned golden.

The glorious smell of cooking pancakes, hot batter and sugar and the scent of freshly squeezed lemon always whisked Poppy straight back to childhood. One of the few memories she had of Alice's mother was of herself, Alice and Rose all crammed into the small kitchen next door watching Patsy Bennett cook pancakes. Sometimes she would let them have a go at tossing them, putting her hands around their tiny fingers on the handle of the pan and helping them flip them in the air. Lots of them landed on the floor, but Aunty Patsy, as Poppy and Rose had always called her, never seemed to care. Poppy wondered if Alice's memory would flick back too, when she saw Charles' offering.

Encouraged by Taylor, Charles went for the pancake-tossing shot. He flipped and caught the first pancake expertly. But he almost dropped the second one because he hammed it up so much, pulling faces and hopping about. It was very entertaining and would make fantastic television.

Alistair, the lawyer, who'd chosen to cook the Italian dish, came the closest to not completing the cooking in ten minutes. He may have been a master of timing when he was in court, but he was completely out when it came to cooking spaghetti, although, to be fair, even producing spaghetti al dente in the time allowed was always going to be a challenge.

As the kitchen filled up with the heavenly scents of cherry tomatoes and garlic sizzling in a pan on the hob, Alistair's spaghetti still wasn't done. He tested it several times and shook his head and then finally confessed that he only knew it was cooked at home if he threw a bit at the wall.

'If it sticks, I know it's done,' he said, his brow beginning to prick with sweat as the pan bubbled on and on and on and he poked dubiously at the spaghetti with a fork.

Taylor encouraged him to throw as much spaghetti at the wall as he liked, which he did, hooking out strand after strand and hurling it from his fork on to the pristine walls and causing much hilarity with the crew.

Poppy caught sight of Mr B, looking furious in the background, but he managed to restrain himself from rushing on to set and demanding this abuse of his kitchen stop immediately. She had no doubt there would be no such restraint from him once filming was finished. She would have to make sure the kitchen was restored to its former spotless state and not just the bits that were beneath the scrutiny of the cameras.

Unfortunately, thanks to the amount of spaghetti that ended up either on the floor or being stuck to the wall, there was very little left in the pan. So when Charles finally proclaimed it to be perfect and served it up, it didn't matter how much he spread it out on the plate, it looked like the kind of portion you'd give someone on a very strict diet.

'Nouvelle cuisine,' he said confidently, arranging the pan-fried garlic and cherry tomatoes on top and standing back just as the timer buzzer went off.

Poppy hoped Alice would agree. She had always had a good appetite. She might not be too impressed with what looked like about eight strands of spaghetti.

Dave was struggling to get a good hero shot too.

Then it was Phil's turn. Poppy realised as she watched him combining his pre-measured ingredients of sugar, flour, milk, cocoa powder, olive oil, vanilla extract and a tiny pinch of salt from the various chopping boards and dishes into a glass mixing bowl that, despite her previous reservations, he had chosen wisely. He couldn't really go wrong. All he had to do was combine the ingredients thoroughly, tip them into the large mug he had requested and then pop them into the microwave. He set the timer for two minutes. Then he whisked out the mug with an oven glove and stuck a skewer through the middle. It came up clean.

The whole kitchen now smelled deliciously chocolatey. Alice loved chocolate cake. Poppy's mouth was watering too and Phil hadn't even broken into a sweat. He stood back with a flourish and glanced at the timer on the gleaming work surface beside him. 'Anyone else fancy a chocolate cake?' he asked, looking around the kitchen. 'I've got time to make another one, I reckon.'

Taylor clapped her hands and egged him on, even though they'd stopped filming. Poppy thought she heard someone whisper, 'Cocky git,' but she couldn't have said who it was.

Mr B appeared to be taking a close interest in Phil's session. Was he hoping he'd make a mistake? There clearly wasn't a lot of love lost between Phil and Mr B and she remembered the discussion she'd had with her crew the previous night at dinner.

At least the crew had heeded her warnings. If there had been any April Fool's pranks, they hadn't disrupted her schedule. It was now just before six thirty. They were perfectly on time. Other than Alice's false start this morning, the entire day had gone like clockwork.

* * *

'So here it is, Alice.' Taylor Stanton's warm voice filled the studio. 'The moment you've been waiting for. Our contenders have all been cooking their little hearts out in the kitchen in an attempt to curry favour – did I just say curry favour?' She laughed. 'I'm pretty sure we don't have any curries.'

'It would be very hard to cook a curry in ten minutes,' Alice agreed. She was now sitting at the table with its white tablecloth and a newly replenished vase of freesias.

Taylor was standing by her side. 'What we do have, though, is a selection of tempting titbits. And it just so happens that two of our lovely Dorset gentlemen have cooked savoury courses and two have cooked desserts.' There was a beat while she listened to her earpiece. 'We're going to start you off with the first of the savouries. And I've just been told Liam is ready to bring in his signature dish. Welcome back, Liam,' she added as the jib camera followed a nervous-looking Liam as he crossed the room towards Alice's table, holding his stainless-steel cloche aloft.

To heighten the suspense, the dishes were being served up beneath the traditional silver domes. When the show was aired, the viewer would find out what each signature dish was at exactly the same time as Alice did. There would then be cutaways to the cooking scenes on screen so viewers could see the cooking process.

'You look terrified,' Taylor remarked. 'Are you worried Alice won't like your signature dish?'

'I was more worried about dropping it before I got here,' Liam quipped back, as he leaned over and put his platter on the table in front of Alice. He lifted up the lid on the silver dish and stepped back. 'May I present my signature dish, salsa-simmered salmon.'

Alice took a forkful from the steaming plate – they must have microwaved that well. For a moment, there was silence as she tasted it. Then she swallowed and put down her fork. 'Absolutely delicious,' she said. 'Top marks.'

Liam looked delighted as he exited.

Alistair was next. Alice raised her eyebrows at the miniscule portion of spaghetti. The cooked cherry tomatoes had shifted about in transit, which didn't help, and they were now blobby red messes on the edge of the plate.

'It wasn't meant to be nouvelle cuisine,' he told her as his expressive black eyes met her blue ones apologetically. 'I can never tell when the darn stuff's cooked unless I throw it at the wall. I had to keep testing it.'

'You threw the rest of my spaghetti at the wall?' She regarded him seriously.

'I'm afraid I did. Yes.'

For a split second neither of them spoke and then Alice snorted with mirth and Alistair gave a great belly laugh and the two of them collapsed into fits of giggles. Alistair was slapping his thighs and howling in a way that was gorgeously uninhibited and Alice was crying with laugher.

It was so contagious that it set the entire crew off and Poppy thanked her lucky stars they weren't using handheld cameras now or they wouldn't have had any decent footage. Even the super-professional Dave's shoulders were shaking, she saw when she finally called cut.

Charles was the third contestant to present his dishes. He brought his pancakes in next, simply garnished with lemon and a sprinkling of sugar.

'This was one of my mother's favourites,' he said, as he revealed them.

'It was my mum's favourite too.' Alice blinked a few times and her eyes were shiny and Poppy knew she was remembering the same scenes from their childhood that she had recalled earlier.

Alice took a forkful and proclaimed the pancake to be beautifully light and fluffy. Charles was the third contestant to go away looking delighted and Poppy found herself thinking that if she achieved nothing else with this show she had made a few people happy and maybe boosted their confidence for future dating experiences. That was a claim that *Naked Attraction* made. It wasn't just about hitching up with someone, it was about getting a confidence boost. If you could swap banter on prime-time television you could definitely do it on a first date.

She wondered if Alice had made up her mind yet about the two finalists. It was a pretty close thing between these three. And Phil was yet to come with his chocolate cake finale. Taylor was announcing him now.

'Welcome back to Phil, the maître d'. This must be a bit of a busman's holiday for you, Phil,' she said as Phil walked straight-backed and beautifully poised towards Alice's table.

'I'm not sure whether that gives me an advantage or not,' he said. 'I guess that means I'm not so likely to drop it...' And then he tripped.

There was a collective gasp as the cloche wobbled and after that everything seemed to happen in slow motion. Alice half-rose from her chair, her hand over her mouth, her eyes wide.

Phil, even as he stumbled for a few more jerky, uncoordinated steps, somehow managed to keep the serving dish upright. At the very last minute, just as disaster seemed inevitable, he righted himself again. The room breathed a sigh of relief.

'Famous last words,' Phil said, as he stood upright once more. He still didn't look ruffled. He was smiling. 'I meant to do that,' he added.

And although his words were light-hearted and clearly not supposed to be taken at face value, Poppy wondered if he had. If the whole thing had been a brilliantly staged device. He was an actor after all and he'd just put himself firmly in the spotlight. No one would be forgetting Phil Grimshaw in a hurry and she had to admit it would be great drama for the show.

Alice was looking at him in admiration. From where she was sitting, it would have looked even more dramatic. 'I'm not used to having men throwing themselves at my feet,' she said, gazing up at him as he reached the table. It was as if she was suddenly seeing him for the first time and she clearly liked what she saw.

'But is Phil's cooking as impressive as his reflexes?' Taylor

Stanton joked as Phil presented his dish, and Poppy had a feeling that she too suspected Phil of some sleight-of-hand trickery.

'It certainly smells heavenly,' Alice announced as she took a forkful of the dark sponge from the top of the mug. 'I love chocolate cake. Nice presentation too.'

She put the sponge into her mouth and chewed, her eyes expectant.

There was a beat. Poppy was just preparing to call cut after the final reaction shot when Alice's countenance changed completely. Her face morphed into an expression of revulsion and she gagged. Her hand was over her mouth again, but it wasn't quite enough to hide the fact that she was spitting out cake. Crumbs of it flew out between her fingers, speckling the tablecloth and landing on Phil, who was now standing opposite her, looking shell-shocked.

'Cut,' Poppy yelled in horror. Shit, what the hell had just happened?

17

Poppy and Dave abandoned the gallery and were in the studio in seconds. Even from the door, Poppy could see there was nothing staged about Phil's shock this time. He looked almost as horrified as Alice. To his credit, he seemed much more concerned about her than the fact she had just spat a mouthful of his carefully created signature dish back at him.

'Are you OK?' He was now hunkered down by the table, looking at Alice with great concern.

'I think she's OK, she's not choking.' Taylor was already pouring out a glass of water and offering it to Alice.

She took several gulps. 'I'm so sorry. But what the hell was in that?'

'Chocolate cake ingredients,' Phil said. 'Sugar, cocoa power, the usual stuff. No nuts. Nothing like that. You're not allergic to anything, are you?'

'No, I'm not. It was the taste... it's foul... ugh.'

Some of the camera ops had stepped closer and Kate was frowning. Everyone was staring at the white mug with its oh-so chocolatey concoction peeking over the top. It had risen well and looked anything but foul. What on earth was going on?

As Poppy and Dave approached and before anyone could stop him, Phil stuck his fingers into the mug, pulled off a small piece of cake and put it in his mouth. He didn't spit it out, but he did screw up his face.

'It's salty,' he said. 'Some bastard must have swapped the sugar for salt.' His face was thunderous.

Poppy looked around for Corinna, who was coming over to the table with both her hands spread out in a question which her face echoed. Could it have been another contestant? Poppy didn't want to even think that. Surely not – even as an April Fool. But what other reason could there be for sabotaging Phil's signature dish? It wasn't as if there was big prize money at stake – this wasn't *Who Wants to be a Millionaire*. Besides, whoever had done this must have known it would come out. Unless they'd miscalculated – maybe they hadn't bargained on how much difference a little bit of salt would make. Maybe they'd presumed the dish would be spoiled but not inedible.

'I'm really sorry,' Alice said. 'I shouldn't have spat it out. It was such a shock.'

'It would be,' Dave said, anger in his words, 'if you were expecting sugar and you got bloody salt.' He looked almost as furious as Phil. What was that about?

Dave met Poppy's eyes fleetingly. He didn't like Phil, that had been plain from the outset, but surely he wouldn't do something like this. Poppy felt ashamed for thinking it, even for a second. Of course he wouldn't. Tricks did get played, but this was a bit more than a trick aimed at Phil. It rebounded on the whole crew in time and money.

'We didn't do the prep,' Corinna was saying.

'Yes, I know. Mr B took charge.' Poppy suddenly remembered Mr B's insistence that they use his staff.

Horrified, she glanced at Phil, who had clearly cottoned on to what was happening. There was nothing composed about him now, he looked thoroughly rattled.

'So, let me get this straight. Mr B prepared the ingredients for my signature dish?'

'Yes. He was adamant that his kitchen staff do it. Something about needing a food hygiene certificate.' Too late, Poppy realised why the chef had been so determined to help.

Phil didn't speak, he was obviously struggling to contain his emotions. Then he lost the battle. Without another word, he stomped across the studio, his shoulders set and rigid, and disappeared through the far door beside the stage.

'I wouldn't want to be in Mr B's shoes when he catches him,' Mike said, reaching into his pocket and producing a packet of two fruit biscuits which the hotel left with the tea-making things in the rooms. He opened them and offered one to Alice. 'Better than the taste of salt.'

'Thanks,' she said, taking it.

Mike nibbled absent-mindedly at the other one. 'I guess we'll need to make another cake before we go again.'

'At least it won't take long,' Dave said.

'Could someone please track down Phil?' Poppy said, gathering herself. 'The last thing we want is him coming back with a black eye.'

'I'd put my money on Mr B having the black eye,' Corinna replied, and there were a few sniggers. She glanced at Poppy apologetically. 'I'll go.'

'Thanks,' Poppy said. Thank God they were using so many cameras. With luck they would get away with just reshooting the last bit of action. She wanted to keep in Phil's 'almost trip'. Up until the point where Alice had screwed up her face, everything had been pretty much perfect.

She bent forward to speak to Alice, who still looked upset. She must have felt as though the trick had been aimed at her personally.

'None of this is your fault. Just someone playing silly buggers. We'll reshoot it – it's not a problem.'

'I'm fine. Don't worry. We'll laugh about it one day,' she said, flicking a strand of blonde hair behind her ear.

Dave moved closer to the table and he patted Alice's shoulder reassuringly. 'You're doing great, girl.'

Poppy spotted Phil coming back into the studio just as Corinna was about to exit it. To her relief, he didn't look as though he'd been fighting. But then he hadn't been gone very long.

'Did you find Mr B?' she asked.

'Nope. He's gone to ground like the rat he is.' He paused to wipe sweat from his forehead. It was the first time she'd seen him look really ruffled since they'd met. It was actually refreshing to see him disconcerted. He was human, after all, and not that polished act he put on, which seemed to fall into one of two categories: maître d' or sex god.

He put his hands in his pockets and looked at the ground and then back up into her eyes. 'I'm truly sorry for holding things up. It's a very long story, but Mr B and I have an ongoing feud.' He rubbed his neck distractedly. 'Feud's too strong a word, but – well, the bottom line is that I think this was a pop at me. To be honest, it's probably my fault. It was payback for something I did to him last year.'

Everyone was staring at him. There were a few raised eyebrows and some rueful grins, but no one chuckled. Practical jokes were cool, everyone was up for a practical joke, but deliberately sabotaging filming and mucking up the schedule – that was a cardinal sin. Phil's cheeks had flushed a dull red. He would know it too.

Poppy bit back the scathing retort she'd have liked to make. At least he'd had the decency to take the blame and apologise. She admired him for that. 'Let's put it behind us and get on.'

Phil clasped his hands in front of him. 'How can I put it right? Should I go and make another cake?'

'That would be a good start.'

* * *

Take two went like clockwork. The cloche was lifted from the chocolate mug cake. Alice proclaimed it to be her favourite and complimented Phil on the presentation. She took a forkful of cake and this time her expression was one of pleasure. If anything, she looked even more delighted than she'd have been in the first place.

After she'd called cut, Poppy remarked on this to Dave, who was sitting beside her in the gallery.

'That'll be the relief of it having sugar in it this time!' he retorted.

'Yes,' she said, slightly aback by his tone. 'Corinna got the ingredients ready. I told her to taste everything personally. No chance of a mistake then.'

There was a little silence. Dave picked up a clipboard and chewed the end of a pen. Poppy could feel his gaze.

'What?' she said.

'You thought it was me, didn't you?'

She knew there was no point in denying it. He had always been as observant as hell. She dropped her gaze. 'It crossed my mind just for a second. Then I came to my senses.' She could feel her face heating up in the small space. 'I'm sorry. I know you wouldn't do anything like that.'

A beat. 'Apology accepted.' He drum-rolled his fingers on the edge of the clipboard. He only ever did that when he was pissed off. 'This is a big deal for you. On all sorts of levels. I know you're stressed. But I just want to make it clear that I would never pull a stunt like that.'

'I know.' She felt terrible now.

For a moment, they sat in a silence that was only slightly less awkward than it had been before. Then they both spoke at once.

'I hope she's OK.'

'Did anyone track down Mr B...?'

She gestured for him to go first and he put the clipboard down. 'To answer your question. The consensus seemed to be that Mr B had gone home. But he wasn't supposed to be in tonight anyway. Tonight's dinner was prepped yesterday and his staff will presumably serve that up.'

'Yes. But he'll have to come back at some point. With a bit of luck, they'll keep their differences out of my studio. I think they will. Phil seemed embarrassed.'

'So he should.' His eyes darkened. 'Alice bore the brunt of that trick, whether it was aimed at her or not, and I'm not entirely taken in by that Amazonian-princess super-cool front she puts on.' He raised his eyebrows. 'She's a lot more insecure than she looks. Or am I barking up the wrong tree?'

'You're not. No.' He was spot on. But she was surprised he'd seen it. Not many people saw through Alice's beautiful armour.

'Bloody imbeciles.' He was drum-rolling his fingers again and Poppy thought suddenly, *Oh God, that's what it is. He really likes her and he's pissed off that the salt trick upset her.*

A flashback of them dancing at Rose's party shot into her head. She remembered their heads close together, that intimate way they'd leaned in, laughing together. She had registered it then in her half-inebriated state, but she hadn't thought about it since.

It also explained Dave's antagonism towards Phil. He didn't like the maître d' because he saw him as a rival. Half a dozen jigsaw pieces slotted into place and suddenly his attitude made sense.

'I don't suppose the maître d' will get into the final now,' Dave said, and Poppy knew she wasn't imagining that flash of satisfaction. 'Not after today's little performance. I know it wasn't his fault, but that must have left a bad taste in her mouth. Literally!'

Poppy wasn't so sure. Alice had a strong sense of justice and she might feel more obliged to put Phil through now she knew he'd been the victim of a sabotage attempt. It probably wasn't the best moment to tell Dave this, though. He clearly thought his rival was out of the way.

'Talking of dinner,' she said, suddenly desperate to move on, 'we'd better head over to the restaurant. While they've still got something left.'

* * *

The restaurant was full by the time they got there, but Alice had saved her a place on a long table by the window overlooking the terrace that was reserved for film crew, and Alice was as far away as possible from the contenders' table to help make sure they didn't mix. Corinna, Mike, Lenny and Si were already seated. There wasn't room for Dave. 'It's fine,' he said, as he headed off to find a chair somewhere else.

Poppy was relieved. She knew he hadn't been guilt-tripping her earlier – he'd just been justifiably pissed off she'd thought even for a second he might have pulled the salt stunt. But she could do with avoiding him for a bit. She could really have done with skipping dinner altogether and sneaking off to her room and lying down in the dark, she was exhausted, but she wanted to make sure Alice was OK.

She sat down beside her. 'Hey. Thanks for saving me a seat. We can have a catch up.'

Fat chance of that. It was way too noisy for a conversation. There was a fair amount of banter about the salted-cake fiasco going on and Poppy caught the occasional snatch of conversation about it on other tables too. Everyone seemed to be of the opinion that it was Mr B who was responsible, partly because he had disappeared.

Tonight's menu choice was salted fish served with sugar snap peas.

'Watch the food, mate,' Poppy heard a camera op on the table next door say. 'It'll probably turn out to be sugared fish and salt snap peas.'

There was a burst of laughter.

'It's probably safer to go for the vegetarian lasagne,' said Mike, who had obviously heard the exchange.

'What about the bread and butter pudding?' Si asked. 'I've never understood how bread and butter can go in a pudding anyway. Isn't that supposed to be a savoury thing?'

Mike looked at him with disdain. 'You can put marmite on it. Or you can put jam on it. It's either/or. Don't you kids know anything, these days?'

Si scrunched up a paper napkin and threw it at him.

'Bread and butter pudding. Is that for dessert?' Corinna asked. 'That's my all-time favourite. My mum does the best one in the world.' She sniffed the air expectantly. 'I really hope we're getting that.'

Poppy let the banter wash over her, even though a part of her wished they'd stop talking about it. As far as she was concerned, the sooner they put it behind them the better. At least Alice seemed to be taking it in her stride.

* * *

They were halfway through the meal, which turned out to be gorgeous, even though Poppy had lost her appetite a bit, when she saw Clara heading purposefully towards their table. Clara hadn't been around for the salted-cake fiasco. She'd been out at a meeting.

She came to a halt by Poppy's chair. 'I've just heard about what happened earlier. I wanted to catch up with you and apologise.'

'It's fine, there's no harm done,' Poppy said, as she met the manager's concerned eyes. 'It's not your fault.'

'But you were obviously held up.' Clara's hands were clasped in front of her. 'That costs money.'

'We weren't held up for long.'

'So was it the chef who sabotaged the cake?' Mike asked. He never minced his words and his clear voice carried, which resulted in the room hushing as several people waited for Clara's reply.

'I can't be completely sure.' Her eyes told a different story. 'But someone at the Bluebell Cliff is responsible, which makes me responsible. I can only apologise. Could I offer you a complimentary bottle of wine? Per table, I mean.'

'That's not necess—' Poppy began, but her words were drowned out by a cheer, as by now half of the restaurant had tuned in and were listening. She met Clara's gaze. 'Thank you,' she mouthed.

She'd been going to add that maybe they should have the

complimentary wine on the last night – she didn't want hungover crew – but she supposed a bottle of wine between six people, which was how most of the tables were set up, couldn't do much harm. They were all adults.

* * *

At half past nine, when everyone was on coffee, she leaned across to Alice. 'Shall we go somewhere a bit quieter for a catch-up?'

Alice picked up her cup and saucer and stood up and the two of them excused themselves.

A few moments later, they were out on the terrace, which was quieter than the restaurant, although a cluster of people who'd come out for a vape were chatting and laughing at a table. A mix of synthetic sweetness wafted on the faint breeze. Poppy chose a table out of earshot of them and she and Alice sat down. No one would disturb them out here. They'd assume they were talking shop.

It was dark, but a moon path stretched out across a ruffled sea. Stars were beginning to pinprick the navy sky above and the sea air was refreshing after the stuffy heat of the restaurant. It was surprisingly warm.

Poppy noticed all the tables had flickering tea-light candles inside glass jars. That was a nice touch. Who changed all that lot? When she looked at one properly, she realised it was electronic.

'I just wanted to make sure you were OK?' she said, leaning across to touch Alice's hand.

'Of course I am. Practical jokes aside, I've loved today.' She caught hold of Poppy's fingers, her eyes bright in the glow of the electronic candle. 'I was more worried about ruining the filming than anything else. Thank you so much for asking me to be part of it.'

'You haven't ruined anything. And it's me who should be thanking you. You've been brilliant. I'm so glad you're enjoying it. It comes across on camera. You're an absolute natural. Even Dave mentioned it.'

'Did he?' Alice looked pleased. 'He's lovely, isn't he?'

'Yes.' Poppy wondered whether now was the moment to mention that she was pretty sure Dave had a thing for her sister. No, it probably wasn't. It might muddy the waters when it came to Alice's choice of men. Oh, the irony that Alice might end up having a relationship not with one of her hand-picked suitors but the cameraman who was filming them. Breaking all her own rules and with a quick peek over her shoulder to check no one was in earshot, she said quietly, 'So, have you made up your mind then about the two finalists? Do you know who you're going to pick?'

'Poppy Allen, you expressly told me to keep that information to myself.' Alice's eyes danced with amusement. 'Do you really want to know?'

Poppy struggled with herself. 'No, I suppose I don't. You're right. Don't tell me.'

'OK, I won't.' Alice yawned. 'I'll tell you one thing I do know though, angel.'

'What's that?' Poppy yawned too. It was catching.

'Your dad would be so proud of you.'

Poppy stilled. 'Thank you, honey. I wish he was around to see what I'm doing. He'd have loved today. Your mum would be really proud too. Seeing her little girl all grown up and starring in a TV programme.'

Before Alice could reply, a flicker of movement high up in the sky above the sea caught both women's attention. A shooting star had just flared its incandescent trail through the dark. It had been so quick that Poppy wasn't sure if she'd imagined it. But she could feel goosebumps suddenly on her arms.

'Hey, did you just see that?' Alice asked, reaching over and catching her fingers.

Poppy felt her throat close. 'I did. It was really there, wasn't it?'

'It really was.' Alice's eyes were wide with wonder and for a moment Poppy was thrown back to the past – she and Alice sitting in the cosy darkness of her bedroom holding back her My Little Pony curtains so that they could look out at the stars. Alice had told her once that when someone died they never went completely away, they became a star – high up in the sky, looking down at their loved ones. 'They're up there, keeping an eye on us.' Alice's voice came out cracked with emotion. 'Your dad... and my mum. They're probably together now, raising a glass to the pair of us.'

Poppy smiled. 'Dad's will have IPA in it.'

'Mum's will be a G&T, complete with ice and a slice.'

They hugged and Poppy knew they were both a bit teary. A mixture of exhaustion and the shooting star, which had been such perfect timing, on so many levels. A sign from their gone-but-never-forgotten parents, if not the universe itself, that all was exactly as it should be.

'We should get to bed,' Poppy said. 'It's getting cold.' They stood up in unison and walked back across the terrace into the hotel.

It was quiet as they climbed up the beautiful ornate staircase that led to the first-floor bedrooms. They hugged again outside Poppy's room, which they got to first.

'Sweet dreams, Alice,' Poppy said softly as they drew apart.

'Sweet dreams, angel.'

18

The next day started badly because one of the external camera assistants phoned in to say she had a bad migraine and might not make it in. Poppy told Dave, who said they would manage without her. Then they had a problem with one of the lighting rigs, which turned out to be down to a fuse. Lenny sorted that out himself. Then, one of the young sound technician assistants had a call to say she was needed urgently at home because her mother had just been involved in a car accident.

'Don't worry,' Poppy told her, looking at her anxious white face, 'I'll get someone to run you to the hospital. You've had a shock, you shouldn't drive.'

All of this happened before breakfast. By the time Poppy walked into the restaurant ten minutes before it was actually open, she was already feeling frazzled.

Corinna beckoned to her from a table close to the 'staff only' door, where she was sitting with Si and Dave.

'Please don't give me any more bad news,' Poppy said when she reached them. 'Tell me something nice.'

'It's not exactly bad news,' Corinna replied, running a hand through her slightly dishevelled hair in a futile attempt to flatten it down.

'What do you mean, not exactly?' Poppy pulled out a chair.

'There's been something kicking off in the kitchen,' Si filled her in. 'Pots and pans being thrown about too, by the sound of it. What my grandad would call "a right old barney".'

'Kitchens are stressful places,' Poppy said.

'Yes, but—' Corinna put a finger to her lips. 'Hang on – they're shouting again. We think it's Phil and Mr B.'

The door was closed, but they were right. There were raised voices. And it did sound like Phil's deep voice and Mr B's slightly higher one.

'It was a low stunt to pull – even for you. I wouldn't care, but it wasn't just me you pissed off. You impacted on the whole crew. It was bloody unprofessional. You do realise that's disciplinary material. It reflects badly on the whole hotel.'

'I've told you. I wasn't here. I'm not responsible for zounderkites.'

'What's a zounderkite?' Corinna mouthed.

Everyone on the table shrugged.

'I'll give you bloody zounderkites – this was sabotage and you know it, you bastard.'

There was the crash of metal against worktop. As though someone had slammed something down hard. Then another crash before the door flew open and Mr B, moving considerably faster than Poppy had ever seen him move before, flew out into the restaurant in his chef whites.

'Greetings,' he said, looking slightly startled to see a table of people on the other side of the door but not lingering to chat. He darted behind the table next to theirs to avoid Phil, who was in hot pursuit and carrying a heavy-looking metallic-grey frying pan raised high above his head like a weapon.

Phil stopped short too when he saw Poppy and Corinna. He lowered the frying pan and held it awkwardly in front of his chest. From weapon to shield. It flashed as it caught the sunlight flooding through the windows. 'Good morning, ladies.'

'Morning,' Poppy said, glaring at him. 'Shouldn't you be in make-up?'

'I'm just on my way. I was just, er...' He put down the frying pan and threw one last furious glance at Mr B, who stayed where he was with the table in between them, blinking and looking mightily relieved at this turn of events.

Nothing else was said. Phil disappeared. Mr B picked up the frying pan, polished it with the tea towel he had in his hand and went back into the kitchen.

Poppy met Corinna's eyes and suddenly they were both snorting with laughter.

'You couldn't make it up,' Dave said, glancing around the restaurant, which had started to fill up with yawning crew members. Poppy wondered if he was looking for Alice. Perhaps he was hoping she'd witnessed that little incident and would now definitely kick Phil out of the final. She gave herself a mental shake. She was probably overthinking things, having finally cottoned on to what was going on.

She glanced across at Dave. 'Hi. Sleep well?'

He nodded slowly, but he didn't seem in the mood to talk. When she'd thought about them doing this project together, she had envisioned him being by her side. She'd imagined them talking about the funny bits and pieces that happened during the day. Laughing about things that inevitably went wrong. She'd imagined them discussing shots that had worked, shots that hadn't – just as they usually did when they worked with each other.

But it wasn't panning out like that and she felt a wash of

disappointment. Maybe she'd expected too much. Or maybe he was still sore because she'd suspected him of having something to do with the salt. God, she must have been stressed to have thought that.

Mike arrived at their table and she got sidetracked telling him about the young sound technician who'd gone to hospital.

'We can manage without her. No worries. Everything should be set up pretty much as we need it from yesterday.' More quietly, he asked, 'You all set for today?' It was the closest the brusque, straight-talking sound man would ever get to asking if she was OK. But she could see the kindness in his eyes.

'All is good, thanks, Mike.'

* * *

The walk-throughs and rehearsals went smoothly. Alice was on good form. She and Taylor were chatting about an event Alice was involved in at Chelsea, which was where Taylor lived. Charles looked cheerful. Phil looked brooding and serious again, but it was all going on behind those dark eyes. Alistair looked nervous and Liam was flirting with Corinna.

At 10 a.m. Poppy sat beside Dave in the gallery and she hoped for his sake that Phil didn't make it through to the final.

'You ready for the off?' she said, adjusting her headset.

'Ready when you are, boss.' He said something to his lead camera and glanced back at her.

'Three, two, one... action.'

* * *

'Right then, Alice my darling. It's *Date for a Day* Decision Time. Which two contestants are you sending home and which two will be in your final? Which two impressed you the most with their culinary masterpieces and which two were dinner disappointments?' Taylor clapped her hands. She looked as excited as if she'd just been told she'd won the lottery and her enthusiasm was infectious.

Alice's eyes shone. 'I would like to say that none of them were dinner disappointments. I loved everything they cooked for me. So this is really hard.' Her gaze swept from contestant to contestant and the cameras zoomed in on the men's faces one by one.

Liam looked hopeful. Alistair's expression was inscrutable. He'd be a formidable adversary in court. Charles studied his fingers and Phil looked a little resigned.

Taylor looked at Alice. 'So, in no particular order, who's the first Dorset gentleman who'll be going through to your final, Alice? Who will you be asking to serenade you with their party piece?'

'The first man who I'm putting through to the final is Alistair,' Alice said in her clear confident voice.

The human rights lawyer nodded and the smallest smile played over his mouth as camera two zoomed in on his face. He had just the right amount of pleasure and humility, Poppy thought, pleased. *Good choice, sis.* She sent out a silent message of approval.

'So, I'm guessing Alistair's nouvelle-cuisine portion of spaghetti whetted your appetite for more?' Taylor joked.

'Indeed it did. I've always been a fan of Italian food.'

'Congratulations, Alistair.' A beat. 'So tell us the name of your other finalist, Alice.'

Alice's gaze swept over the remaining three contenders, lingering the longest on Liam the lifeguard, who smiled at her before lowering his eyes.

'My other finalist,' Alice said, 'is... Phil. I've always been a fan of chocolate cake too.'

Phil looked stunned as the camera zoomed in on his face. Another genuine reaction, Poppy observed.

All four contestants were now clapping politely as the two finalists' red hearts flashed and the other two dimmed to nothing.

'And cut,' Poppy said, not sure whether she was pleased or disappointed that Alice had gone for Phil. She glanced at Dave to try and gauge his reaction. Would he be pissed off?

'There we are then,' was all he said. 'Just the party pieces to go. Are either of them using the amphitheatre?'

'Alistair wants to read a sonnet – it could be inside or out, but the amphitheatre would be good. It's great weather for it.'

'And the other finalist?' He sounded as though he couldn't bear to say Phil's name.

'Phil's using the grand piano. He's playing "Scarborough Fair".'

'Maybe we should get someone to stand guard over it then,' Dave said idly. 'Just in case Mr B decides to dot the keys with superglue.'

Poppy looked at him in horror and his mouth quirked.

'Just kidding, boss.' He leaned across to her and his face softened. 'Don't look so worried. It's going well.'

'It is,' she said. 'I guess I'm a bit on edge. After yesterday. I haven't quite got my sense of humour back.'

'Not altogether surprising.' He made some more notes on his clipboard. 'It would be handy – when we start filming the rest of the series – to get a vision mixer in here. Save us being jack of all trades.'

'Don't you mean *if* they approve the rest of the series.'

He gestured towards the monitors. 'It looks pretty damn good from where I'm sitting. They'd be mad not to.'

'We both know that's no guarantee.'

'Hey, think positive.' He smiled. 'Which party piece do you want to do first? Outside or in?'

'Let's do the amphitheatre at one o'clock because I think that might be the most complicated – excluding any possible piano tampering, that is. Then we can do the piano piece at two o'clock.'

'Sounds good. Amphitheatre on location – same team as the kitchen shoot.'

'We'd better get cracking on the rehearsals.'

* * *

'That was a surprise,' Poppy said to Alice when they caught up at lunchtime in the catering-van queue. They both got chorizo and salad paninis and took them to the same table they'd sat at last night on the terrace.

It was a cool blue day but with a definite hint of spring under-laying the chill and there were flowers growing in the rose beds, clusters of violet, sunshine yellow and pink, their sweet scents drifting on the air. Poppy wondered if the bluebells were out yet. She would go and see when she got a spare second. It seemed like a hundred years ago that she and Dave had strolled down to the copse.

'I thought you were going to pick Liam,' Poppy added as she and Alice sat down.

'Instead of Phil. Yes, I know, it was a close call. I almost did, but I didn't want to be put off Phil because of what happened.'

'What they didn't realise was that if they tried to push you one way, you'd go the exact opposite,' Poppy said.

'Got it in one,' Alice stuck her chin out. 'I don't like being manipulated. So their little trick backfired. Was it the chef who swapped the sugar for salt?'

'I think it might have been.' Poppy told her about the frying pan incident at breakfast and Alice's eyebrows shot up in disbelief. 'So there is a hot-blooded man beneath all that brooding, controlled stuff. How interesting.'

It was hard to tell from her expression whether she approved or disapproved. Poppy was about to ask when Alice went on thoughtfully.

'Phil reminds me of someone. He has from the moment I saw him.'

'Is it Aidan Turner?'

'No. Although I can see what you mean. No, it's someone closer to home. He reminds me of your ex. Stephen Knight – looks-wise, I mean. He had that whole brooding and mysterious thing going on too. Well, he did before he let himself go, didn't he?'

'Yes.' Poppy's heart felt as if it had stopped beating. 'I guess he reminds me a bit of him too,' she acknowledged, and she wondered suddenly if that was why she'd been drawn to Phil all along. 'Although definitely not in personality. For a start, Phil put his hands up and apologised for the cake incident.'

'That's true. Your Stephen wasn't big on apologies. Or humility.'

'Or being accountable for his actions.' She met her stepsister's steady gaze. 'When this is done and dusted – and you are hopefully sorted out date-wise – I am going to dip my toe back in the water too.'

'Are you now? Anyone I know?' She arched her eyebrows.

'Well, it certainly wouldn't be Phil Grimshaw, if that's what you were thinking. I'm not sure I'm up for the dark and brooding type any more.' Not entirely sure that was true either, Poppy crossed her fingers in her lap. Before either of them could say anything else, Poppy was diverted by a phone call. It was the young sound technician to say that her mother wasn't as badly hurt as they'd originally thought but that she was going to stay with her, if that was OK.

'You stay as long as you need to,' Poppy told her, glancing at Mike, who was sitting at a neighbouring table tucking into what looked like an all-day breakfast. 'We're fine.'

She'd also noticed a phone message on her phone from her mother that gave her a bit of a start.

Hope all is going well with the filming. Kenny and I saw God last night.

Poppy showed Alice her phone. 'This just came through from Mum. Any idea what she's talking about?'

'She's still got the predictive text on by the look of it. I got one from her a few days ago asking if I knew of any slimming classes. When I phoned to ask her why she was going on a diet, she told me she meant to put swimming, but her phone had changed it. She probably doesn't know how to turn the predictive text off.'

'Or she's left it on because she finds it amusing.' Poppy looked back at the text. 'I wouldn't put it past her. That's assuming she hasn't decided to give the church another chance. Mind you, I didn't know she wanted to go swimming either. She's not exactly a fan of water.'

'I thought that too. But when I asked her, she said that's exactly why she wants to go now. She said there were so many things she hadn't done in her life – learning to swim being one of them – and she wanted to put that right.'

'Did she? Wow, well good on her. Learning to play the piano and learning to swim. No wonder she doesn't have time to read any more.'

'At least she's keeping busy. And she did sound happy.'

'That's the main thing.' Poppy decided to ring her mother at the end of today's filming and find out what was going on. She also wanted to ask her if she'd ever heard of the word 'zounderkite' which, according to her online dictionary, was a Victorian word for 'idiot'. Mum was an expert on the origin of words. She may have decided to give up reading but that didn't mean she didn't still love the language. Words were a massive part of her world – they always had been – and besides, it was high time they had a proper catch-up.

19

The sonnet Alistair had chosen to read was one he said he had written himself, especially for Alice. He requested that he read a different sonnet at rehearsal because he felt it would lessen the impact if Alice heard his creation twice.

Phil, on the other hand, had been happy to play 'Scarborough Fair' at the rehearsal. He'd said he needed the practice.

Alistair was hot favourite to win. Most of her crew thought that Alice had only put Phil through as a gesture because he was the underdog and, while Poppy knew it was slightly more complicated than this, she was pretty sure that Phil thought this too. Straight after the rehearsals, during which he'd limped through a not very good rendition of 'Scarborough Fair', he had sought her out.

'Thank you for giving me the opportunity to be here,' he'd said. 'And I'm sorry again about the incident yesterday.'

'I appreciate your apology,' she'd told him. Then she'd had to escape, because no matter what she had said to Alice at lunchtime she couldn't be around Phil for long without feeling that same supercharged chemistry she'd felt when she'd first met

Stephen. Maybe Phil was her type, after all – she really couldn't make up her mind.

Poppy had decided to shoot Alistair's amphitheatre party piece 'on location' in the same way as they had shot the cooking of the signature dishes with just a skeleton crew and handheld cameras. This meant the only people present were Poppy, Dave, Mike and two other camera ops. And, of course, Taylor and Alice, who sat side by side in the raised stone seats with the backdrop of the sea in the distance when a cameraman panned out behind them.

Alistair looked very impressive, standing still and tall in front of a wooden podium which they had borrowed from the Bluebell Cliff. His face was serious as he launched into his sonnet, which began with the words, 'I could compare thee to a summer's day...

But that's been done, so let's not head that way...'

It went on in a similar vein, corny but powerful. It was a mixture of poignancy and humour and it made both Alice and Taylor look at him with affection, and Poppy thought, *no wonder he only wanted to do it once.* If anyone had picked at the rhythm or looked at the structure too closely, it would probably have fallen apart.

After he'd finished, Alistair gave a little bow and Alice applauded with great enthusiasm. Poppy could see her sister had really warmed to this man, who was such a mix of passion and focus but whose sense of humour was clearly in great working order too. She didn't think there was much that Phil could do to pull this out of the bag now. No matter how wonderful his rendition of 'Scarborough Fair' was, and it hadn't been all that great in the rehearsal, she didn't think he'd be able to compete with Alistair Long.

The lawyer and her sister were undoubtedly well matched. Both of them passionate about their jobs, totally focused, and yet able to have fun too. Alistair would be good for Alice. She pictured him at curry nights, making Kenny laugh and charming her mother and having serious conversations with Micky about law. Alistair would fit right into the family. Having Phil there could be awkward.

* * *

Back in the studio once more at the Bluebell Cliff, Dave and Poppy were in the gallery as they got ready to film Phil on the piano. This time, with the benefit of a full studio at their disposal, Alice and Taylor would be filmed standing up alongside him.

Phil had dressed up for the performance by adding a black bow tie to his white dress shirt. He looked every inch the concert pianist – even if he didn't play like one.

'Before I begin,' he said, 'I'd just like to say that I'm not really a pianist. I dabble a bit, but I have learned this one song in order to play it here today. And it's called, "Her Name is Alice".'

'I thought he was playing "Scarborough Fair",' Dave hissed from his place beside Poppy in the gallery.

'So did I.' Poppy was more intrigued than annoyed.

Neither of them spoke as Phil sat down at the piano and bowed his head slightly over the keys. He played a cut-down version of the classic piano piece. It wasn't quite note perfect. Clearly, he hadn't lied about not being a pianist, but if anything it was more beautiful for being flawed.

When he stopped playing and turned from the piano stool towards Alice, and camera one zoomed in for her reaction, both Dave and Poppy could see that she had tears in her eyes. Even the hard-headed professional, Taylor Stanton, who must have seen most things, looked moved. They both clapped for a long time.

'Give me strength,' Dave said, when Poppy had finally called cut. 'How many more tricks has that bloody waiter got up his sleeve?'

'I don't think he's going to need any more, Dave, is he?' Poppy pushed her uneasiness aside. This was Alice's call, not hers.

'Sadly, I think you might be right.' He didn't look at her. He was busy making notes, but when he did turn back, his eyes were darker than usual.

'Do you need a bit longer, Dave, or shall we go straight on to the reveal of the winner?'

'Let's get it over with.'

* * *

'Three, two, one... action.'

'OK then, Alice my darling. This is it. It's *Date for a Day* Decision Time. Our two finalists have done everything they can to impress you and the only thing left to do is to pick your winner.' Taylor looked at Alice. 'I just need one thing from you now. I need the name of the man you would like to accompany you tomorrow on your Date for a Day.'

Camera one focused in on Alice's face as her gaze flicked from Phil to Alistair and back again. There was a pause that couldn't have been more perfect if they'd asked Alice to time it. Everyone in the studio was silent as the sense of expectation rose.

Alice took a deep breath and with one more lingering look at each of the two finalists, she said. 'The name of the man I'd like to accompany me tomorrow on my Date for a Day is... Phil.'

Alistair clapped cheerfully like the good sport he was. Phil looked delighted. Taylor was clapping too, enthusiastically. All that was left was for Phil to walk across to Alice and take her hand and Poppy would have her wrap.

Poppy didn't dare look at Dave as Phil took Alice's hand in his and then planted a kiss on her upturned palm.

Her sister was clearly enamoured and Poppy was hugely relieved that she hadn't given Alice an inkling of how she herself felt about the maître d' when they'd chatted. She could feel the chemistry sparking between Alice and Phil even via the monitor and she was really pleased for them.

There had been a few surprises along the way – more than even she had envisaged – but, overall, Poppy knew, with that instinct that had taken her years to develop, that the pilot had been a success. The rushes so far had been brilliant. It was the best it could possibly be. The date itself couldn't fail to make good television, set as it was against the beauty of the Dorset coastline, but that would only take up a tiny part of the fifty-minute pilot. The hardest part was done. 'Cut,' she said, 'we have a wrap,' and the studio cameras stopped rolling.

For a few moments, there was silence in the gallery. Then Dave reached across and touched her shoulder.

'Well done, boss. I think that went pretty well.' Whatever he thought or felt, he was back in professional mode.

'Me too.'

He looked at her carefully. 'Are you OK? Are you happy with that outcome?'

'Of course. I am. Why wouldn't I be? I'm thrilled for her. And it's made a super pilot. We've got some fabulous sequences.' She was aware she was gabbling, but she couldn't seem to stop. 'We shouldn't have too much to reshoot from yesterday. I just need to check and see if we have any gaps.' She broke off.

Dave was looking at her with that annoying knowing expression he had, which meant he was taking everything she said with a pinch of salt. *Salt being the operative word*, Poppy thought as she bit her lip and turned back to her clipboard of notes. How was it that he saw through her so easily? She supposed that was what good friends did.

There was a light tap on the door of the OB. Poppy got up as it opened and Alice popped her head around the gap. 'Am I interrupting?'

'No. Come in.' Poppy was glad of the interruption. She couldn't bring herself to look at Dave for some reason.

Alice jumped up lightly into the truck, bending her head to avoid being knocked out. She looked starry-eyed. 'I just wanted to say thank you. To you too, Dave.' She glanced at the director of photography. 'I've had the best time.'

'Despite the hiccups,' he said.

'Despite the hiccups.' She leaned across to where he was sitting and, in typical impulsive-Alice fashion, planted a kiss on his cheek. 'Thank you.'

'Better not let your new bloke see you kissing another man,' he said, looking pleased, nonetheless.

'I won't tell him if you don't.' Her laugh pealed out, lightening the atmosphere in the truck.

Poppy couldn't help smiling too. It was brilliant seeing Alice so happy. 'Are you looking forward to your date?' she asked.

'I really am.' Alice fidgeted. 'Do you fancy a walk?' She was clearly itching to discuss something.

'Did you want to get changed first?' Poppy eyed the beautiful blue dress and her sister's shoes.

'Oh, I don't mean far. Just on site. We could go and check out those bluebell woods you mentioned.'

Suddenly there was nothing Poppy wanted to do more. She grabbed her jacket from the back of her chair. 'Catch you in a bit, Dave.'

'Sure.' He turned slightly so she couldn't see his face, but she had a feeling he was glad she and Alice were disappearing. If he did like Alice as much as Poppy suspected he did, it must be quite galling knowing that he would be filming her cavorting with another man for most of the following day.

* * *

A few minutes later, Poppy and Alice were on the path at the entrance to the bluebell woods. The same scent of mustiness that she remembered greeted her as they stepped beneath the trees. The silver birches were more fully in leaf than they'd been even ten days ago, so there was more of a contrast from the clifftop sunshine into the dappled shade.

There was a fragrant newness as ferns unfurled from the earth. It had been a very mild spring, which Dave had said meant the perfect conditions for an early showing of bluebells, but the woods looked much the same. There was the odd flicker of blue as a pioneer peeked out from the green, but it would be a few weeks more before the bluebells were in full swing. She commented on this to Alice.

Her stepsister replied, 'I suspect I might get the chance to come here more often if I end up going out with Phil. That's what I wanted to talk to you about.' She turned towards Poppy, her eyes lit with questions, eager as a child's. 'What do you really think of him? Tell me your honest opinion.'

An image of Phil's dark, brooding looks leapt into her mind and she pushed it aside. 'From what I've seen of him, I think he's... nice,' Poppy said, choosing her words carefully.

'*Nice.*' Alice whirled round. 'Never mind nice. Do you really not think he's hot?'

'Um... yes, I suppose he is. I hadn't really noticed,' Poppy gabbled.

'You liar.' There was a little silence, broken only by the sound of a squirrel skittering around somewhere up above and the scrape of claws on a branch.

Poppy met her stepsister's eyes, which were sparkling. So she wasn't taking this too seriously. 'OK, I obviously noticed enough to think he was quite hot. But he is more your type than mine.'

'Even though he reminds us both of Stephen.'

'The last thing I want is another Stephen.' Poppy took a deep breath. Phil Grimshaw wasn't the only one who could manage a bit of poetic licence when the occasion warranted it. 'I might have gone for the dark and brooding look once.' She decided not to mention the gorgeous voice. Best to leave that out of it. 'But not any more. I'm not sure I even have a type.' She met Alice's gaze squarely. She was warming to her theme. She was starting to believe there had never been any chemistry between her and Phil herself. 'In fact, going back to what you said yesterday when you described your Dorset gentleman, I think you were right. It's not about looks, it's about personality. Kind would be quite high on my list too.'

Alice narrowed her eyes. 'OK, no more interrogations. I believe you. I just wanted to make sure I wouldn't be treading on your toes – with Phil, I mean. That you definitely weren't interested in him yourself. I thought once or twice that I'd seen something on your face when you two were chatting. And it would be awful, wouldn't it, if I ended up going out with Phil and bringing him home for curry nights and things – if that was the case.'

'You imagined it.' Poppy closed that line of conversation down. 'Anyway, aren't we getting ahead of ourselves? You haven't even been out on a date with him yet. He might turn out to be scared of water or a rubbish horseman.'

'He likes water,' Alice said. 'He was brought up by the sea, just like us.'

They had come out the other end of the copse now and they

found themselves on the Bluebell Cliff's boundary, overlooking the coast path. The occasional gorse bush was dotted with yellow and its sweet coconut scent drifted on the breeze. A late-afternoon dog walker looked surprised to see them suddenly emerge from the woods. They must make an odd pair, Poppy thought, two women, one dressed in a pastel blue dress with television make-up and heels and the other in skinny jeans and biker boots.

The dog walker called a greeting and pulled his woolly hat more firmly down over his ears and Poppy and Alice waved back and paused to look at the sea. There was a great view from up here – the sweeping curve of the bay with its blue waters and the milky hues of the sky above it. In the distance, they could see the white sail of a yacht skimming close to the shore past the golden strip of beach.

'Apparently, Phil rides well too,' Alice continued. 'He told me that just now. He learned because it's a good thing to have on your acting CV. The more you can do, the more options you have. That's why he can also play the odd tune on the piano. Actors need to be a jack of all trades, don't they?'

'Yes, they do.'

'He's a bit like me in the sense that he doesn't like to waste time,' she went on. 'He's a fan of living live to the full. He's never tried waterskiing though. Oh and he also told me he was scared of spiders. And rats. I'm with him on both counts.'

'You won't have anything left to talk about at this rate,' Poppy quipped before deciding that made her sound almost as snidey as Dave.

Poor Dave. Judging by Alice's lit-up expression, she was already completely sold on the idea of Phil as a boyfriend. Dave wasn't going to get a look-in.

She touched Alice's arm. 'I'd better be getting back. I just want to confirm a couple of things for tomorrow. And I want to phone Mum for a catch-up.'

'Yes. Good idea.'

They strolled back on the path through the woods, Poppy striding a couple of paces ahead, her mind already on the next day.

They were almost out of the woods when it happened.

Poppy heard a squeal from behind her, followed by a small cry of distress. She turned immediately and saw Alice bending down, rubbing her ankle.

'Are you OK? What happened?'

'I fell off my heel. It's all right. I'll be fine in a sec.'

Poppy could see immediately that Alice was not fine. Her face had gone a sickly white colour and she was still half-crouched, holding her ankle.

'Bollocks,' she said, looking up at Poppy through anguished eyes. 'I've got a horrible feeling I've done something to it.' She straightened slowly and Poppy looked at her ankle. Even from this distance, she could see it was already puffing up.

Taking the two steps that separated them, she bent down for a closer look. 'It doesn't look good.' She stood up again. 'Lean on me for a minute. Catch your breath.'

Alice did as she was bid and Poppy could see she was close to tears.

'What a stupid thing to do. I should have listened to you and changed my shoes. But I didn't bring any flatties with me and it's not like I'm not used to heels.'

'It could have happened to anyone. There are so many tree roots.' It was true, they snaked everywhere like little tripwires, hidden by the new spring growth. 'Can you put any weight on it?'

Alice tried and her face screwed up in pain. 'Shit. No, I don't think I can.'

'OK. Don't worry. Don't try again.' With the arm Alice wasn't clutching, Poppy hooked her phone out of her pocket. 'I'll give Dave a call. Maybe if he was on one side and I was on the other you could lean on us both. Would that work?'

Alice nodded miserably. 'I'm so sorry, Poppy. I've mucked everything up, haven't I?'

'No, of course you haven't. Don't even think it.' Poppy tried Dave's phone, but it went straight to voicemail. She left a message asking him to call her urgently.

'How am I going to waterski tomorrow? I don't think I can even walk back to the hotel.'

'Forget about tomorrow. We can easily reschedule it. I'll—'

Dave phoned back before she had finished the sentence. She explained the situation as quickly as she could.

'He said stay where we are,' Poppy told Alice, who gave her a watery smile.

'Like we're going anywhere. I can't believe this.' She had started to shiver a bit. A mixture of shock and pain and the cooling air, Poppy thought, taking her jacket off and offering it to her.

Alice took it gratefully. 'Maybe if I get an ice pack on it quickly,' she said, taking another experimental step and then stopping abruptly. 'I've always healed quickly. I've got a great moon system.'

Poppy shook her head, acknowledging their old childhood joke with a sympathetic hand squeeze. 'I know, honey, but I think on this occasion we might need more than a good moon system. More like a miracle.' She was about to add that she'd actually like to run Alice to A&E to get an X-ray. Just in case. But she knew she was going to have trouble with that. Alice had hated hospitals ever since her mother had died in one. She point-blank refused to go near them. Once, when she was away at uni, she had spent an agonising evening with abdominal cramps – which several of her uni mates had been convinced were the onset of appendicitis but which had luckily turned out to be a touch of food poisoning – refusing to go to hospital. She had only told Poppy this several days later.

Poppy saw Dave hurrying past the amphitheatre towards them. He was carrying what looked like a walking stick in his hand. Where on earth had he got that from?

'It was in Clara's office,' he explained when he reached them, slightly out of breath. 'I saw it the other day when I was in there chatting. I thought it may come in handy.' He turned towards Alice. 'How are you, sweetheart? What would you prefer? A stick – or a fireman's lift from yours truly?' He grinned at her.

'Definitely a stick,' she said, eyeing the shiny, silver, metal dog's head on the end of the polished wood. 'Especially a flash stick like that.'

'That's what I thought. The other option was a wheelbarrow. That crossed my mind, but I thought you'd prefer not to ruin that posh dress.'

His words were matter of fact but his eyes were tender and Poppy felt a rush of affection for him. That was so typical of Dave. He never made a drama out of anything. He managed to inject a little humour into situations, even when that seemed impossible, which had the effect of being wonderfully grounding. She watched him reassuring Alice with a little ache in her throat. It was a shame. She could imagine Dave at their curry nights too – somehow, he fitted into the gap by Alice's side so much better than Phil did.

'Does anyone beside Clara know what's happened?' Poppy asked him now.

'No, boss.' He turned to her, brusque again. 'I thought I'd leave that one to you.'

'Thanks,' both she and Alice said in unison, as they set off very slowly. After a couple of false starts, Alice realised the best way to go forward was if she leaned on Dave with one hand and supported herself on the stick with the other.

Poppy walked on the side with the stick, just in case, feeling surplus to requirements.

20

When they'd got back to the hotel, a concerned Clara had met them and taken them straight into her ground-floor office where they had made Alice comfortable with a chair, an ice pack and a footstool.

As Poppy had suspected, Alice refused to go to A&E. 'I'm certain I haven't broken it,' she said stubbornly. 'It would hurt more than this if I had. Besides, I'll be much better off here putting it up with an ice pack than sitting at the hospital waiting for someone to tell me to go home and put it up with an ice pack.'

This was actually a fair comment, Poppy knew.

'It might be OK by morning,' Alice said, but even she, with her iron will and stubborn determination, hadn't been able to prolong this charade for long. 'OK, a few days,' she conceded, biting her lip and looking close to tears again.

Poppy crouched down by her chair. 'We will reschedule the filming for when you're completely better.'

'I'm so sorry.'

'It was an accident. It wasn't your fault, honey. Please don't worry. I have insurance for accidents.'

Then Dave and Poppy had a brief confab out of her hearing and everyone else's on the terrace of the hotel. Not that other people didn't know. Corinna and Kate had seen them hobble in. The whole crew would soon know what was going on.

Poppy bit her lip, the enormity of the situation only just hitting her. A list of tomorrow's arrangements scrolled through her head. The boat, the horses, the permissions, the crew. 'I need to start cancelling things,' she told Dave. 'While we've still got a bit of the business day left.'

'Do you want me to tell the crew?' he asked.

'Yes, please. That would be helpful.'

'How about Phil?'

'Yes, please.'

For once he didn't make light of the situation. He just got up, cleared his throat and said, 'Consider it done.'

* * *

The rest of the day was a subdued affair. The derig of a studio usually had a bit of an anticlimactic feel. But even more so tonight, although Poppy was aware that her entire team were doing their best to keep up her spirits.

'At least we got a wrap with the studio stuff,' Corinna said. 'It would have been worse if it had happened yesterday.'

'That's very true.'

Even Mike, who wasn't known for his tact and sensitivity, patted her shoulder. 'Keep your chin up. You've done a great job.'

'Thanks, Mike.' She was grateful to them for being so nice. This affected them too. Rescheduling put everyone out. Luckily, she'd managed to get hold of everyone she needed to and they'd all been understanding. It was no one's fault. These things happened. They were happy to reschedule whenever she let them know.

After they'd had dinner, Poppy drove Alice back to Poole in Alice's car despite her protestations, with Dave following in his so he could take her back to the Bluebell Cliff again.

Alice's penthouse apartment, although it had a lift, was not the best place for someone who only had the use of one foot, so after some discussion they'd arranged for her to stay with the parents.

'You know Mum will love having the chance to spoil you,' Poppy had told her. 'And you're always saying you'd like more quality time with your dad.'

After a token argument about being independent, which she clearly couldn't be right now, Alice had given in gracefully. She could put very little weight on her ankle, so it was by far the best thing to do. Clara had let Alice borrow the walking stick. It had been unclaimed lost property from about a year ago, apparently, so she didn't think anyone was going to miss it.

With the help of the stick and Kenny, and Dave and Poppy bringing up the rear with Alice's bags, Alice was welcomed as though she was a prodigal daughter.

Aware of Dave hovering just outside the front door in the pool of light that spilled on to the garden path from the house, Poppy kissed her sister goodbye. 'Look after that ankle of yours and give that moon system a chance to work. And show Mum how to use her phone properly while you're here.' She knew it was a feeble attempt to lighten the moment, but Alice manged a small smile.

'I will.' Alice blinked a few times. 'And I'm so sorry again.'

'Hey, you have nothing to apologise for. I'll see you on Friday.'

'Friday?'

'It's the fifth of April. The first Friday of the month. Curry night. Surely you hadn't forgotten.'

'I had – what with all the excitement. Yes, see you then. And thank you and—'

Poppy shut the door firmly in case she was planning on apologising again, and she and Dave walked back to his car.

For the first part of the journey, they drove in silence. Then Poppy said, 'What did Phil say? I meant to ask you earlier.'

'He was fine about rescheduling. Concerned about Alice too – as everyone is, but fine. Poor bugger must be disappointed.' He sounded as though he was genuinely sympathetic.

'Yes. Thanks.' She hesitated. 'And thank you for this too, Dave. I don't know what I'd do without you sometimes.'

'I'm happy to help.' A beat. 'That's what friends are for.'

They lapsed into silence again and when they pulled up in the darkening car park of the Bluebell and got out beneath the starlit night, Dave said, 'I know this hasn't gone completely as we planned, but what we've done is really good. Don't lose sight of that.'

'I won't. Thanks.' They were standing face to face and, on impulse, Poppy stood on tiptoes and kissed his cheek.

He stiffened slightly, then said, 'Come on, let's get back in and see if the bar's still open. I think I'm in need of a nightcap.'

'Me too. And I'm buying.'

* * *

Poppy had never been more in need of curry night than she was when Friday came. She was really looking forward to being wrapped in the warm security of her family. She was even looking forward to seeing Lennox and hearing about his sock scenarios and catching up with the latest on Micky's baldness treatments. Not to mention seeing how Alice was – who had insisted on the phone that she was a million times better and would be going jogging again in a couple of weeks. Poppy didn't believe that for a second.

But it was odd how it was the little things that mattered the most, she thought, as she walked up the path to the familiar black-painted front door.

A quick scan of the cars outside told her she was last to arrive. She'd had a busy day and the door was slightly open, a wedge of warm light visible in the hall. As she approached, she heard raised voices on the other side.

'Like I said, I left in time. The car wouldn't start. How's that my fault?' It was Lennox, Poppy realised, hesitating.

'It never is your fault, though, is it? That's exactly my point.' Dana sounded annoyed. 'You're just...'

Poppy coughed loudly and pushed open the door, not wanting to walk into the middle of an argument but not wanting to eavesdrop on one either.

'Hey, you two.' She put on her best smiley face. 'Lovely to see you. I'm not last, am I?'

'We thought we were,' Dana said, rearranging her face from cross to polite and not quite pulling it off. 'Thanks to him.'

Lennox didn't bother with polite. He was still scowling. 'Now we are here, maybe we can get inside.'

The tension fizzed down the hall alongside them and Poppy escaped into the kitchen, where her mother was fussing around with a tray of glasses.

'Hello, darling. Just in time to take these in for me.' She came across and kissed her on both cheeks. 'Rose was coming back for them, but she must have got sidetracked.'

Poppy took the tray, pleased to see her mother looking happy. She had always been at her best when she was looking after people. She was probably enjoying having Alice here. Particularly as Alice had always been the most independent one of them all.

When Poppy walked into the warmth of the conservatory, she found Alice holding court. She was sitting on one of the armchair rockers with her foot propped up on an orange cushion, wearing a pair of narrow, fur-ruffed slippers, while Jack, Rose, Micky and Kenny sat around listening.

'He didn't quite fall at my feet,' Alice was saying, 'but it was a close thing. I have no idea how he managed to keep hold of the serving dish. Anyone else would have dropped it.'

Rose and Jack were shaking their heads in amused disbelief and Micky's eyebrows were arched higher than usual.

'That's obviously where I'm going wrong,' Micky said. 'I thought falling at women's feet went out with Emmeline Pankhurst. Modern women don't really want that kind of thing, do they?'

'Modern women like romantic gestures,' Rose said, sliding a glance at Jack. 'And this Phil does sound very romantic.'

'Oh he is...' Alice broke off and looked at Poppy. 'I can't wait until we can do the horse riding on the beach. I mean, if that's not the height of romance, what is?'

Kenny rubbed his daughter's arm. 'I don't want you riding any horses until you're completely better.' He looked up at Poppy for confirmation. 'Isn't that right, love?'

'Totally right,' Poppy said, putting the tray of glasses on the table. 'Don't worry, I won't let her do anything reckless, I promise.'

'If you ask me, getting on a horse is reckless whenever you do it.' Lennox came into the conservatory. 'And I've never understood the romance bit. Horses are great, hairy animals with massive feet, and they poop a lot. What's romantic about that?'

Dana, who came in behind him, said, 'For once we are in agreement. Horses might look romantic from a distance, but get close up and it's a different story. Like a lot of things in life.' She gave Lennox a pointed stare.

Poppy wondered if she was the only one who'd noticed it. There was definitely something wrong between those two. It was a shame. She had always thought that Dana and Lennox were the perfect match. Despite the fact that on the surface they were chalk and cheese. Dana was the archetypal sensible, responsible schoolteacher and Lennox was the big kid who larked about and never took anything seriously. Dana was so sensible, Lennox was so – not. But it had seemed to work out for them. Or at least they'd rubbed along happily enough for the last ten years.

Poppy dragged her attention back to Alice and Kenny. 'Has she told you she was a total star? She wowed everyone. It went brilliantly.'

'Until the point I bust my ankle.' Alice's face shadowed.

'As I said, we can simply reschedule. We have the technology.' Poppy waved a hand dismissively as if rescheduling was of no consequence at all. The last thing she wanted was for Alice to go off on another guilt trip. 'And how is that ankle?'

'The swelling's completely gone.'

'It comes up again if she walks on it too much,' Eleanor said, coming into the room with the curry-ordering notepad and a pen.

'And she limps when she thinks no one is looking,' Kenny added. 'So it's not as recovered as Alice would have you think. Is it, my love?'

Poppy noticed that his daughter didn't contradict him. 'There is no rush,' she said, glancing at Alice carefully and seeing the telltale signs of tiredness beneath her make-up. Her stepsister had been more shaken up by the injury than she was letting on. Like Poppy, she was as independent as a lioness and she wasn't used to being out of action. 'Far better that you're completely right before we reschedule,' she told her. 'And can I just put in a plea that you don't tell anyone outside these four walls about the outcome of the show? Or too much of what went on in it until it's aired. I should have told you that before.'

Alice clapped a hand over her mouth. 'Sorry.'

'That goes for the rest of you too.' Poppy made zipping motions across her lips. 'Keep it between us, eh? No mention of names or who won the date until after it's been on.'

They all agreed solemnly, and Poppy knew they would keep it to themselves. Even Lennox was quite good at being discreet if you expressly asked him to.

* * *

The evening went by in much the same way that every curry night did. They ate too much curry and demolished a Jamaican lime and coconut cheesecake and a sticky toffee pudding that Micky had bought from some upmarket shop. There was lots of chatter and catching up on what went on in everyone's life and the usual banter about the flatbed truck which was a 1960s Bedford and was, apparently, going to be sold for a handsome profit when it was ready. As usual, Kenny joked about them going to see his big ends.

'We can all go and look at it when it's done,' Micky said. 'If that's OK, Kenny?'

Their long-suffering stepfather agreed that it was.

Poppy discreetly checked Micky's bald patch in the hall when he asked her and declared it to be definitely smaller than it had been last month. In truth, she couldn't see much difference at all.

Eleanor updated them all about her piano lessons – she was finding it fun, but frustratingly slow, she said. This wasn't helped by the fact that she didn't have anything to practise on yet. She said she wanted to be sure she was going to carry on before she made what was going to be such an expensive investment.

Poppy and Rose exchanged glances. Poppy knew that up until that point they had both been of the opinion that after a couple of false starts this was the hobby that would stick. Maybe not then.

'I thought now I've got more time, I might also give swimming a second chance,' Eleanor said conversationally. 'Did Alice tell you?'

'Yes,' Poppy said, remembering the swimming/slimming text. 'That sounds fun.'

'But I've decided to wait until the summer when it's warmer.'

'I got a weird text from you the other day, Mum,' Rose said suddenly, reminding Poppy of her own God text. 'About you and Kenny seeing God. What was all that about?' She fiddled with her phone and then handed it over. 'Have you decided to give the church a second chance too?'

Eleanor looked puzzled as she squinted at the phone. She blinked a few times and then, when Rose made the text bigger, her face cleared and she laughed. 'That should say Gord. Gord Grainger, my piano teacher. It's that predictive text thing again. We went to see him doing a recital at the community centre. That's what put me off the piano, to be honest. It was sublime, wasn't it, Kenny? I will never be that proficient. It's just too difficult. I've realised I don't have a musical bone in my body.'

'Never say never,' Rose said. 'It's always possible to learn something new.'

'But I'm nearly sixty. I think you need at least a modicum of talent if you learn something when you're older.'

'Sixty is the new fifty,' Alice announced.

Eleanor looked sceptical.

'I can show you how to turn the predictive text off, if you like?' Micky offered.

'I know how to do it,' Eleanor said, 'thank you.' And that brought the conversation to an end, although Poppy still felt slightly unsettled for some reason.

Rose and Jack were excited about a new business venture they had.

'Rose is going to do some webinars on personal training,' Jack told them. 'We've been doing some research and we reckon they're a great way to expand her business and ultimately do some online courses. That way, we can get a passive income stream going and—'

'Hang on.' Kenny put up a hand. 'Before you go too much further, for the benefit of your mother and I, can someone please explain what a webinar is?'

'It's a seminar on the web,' Alice told him. 'You use an online platform to talk to an audience who pre-book to see it. In Rose's case, I imagine it's how to get fitter and develop a healthy lifestyle, is that right?'

Everyone looked at Rose.

'Precisely,' she said. 'It's new to us too, but it's very current and it could be profitable because you can charge a reasonable amount for people to come and you can also record and sell them, which could lead to all sorts of other opportunities. My aim is to get a bigger online presence and ultimately work for myself.'

'It's a different world,' Kenny remarked, looking at Eleanor.

'I know. Look away for five minutes, especially when it comes to technology, and the world leaves you behind.'

There was something in her voice that made Poppy glance at her. Regret maybe? Before she had a chance to ask her anything, Jack leaped ahead.

'If we can get it going, we can set up a passive income stream – which basically means,' he looked at Kenny again, 'that we can earn more income without actually doing any more hours. It's the way to go.'

'It sounds ideal.'

'You could do it too,' Rose said.

Kenny tugged his beard. 'Mmm, I could just see myself doing a web-a-wotsit on mechanics for beginners.'

'You don't need to get too technical. You could do one on changing a tyre. Or... I don't know... fitting a spark plug,' Jack said.

'That's not exactly rocket science, though, is it?' Lennox said. 'Surely even a dummy knows that to change a tyre you just unscrew a few wheel nuts.'

Dana glared at him.

No one else took any notice.

'Passive income streams are a good idea,' Alice confirmed. 'If I had a passive income stream, I could be earning money right now while I'm sitting here with my foot on a stool.'

'You'd be amazed what people do webinars on,' Poppy added. 'Not to mention YouTube videos. They can be the simplest things. I once saw a ten-minute video on how to crush up eggshells to feed your chickens. It had over eight thousand views.'

This led to a discussion, fuelled mostly by Lennox, about simple things you might video yourself doing.

'Getting out of bed,' he began. 'Choosing which leg hits the ground first. Left or right. Very important.'

'Well, there is supposed to be a wrong side of the bed,' Dana said.

'Choosing what colour socks to wear,' Rose said slyly. 'Or, indeed, choosing to wear odd ones.'

Lennox glanced at his socks in alarm. 'They are black, aren't they?'

'They are,' Jack told him. 'Ignore her.'

'Cleaning your teeth,' Micky said. 'Electric toothbrush or manual. Making toast. Toaster or grill. Brown or white bread? The possibilities are endless.'

'Anyway,' Rose said, 'getting back to me. We haven't told you the reason we're looking into all of this stuff, have we?'

'Other than wanting to be lazy millionaires,' Lennox quipped. 'Good luck with that.'

'Not quite.' She grabbed her husband's hand. 'Jack and I have decided that we're going to try for a baby.'

There was a little silence as everyone digested this news, and in it, Poppy saw that Lennox's face had changed from jovial to stricken. The look was gone almost immediately, but when everyone else began to say things like 'Good on you' and 'About time', he didn't comment. Dana's smile looked forced too.

Rose hadn't noticed her brother's reaction. She was smiling at their mother, who looked pleased at the prospect of her first grandchild on the horizon. Poppy caught Micky's look across the room. He looked pleased too.

When the hubbub died down, Alice began talking to Jack and Kenny about webinars. Lennox and Dana excused themselves earlier than usual, saying they had an early start. Rose and Jack weren't far behind them and finally it was just Micky who volunteered to stay and clear up, as he so often did.

'I'll help you,' Poppy said, having instructed Kenny and her mother to put their feet up. As she stacked plates in the dishwasher while Micky washed glasses in the sink alongside her, she asked him if he'd seen Lennox's expression.

He shook his head.

'It might be just me, Micky, but I'm worried about those two lately. I overheard them arguing earlier. I'm not sure what about. I wondered if it was worth you having a word with him? Maybe, just ask him if he's OK?'

'He won't tell me anything,' Micky said. 'But I'll try if you like.'

'Thanks. I'll text Dana too.' She and Dana had never been particularly close, but they had each other's numbers and occasionally swapped Christmas present ideas. Poppy felt a little guilty that she hadn't made more of an effort. But it had never seemed necessary to do more socialising with her sister-in-law than their monthly curry nights. 'It's hard to know where being concerned ends and being nosey begins,' she said to Micky now.

'I think it's different for men and women,' he said, picking up a tea towel. 'As you know I tend to err on the side of keeping completely out of it.'

Before she could reply, their mother came into the kitchen.

'Mum, I thought I told you to sit down.'

'I don't seem to do a lot else lately, darling. Were you just talking about Lennox?'

'Yes, are you worried about him too?'

'I am, but only because I've just noticed they're still sitting outside in the car. I'm not sure why, but they've been gone twenty minutes or so, haven't they?' She glanced at the kitchen clock.

'Maybe it won't start. Earlier on, I overheard a conversation...' Poppy broke off. 'I'll go and see.'

Seconds later, she was outside, but it was only when she'd already rapped on the passenger window that she took in the fact the glass was steamed up. If the car wouldn't start then surely they'd just have come back in again to ask Kenny to take a look.

It was too late to backtrack. As she stood there awkwardly, the passenger window slid down. Dana was sitting there and Poppy could see, even in the dim light, that her face was mascara-streaked with tears.

21

'Is everything OK?' Poppy asked, even though it patently wasn't. 'We were worried you may have car trouble or... something.'

'It won't start,' Lennox said in a voice so devoid of his usual cheeriness that she was shocked. 'My fault, as is everything else in the world. No need to bother Kenny.'

'I'm so sorry,' Dana said.

'Don't you dare apologise for me,' Lennox thundered.

'I wasn't. I truly wasn't.' Dana gave up the pretence of anything being OK and burst into tears again and, on impulse and because she didn't know what else to do, Poppy opened the car door and hunkered down beside her sister-in-law.

'Hey,' she said. 'I know that it's none of my business and feel free to tell me that, but if I can help...?'

'You can't,' Lennox said. 'For once, Perfect Poppy can't help.'

Feeling a little shocked by his tone but distracted because Dana had now got out of the car, Poppy glanced at him and then turned back to her sister-in-law. 'Do you want to come back inside for a minute?'

'I don't want to cause a fuss...'

'Oh, great,' Lennox huffed. 'That's all we need. A family intervention.'

Dana shook her head and Poppy looked at her brother. 'No one said anything about an intervention. If you'd rather I just went away and left you to it, then just say.'

'We would.'

'Lennox, we can't exactly sit here all night, can we?' Dana leaned back into the car. She turned back to Poppy. 'We've just discovered the RAC has lapsed when we called them.'

'My fault too,' Lennox said bitterly, and drummed his fingers on the steering wheel.

'I can give you a lift home, if you like? Or I could get Kenny?' Poppy suggested.

'I'll get him.' Lennox swung open the door and got out, stomping up the garden path to the house.

'Let him go,' Dana said, glancing after him. She sniffed and retrieved some tissues from her bag and wiped her face. 'Would it be an awful imposition to take you up on your offer? I'd like to go home. I can't really face...' She shrugged and didn't finish the sentence. But it wasn't hard for Poppy to empathise. The last thing any woman would want, let alone someone as private as Dana, would be to continue what was obviously a domestic in front of her in-laws and extended family.

'I'll just get my keys,' Poppy said. 'And say goodbye to the folks.'

Dana hugged her arms tight around herself. Every inch of her shouted *please be discreet*, but Poppy was good at being discreet. She would let Lennox give Dana's excuses.

A few minutes later, they were winging their way towards Lennox and Dana's house, which wasn't far from her parents', a bungalow in a tree-lined road in lower Parkstone. Poppy couldn't remember the last time they'd come here, she thought as she parked her Jeep outside.

'Will you be OK?' she asked.

'I will. Thank you.' Dana hesitated. 'I owe you some kind of explanation.'

'You don't, honestly.'

Dana put up a hand. 'I do. And, to be frank, I could do with talking to someone.' She swallowed. 'It's not as bad as it looks. We're fine most of the time, but it's this baby thing.'

She hesitated again and Poppy said gently, 'I guessed as much. I saw my brother's face when Rose and Jack made their announcement. But if you're not ready, honey, you're not ready. He'll have to wait.'

'It's not me who's not ready. It's Lennox.' Dana shook her head. 'Oh, he thinks he is. He thinks it's all going to be everyone in the bar wetting the baby's head and congratulating him and blue romper suits and football at the park. He hasn't got the faintest idea about the realities. The endless sleepless nights, the emotional exhaustion, the cost. He's like a great big, overgrown bloody kid himself. He's just given up yet another job because he doesn't get on with one of the barmaids. It's what he does every time. When he gets fed up, he doesn't try to resolve anything. He just walks away. You can't walk away from a baby.' She got another tissue out of her handbag and blew her nose again. 'Frankly, I'm terrified, Poppy. I can't see him ever being responsible enough to be a parent. He doesn't live in the same world as the rest of us.'

'He never has,' Poppy said slowly, unpicking all this and realising she wasn't surprised that Dana thought that. Lennox was exactly as she had just described. She wanted to say something in his defence, but now that Dana had started to unburden herself she didn't want to stop her from talking.

'My family's very different from yours. I don't know if Lennox has ever told you, but there's only myself and Mum. My parents got married because she was pregnant, but my dad left before I was a year old. He didn't do babies. He was a travelling salesman – the emphasis being on travelling. I don't think he was very successful at the selling thing. He never gave my mother any maintenance, that I do know, although he used to turn up with presents for me.'

In the dim light of the car, Dana looked at her hands and Poppy knew she was back in the past, reliving her own first-hand experience of what fathers were like.

'Once he turned up with a great big blue teddy bear. It's one of my earliest memories. I think I was about five and he and my mother were arguing about why he'd bought blue and hadn't he remembered he had a little girl, not a little boy? She told me years later that he'd won it at a fair.' She sighed. 'Another time he bought me a make-your-own-jewellery kit. It was full of pink and purple beads. I remember that because Mum threw it at him outside our house and it burst open and there were beads all over the path rolling around. We kept finding them for ages after-wards, stuck in the cracks of the crazy paving.'

'Why was she so cross about that?' Poppy asked.

'Because by that time I was nearly thirteen and she told him I was way past making my own jewellery and that he'd have been better off giving her some money for a new school uniform. That was what her anger was really about, I think. Although, of course, at the time I didn't know that he never supported me. Other than by buying me unsuitable presents.'

'Are you still in contact with him?'

'No. Although he did come to my graduation. He didn't get an invite. Mum would never have invited him, but he was hanging around outside. I never did find out how he knew. Mum told me he had only turned up because he wanted to take credit for me being a success and that it wasn't his to take.' She bit her lip and Poppy grabbed her hand across the handbrake and squeezed it tight. It was such a heartbreaking story.

'Have you told Lennox all this?' she asked.

'I told him bits of it when we first got together. It was one of the things we had in common, not having a father, although of course you lost yours in very different circumstances. I do know that.' She stared out of the windscreen at the street-lit road, back in the past again. 'This might sound a little hard to understand, but in some ways Lennox reminds me of my father. My father had the same happy-go-lucky attitude. Whenever my mother shouted at him, he just shrugged it off and said she took everything too seriously and she should learn to lighten up.'

'Lennox can take things seriously,' Poppy said gently. 'I know he's my brother and I know he generally acts out like a big kid, but there have been occasions when he's stepped up to the plate.'

'Such as...?' Dana said and Poppy knew that what she said next was very important. Dana was right – it was almost unheard of for Lennox to take responsibility and she had to dig deep to find an occasion when he had. But she didn't have to lie. Because the one occasion that she could remember was massive.

'I remember when our dad died, it was Lennox who was upset for the longest. I thought it would be Rose because she was the youngest, or maybe Micky because he's the most sensitive. But it wasn't. It was Lennox.'

Dana shuffled in the passenger seat. It had grown cold since they'd been sitting outside the bungalow, but Poppy hadn't wanted to stop the connection by suggesting they go inside.

'I've got heated seats in here,' she said. 'Shall I put them on?'

Dana nodded and Poppy switched on the ignition and pressed a couple of buttons on the dashboard.

'When Dad died,' she continued, 'Rose was seven, I was ten, Micky was fifteen and Lennox was just sixteen. It was at the funeral, which was at Poole Crem. The service had just finished and we were all standing outside. Rose, Micky and I were with Mum. Lennox was talking to Kenny and Alice. Then suddenly he looked across at us and he came over and he put his arms around us all. His skinny little boy arms. He said we weren't to cry because he was the man of the house now and he was going to look after us.' She paused. 'Rose, cheeky as always, asked him how he planned to do that when he didn't even have a man's job and he said that it wasn't just about having a man's job. He went and hugged her and he promised that whatever happened he would always try his best to make her smile. Because she was his little sister and he thought that's what Dad would have wanted.'

Dana didn't reply. She had gone very still and Poppy knew she was listening intently. As she'd been speaking, Poppy had been aware of the headlights of a car coming into the cul-de-sac behind them. Now in her rear-view mirror she could see the car stopping behind the Jeep. It had to be Lennox. Kenny must have got his car started. The lights dimmed and she could see in the street lights that it was Lennox.

Dana leaned across and squeezed Poppy's hand. 'I've appreciated this chat. Thank you. And thanks for the lift. I'd better go in.'

'You're very welcome.'

Dana got out and Poppy watched her go, but she didn't hang about. She wasn't sure whether she'd made things better or worse. Telling Dana that Lennox had promised always to do his best to make his family smile wasn't quite the same as being responsible, or resolving issues and keeping jobs. It certainly didn't mean that he would take fatherhood seriously, which was what she knew Dana really wanted to hear.

As she drove back to Poole Quay through the dark night, Poppy hoped very much that she hadn't made things any worse.

22

'You won't have made things any worse,' Alice said when they talked about it the next day and Poppy had told her in strictest confidence what Dana had said. 'It probably helped her just to chat. It usually does. Especially if she hasn't got anyone else.'

'It didn't sound like she had,' Poppy said. 'Certainly not on the family front, and Lennox has always said that she's too absorbed in her work at Park Heights to have much time for friends. Being a teacher's a vocation, isn't it, not a job.'

'Yes, it certainly is for Dana. I've heard her mention another couple they see sometimes for meals. I think they're both teachers at Park Heights, but I don't think they're close. You've done as much as you can, angel. Leave it at that.'

Reluctantly, Poppy had to agree with her and changed the subject. 'How does Mum seem to you? I thought she was quiet last night.'

'She probably couldn't get a word in edgeways, what with me babbling on, but, yes, she has seemed quieter lately. I think she was worried about Lennox last night. She'd spotted that all was not rosy with him and Dana too. And I think she'd cottoned on that it was to do with starting families. Not much gets past Eleanor, does it?'

'No. Do you think there's any mileage in you talking to her about getting another job? I don't mean as a way of filling in time, I mean something on the same sort of level as the library. Something where she could use her intellect.'

'I'm not sure she wants another job,' Alice said. 'Funnily enough, Dad and I were discussing it yesterday and he seems to think all this trying stuff out – the craftwork, the piano, the swimming – is her way of trying to find another passion. Something that isn't work.'

'Well, that does make sense, I guess. Did she say anything about the prospect of being a grandmother?'

'She said that naturally she'd be delighted to be a grandmother, but that she suspected it would be in nature's time, not Rose and Jack's, and hadn't we heard of that quote, "Life is what happens when you're busy making other plans."'

'Wasn't that John Lennon?'

'A cartoonist called Allen Saunders said it first, apparently.'

'Which reminds me, I meant to ask her if she knows the origin of the word "zounderkite".'

'Zounderkite?'

'Yes, it's a long story.'

'Do you want to speak to her?'

'No, don't worry, I'll text her. Have you heard anything from Phil?'

'Yes, I have, actually.' Her face brightened. 'He phoned and he asked for my address and he sent flowers. He's a sweetie.'

'He certainly is.'

'Before you dash off,' Alice said, 'we need to talk about rescheduling the filming.'

'We're not doing that until you've been signed off by a doctor.'

'Well, for your information, I have a second appointment with my GP on Friday.'

'I thought you didn't believe in GPs.'

'I also know that filming delays have financial implications.' Of course she did. She was a businesswoman. 'But I'm not reckless either. Contrary to the fuss everyone's been making, it was just a sprain and it's healing fast. I'll make sure I have a clean bill of health before I get on a horse or a pair of waterskis. Don't worry.'

* * *

If all had gone according to plan, Poppy would have been spending the following week going through the rushes of her pilot with a script editor, deciding what to put in and what to leave out, which, of course, she couldn't now complete.

Instead, she spent the time finishing up some outstanding paperwork, chucking out some very old accounts that had been gathering dust in her loft and catching up on all the little domestic jobs she never had time for, so when Dave rang her on Wednesday evening, she was really pleased to hear from him. They'd only spoken briefly since the ankle incident when he'd phoned her to ask about Alice.

'Just checking in, boss. How's it all going? How's Alice?'

'Alice is getting there, thanks for asking.'

'And how are you, Poppy?'

She was about to say she was fine but changed her mind and gave him the unedited version. 'To be honest, I feel a bit flat, Dave. How are you?'

'I'm at a loose end, as it happens. How about we go for a pint of cider on the quay and cheer ourselves up? I can be with you in half an hour.'

'You're on,' she said. 'But give me forty-five minutes.' She was covered in dust from rooting about in old boxes of accounts in her loft and her hair could do with a wash. On the other hand, it was only Dave. She didn't need to impress Dave.

* * *

When he arrived, looking spruced up and clean shaven and carrying what looked like a new, but made to look old, tan leather jacket over his shoulder, Poppy was glad she'd at least had a wash and changed her dusty clothes. She'd put her hair up in a French plait so it looked OK and she'd topped up her twenty-four-hour lippie.

'If we go to The Ship, we'll probably catch happy hour,' she told him. 'It's only just gone six.'

'I'm up for that. Shall we walk down? Parking's at a premium round here tonight, so I left the car a few blocks away.'

'Sure thing. I like the jacket.'

'I like the hair. Although you've got something in it – hang on.' He reached forward and retrieved something from just above her ear which made him frown. Probably a cobweb.

'It's a new hair product,' she lied. 'It comes out of the can quite sticky.'

'Right.'

They walked in a peaceable silence along the quay. On their right, the tide was high and the water lapped at the sides of the quay and around the hulls of the boats moored up alongside it. Above their heads, seagulls hunting for fish-and-chip-bearing tourists to rob circled and squawked. It was a lovely spring-like evening and there were couples strolling and late shoppers and the occasional family out for an early meal.

There were several pubs and restaurants on the quay and

Poppy was suddenly aware of the smell of garlic and rosemary drifting from somewhere. Her stomach rumbled.

Dave must have smelled the enticing scents at exactly the same time because he said, 'Are you hungry?'

'I'm always hungry.'

'Shall we grab a pizza? My treat.'

'There's an offer I can't refuse. What about happy hour?'

'I expect Italian restaurants sell wine. Will that do you?'

She nodded happily and they retraced their steps. The prospect of an evening chatting to Dave over a pizza was very appealing. In fact, given the choice, she couldn't think of a single other person she'd rather spend the evening with.

It was only when they were at the door that Poppy realised it was the same Italian restaurant where she'd had her disastrous hen night, although it wasn't called Il Pescatore any more. It had undergone a makeover since then and was now Antonio's.

Poppy hesitated, but it was too late, Dave had just opened the door and they were greeted effusively by a raven-haired Italian. 'Is this your first visit to Antonio's? It is? Follow me. I give you romantic table. This way, please.'

He'd mistaken them for a couple, Poppy thought, amused, as Dave gestured her ahead of him. Moments later, they were sitting at a window table in an alcove that overlooked the quay. There was a red candle in a Chianti bottle decorated with a waterfall of wax. The waiter leaned forward and lit it with a flourish.

It was the kind of place that had dim lighting and red paper serviettes and, to Poppy's relief, it looked quite different to the restaurant in her memories. They'd extended into the back and they now had more tables, as well as a bar area by the till.

The waiter came back with giant menus. 'Can I take drinks order, please?'

They ordered a bottle of wine and he swept away again.

'He's keen,' Dave said. 'So, how hungry are you? Shall we have starters?'

The menu had a huge choice and the smells coming from the kitchen every time someone opened the kitchen door were tantalising.

They ordered whitebait and garlic brochettes to share and two different types of pizzas, also to share, and they drank wine and chattered about inconsequential stuff and he made her laugh with a story about a job he'd just been asked to do. 'Do you remember that fantastic Audi commercial a few years back when all the car parts were lined up in a domino effect? Well, they're trying to emulate that, only on a much lower budget and with the parts of a bicycle, which are considerably lighter. It's hilarious.'

'Is the commercial for a bicycle?'

'No. It's for a hot tub.' He topped up their wine glasses. 'Honestly. You couldn't make it up.'

When they were halfway through their pizza, the conversation turned to Alice and she gave him an update.

'She's going to let me know what her GP says. She's being really sensible. That's one good thing. Realistically, I guess we're looking at rescheduling for the middle of May, though.'

'I'm so glad she's all right,' Dave said. 'She's a lovely girl.'

'You two got on really well, didn't you?' Poppy probed, wondering if she should come straight out with it and ask him if he fancied Alice.

'Yes.' His mouth tightened and he dropped his gaze in that way he did when he was clamming up.

Poppy decided to leave it. It was none of her business anyway.

Around them, the restaurant had filled up. On the table opposite them, a young couple were sitting. She was feeding him a breadstick and they were giggling. Their intimacy was palpable.

Aware that Dave had noticed them too, Poppy sighed. 'I remember those days.'

'When you were a young, idealistic girl who thought candlelit meals were the height of romance and that you just had to find your soulmate and the two of you would live happily ever after.'

It was so close to what she'd been thinking, and so unlike the type of thing that Dave usually said, that she was caught off guard. For a moment she was speechless, thrown back into the past at her hen night, in this very restaurant, when she'd glanced up and seen Stephen standing in the doorway, so hunched and still.

'Who was he?' Dave asked, his gaze on hers. 'The guy who broke your heart?'

She half-expected him to follow this up with some flippant comment that would make her laugh. But his eyes were too serious and he sounded as though he really wanted to know. So she told him about Stephen and Serena.

He listened, with his chin on his hands, his eyes occasionally softening when she faltered and she realised as she was speaking that she had never told anyone the whole grimy story before. Even Alice and Rose only knew bits and pieces of it. She had never told anyone about that young, starry-eyed girl who'd dreamed of such a different future than the one she had ended up living. That girl who had dreamed of the kind of man who was a cross between her father – who had loved her so unconditionally and made her feel so protected and safe – and some other man – faceless until Stephen had come along, with that silken voice, who had a way of making her feel as though she was the only person in the world. Certainly, she had never told a man about the pain of having all her dreams smashed to pieces at her feet. She had never really trusted one since Stephen.

'Oh my God,' she said, suddenly aware that she had been

talking for several minutes and that the last third of her pizza had gone cold on her plate. So had Dave's. 'I'm so sorry. You didn't want to hear all that.' She clapped her hand over her mouth.

'I did want to hear it. Or I wouldn't have asked.'

It seemed a little late to try to qualify it or to retract anything she'd said, or even to make light of it, so she asked a question instead, 'How did you know?'

'I guess because no one is as anti-dating and anti-romance and anti-love for as long or as stubbornly as you've been unless they've been seriously hurt.' His mouth twisted just the tiniest amount as though he'd been going to smile but hadn't quite managed it.

Cottoning on immediately, she said, 'It happened to you too, didn't it? The girl that you told me about once. You and your brother fell out over her and didn't speak for four years. It was her, wasn't it?'

'Yeah. Yeah, it was.'

Poppy waited, while he crumpled up his serviette in his hands and then finally met her gaze again.

'Her name was Evie Wilson. We went out for maybe eight months and I thought she was the love of my life. I also knew in here...' he touched the left side of his chest, 'that she was way out of my league. In fact, I said it to her at the beginning – and she told me that it was nonsense. No one's out of anyone's league. It ended up as a bit of a private joke between us. She called me League Boy.

'I fell for her utterly, totally, completely. I planned to ask her to marry me. The same week as I got the ring, I took her home to meet my family and that's where she met Jonathan, my brother. They clicked instantly. Jonathan said it was the first time in his life he'd ever wholeheartedly approved of a decision I made. And Evie went all flirty and giggly and I knew that I'd lost her. I knew straight away, even before he took her phone number. He said he'd need to have it so he could contact her on my behalf, if ever he needed to. Then, of course, the inevitable happened. Three weeks after I'd introduced them, they were an item.'

'Your own brother – what a bastard!' Poppy was outraged on his behalf. For a split second, she'd seen the total raw pain in his eyes before he'd managed to blink it back inside.

'Brothers. Best friends. There's not a lot of difference, is there? When the people that should have our back let us down it hurts like hell.'

The friendly waiter arrived back at their table, spotted their unfinished pizzas and looked concerned. 'You no like? There is problem?'

'They were great,' Poppy reassured. 'We just weren't quite as hungry as we thought.'

'I get box. You have takeaway?'

'That would be good,' Dave said. 'Thanks.'

'You like coffee now?'

Dave looked at Poppy.

'That sounds great,' she said.

'You'd better finish the wine too,' he added when the waiter had disappeared with their plates again. 'I've had my quota.'

'Have you had any serious relationships since Evie?' Poppy questioned. 'If you don't mind me asking?'

He gave her a look which told her they were beyond those kinds of boundaries. And she knew that they were. It was the oddest feeling, but unburdening herself about Stephen to Dave hadn't made her feel embarrassed at all. She felt lighter than she had for years, as if something very hard and tight had uncoiled inside her. 'Of course I don't mind you asking. I've been on plenty of dates. As I think I might have told you before, I'm good at being a plus-one. But I've never met anyone else who I've wanted to get serious with until...' He broke off as the waiter returned with their coffees and a takeaway pizza box.

'You have good lunch tomorrow,' he beamed, putting the box on the table next to Dave. 'You like bill?'

'Yes, please. Unless you'd like any more coffee. Would you?' Dave glanced at Poppy and she shook her head.

A few minutes later, having finished their coffees and paid – Dave had refused point blank to let her make a contribution – they were outside again. It had grown chillier in the last couple of hours. Stars twinkled from a dark sky and the street lights made a silvery ripple pattern on the water that lapped against the quay.

Poppy shivered – she was only wearing a light jacket – and Dave shrugged off his heavy leather one and offered it to her.

'Won't you be cold?' she asked.

'I'm a rufty-tufty cameraman, remember?'

'Thanks then.'

Even though they didn't have to walk very far back to her flat, she appreciated the comforting heavy weight, that smelled as familiar as he did, around her shoulders.

At her door, she looked at him. 'My turn to ask you if you'd like more coffee.' Then she suddenly remembered that thing he'd said in the restaurant, just before they'd left. '*I've never met anyone else who I wanted to get serious with – until...*'

And she realised that he must have meant Alice. It had been talking about Alice that had led them on to the conversation about heartbreak. Shit. Poor Dave. He finally meets a woman he likes, but he can't do anything about it – because he has to film her on a date with someone else. What a cruel twist of fate that was.

Feeling flustered now and aware that Dave hadn't said either yes or no to the coffee, she began to backtrack. 'I understand if you want to get back. It is pretty late.'

'Sure. Yeah.' He rubbed his neck. 'You take the pizza for your lunch.' He held it between them like pizza-box armour, as though he were worried she might get too close and he might have to push her away like he'd done the last time she'd drunk too much.

'Goodnight then, Dave.' She took the box from him and he looked relieved.

'Goodnight, Poppy.'

23

It was another two weeks before Alice got the all-clear from her doctor and, just to be on the safe side, Poppy rescheduled the filming to take place a fortnight after that. It looked like her estimate for the middle of May hadn't been too far out.

Another thing that happened was that Poppy had an unexpected phone call from Dana. She had just come in from seeing a client when her phone rang and Dana's name popped up on her screen. She hadn't heard from her sister-in-law since the curry night and she answered it with a certain amount of trepidation.

'Firstly, I owe you an apology,' Dana said. 'I should have got in touch before. I've picked up the phone so many times and then I've lost my nerve.'

It was hard to imagine the confident Dana losing her nerve. 'Are you OK?' Poppy asked carefully. 'How are things?'

She wasn't completely unaware of how things were, having spoken to Micky briefly, who'd phoned to tell her that he'd had a chat with Lennox and that their brother had said he and Dana had been doing a lot of talking.

'I'm very much better than I was and a lot of that is down to you,' Dana said.

Poppy let out the breath she'd been holding. 'That's great news.'

'I thought so much about what you said,' Dana went on, 'and I realised you were right. I haven't really given Lennox a proper chance. I know he's a clown and he doesn't take much seriously, but I also know that he really does love me.'

Wow. That was even better news than she could have hoped for.

'He's one of the good guys,' Poppy said quietly. 'And he adores you. And for what it's worth, I think he would be a great father.' That was true. He certainly wouldn't have any problems being on the same wavelength as his kids. Being a big kid himself. She decided to keep that thought to herself.

'He'd probably be better than me at understanding their points of view,' Dana said, echoing her thoughts. 'I know it's a shocking thing to say, but he would probably be closer to them in mental age than me.'

'That's so true,' she said warmly. 'And I'm really, really pleased.'

'Me too. Another thing I realised after our chat was that I can't let the painful past taint my view of men forever. Just because my father was a complete waste of space, it doesn't mean that Lennox will be too.'

'Totally,' said Poppy. 'But I guess we all let the past affect us to a degree.' There was a twang in the region of her heart, which she decided to ignore.

'Please don't say anything to anyone about all this,' Dana added.

'Of course I won't.'

'See you at the next curry night. And thanks again.'

'You're so welcome.'

* * *

The May curry night was much better and much lighter, Poppy thought, than the previous one had been. Possibly because it didn't start with her overhearing an argument and end with Dana pouring her heart out. And also because dear Alice proclaimed herself to be back to full strength and was walking around with no trace of a limp.

To Poppy's surprise, Lennox cornered her not long after she got there and apologised for how he'd spoken to her at the previous one. 'I was a bit of a git, I seem to remember.' He brushed hair back from his receding hairline and frown lines creased his high forehead.

'You were stressed,' she said. 'Because your car wouldn't start.'

'Yeah,' he agreed. 'That's right.'

She knew neither of them were going to mention what had really been going on, but that was OK. For all of his clowning about, in some ways Lennox was as protective of his private life as Micky was.

'That was no excuse to bite your head off, though. Sorry, Popsicle.'

'I prefer Pops to Popsicle, but either is better than *Perfect Poppy*.'

'Sorry, Pops.'

'Your apology is accepted.'

'Cheers.' He grinned and she saw a flash of his usual sparkle. 'I hear the dating show's back on schedule.'

'I hope so.' She held up crossed fingers. It was never worth tempting fate when it came to film schedules. Especially when they were shooting outside and relying on the weather.

Rose and Jack updated everyone on the webinar progress but not, to Poppy's relief, on their baby-making progress. She wasn't sure that Dana and Lennox would be quite up to hearing all about that.

Kenny pronounced that the flatbed truck was going to be sprayed baby blue and it was almost ready. Everyone agreed that they would look at the truck when it was actually baby blue and what an exciting event that would be. Not!

There was a lot of laughter over that, which Kenny sat through politely before tapping his nose. 'You lot won't be so sceptical when you see how much I get for it. It'll be going in *Classic Truck*.'

'"Trucks for a Tenner", more like,' Lennox quipped. 'I've seen that in the classifieds.'

Micky mentioned that he was going to a monthly dinner-club evening organised by someone at the law firm where he worked.

'My little brother's going dinner dating,' Lennox said incredulously. 'Flaming hell. I didn't see that one coming.'

'It's not dating, it's a dinner club,' Micky said, blushing furiously. 'Everyone takes it in turns to host it in their houses.'

'That's just another word for dating. There's going to be women there, aren't there? Or is it men only in this club?' Lennox teased.

'Shut up,' Dana said, throwing him a warning glance, and Lennox shut up. Or at least he switched the focus of his attention from Micky to Poppy.

'At this rate, you'll be the only singleton in the family, Pops. Alice will be fixed up. Micky'll be fixed up. When are you going to bring a nice bloke back for us to interrogate on curry night?'

'When are you going to start wearing time-appropriate socks?' Poppy shot back at him. 'Or are Santa Claus socks in May a thing?'

'They're Homer Simpson socks. Aren't they?' He whipped up his trouser leg to look and Poppy giggled.

'Made you look.' She wet her index finger and drew a line in the air. 'One all, I think.'

'Fair enough,' Lennox said.

'Stop it, children,' Eleanor admonished with her best mock-stern voice, 'and tell Kenny what you would like to eat. Spice Nights will be closed if we don't get a move on.

The curry was ordered and, when it arrived, the chatter quietened a bit while it was eaten. Then Rose and Jack went to get the desserts they had brought and the conversation turned back to Eleanor.

There was no sign of an electric piano yet and, when pressed, Eleanor said that she wasn't quite as sure as she had been that playing the piano was for her. 'As I said before, I think you prob-ably need to start with some form of innate musical talent,' she acknowledged. 'And I don't have any. Gord said I have a good ear, but no sense of rhythm whatsoever.'

'He didn't say that, love,' Kenny interrupted. 'He said your rhythm needs work and a metronome might help.'

'That's what he meant, though, wasn't it?' She shot him an affectionate, but slightly worried look. 'I can even make scales sound disjointed.'

'Scales are difficult to master,' Rose said, and she was joined by several other voices raised in agreement.

'Thank you, everybody, but I think I've decided that music is not the vocation I thought it might be. Now then...' She cut the conversation short. 'Who'd like some more of Rose's delicious charlotte russe? Did you make this one, Rose?'

'Yes, and I put it on that special plastic dish and then popped it into a Waitrose box,' Rose said, rolling her eyes. 'Why would anyone bother making one when shops do it so much better?'

'Not true,' Poppy countered.

Dana was nodding in agreement and a discussion ensued about which desserts were easier – and probably also cheaper – to buy from shops than to make from scratch.

Smooth change of subject, Mum, Poppy noted, deciding to challenge Eleanor when there weren't so many people about.

* * *

At the end of the evening, to both Poppy and Micky's surprise, Lennox offered to help wash up.

'I didn't think you knew what tea towels were for,' Micky said, handing him one.

'What? We're not using the dishwasher?' Lennox took the tea towel from his brother. 'Just kidding. This is me being a responsible adult.' Lennox glanced at Poppy. 'I'm turning over a new leaf, sis.' And Poppy knew that was the closest he would ever get to referencing the chat she and Dana had had the previous month.

Later, at the door, out of earshot of the kitchen, their mother confirmed this. Just before she kissed Poppy goodnight, she said quietly, 'Lennox told me you'd been singing his praises to Dana. Thank you, darling. He's not as confident as he makes out.'

'I know he isn't. Are you OK, Mum? I mean really OK? You haven't seemed quite yourself lately either.' Poppy still felt a vague sense of unease about her mother's state of mind.

'I'm OK, darling. Don't you worry about me. As long as you lot are happy, I'm happy too.'

'I don't mean second-hand happiness, though, Mum. I mean proper, first-hand happiness.'

Eleanor looked jolted and she hesitated for the briefest moment. 'What an odd thing to say. Of course I'm happy. Now, you go and concentrate on getting your filming done and making Dorset famous, and stop worrying about other people for once.'

'All right, I will.' Poppy decided not to press her for now.

Eleanor hugged her and, as they drew apart, she said, 'You're happy, aren't you, darling? You didn't take any notice of Lennox's teasing?'

'I never take any notice of his teasing,' Poppy reassured her. 'Night night, Mum.'

'Night, darling. Love you.'

* * *

Poppy usually slept really well, but that night she woke around 4 a.m. with her head churning like a washing machine on the 'handwash' cycle. She lay in the soft darkness thinking about her family.

She was pleased that Dana and Lennox were back on track. It was brilliant what talking could do and Dana's words echoed in her mind – *'I can't let the painful past taint my view of men forever. Just because my father was a complete waste of space, it doesn't mean that Lennox will be too.'* It had been something like that.

Poppy was still surprised how much Dana had opened up to her. Mind you, she knew she had done the same with Dave. She remembered the expression in his eyes when he'd looked at her across the table. *'No one is as anti-dating for as long or as stubbornly as you've been, unless they've been seriously hurt.'*

He had been spot on, as usual. Lovely, perceptive Dave. He was such a good friend. She hadn't seen him since their night at Antonio's. He was away doing his domino-effect advert this week for the hot-tub company.

It was always so much easier to get perspective on other

people's problems than it was to find it on your own, she thought, her thoughts circling back to her mother.

She still wasn't convinced all was rosy there. But maybe she was overreacting because there were so many other emotions flying about. Perhaps she was imagining problems where there were none.

24

When Poppy had planned her original schedule for filming the date itself, all of the parties involved, with the exception of Phil Grimshaw, would have been staying at the Bluebell Cliff. Herself, Dave, Mike, Si, Alice and Mandy, who did make-up and hair, would simply have got up, had an early breakfast and headed off to the coast. Most of them would have been in the same car too. They'd have had all the equipment they needed for shooting on location with them. Plan B was a little more complicated.

Understatement. She'd arranged that she and Dave would travel in her Jeep together to the first location. Mandy was calling at Alice's apartment, then she and Alice would meet Matt, the owner of the speedboat, on Poole Quay and they'd whizz over in the boat and meet them on the beach on the Studland side. Most of the crew were staying at Bluebell Cliff tonight. Mike was picking up Si because they lived within a mile of each other and they would be meeting them at the first location, which was South Beach. Phil was getting there under his own steam, but Poppy had no doubts about Phil's reliability. When she'd spoken to him on the phone, he'd said the date was the highlight of his year and he was looking forward to it immensely.

Taylor Stanton was only needed for the final reveal – which would take place at the Bluebell that evening. If the series got green-lit, then the reveal that came at the end of each episode would be filmed when they filmed the following episode, when the studio would be fully set up and the presenter on site. Because they couldn't do this with the pilot, Poppy planned to do the reveal on location at the Bluebell and she and Dave had decided to use the lighthouse to do it.

Ostensibly, this was because it was incredibly picturesque – what could be more romantic than a lighthouse? But, in reality, it was because they could shoot the reveal effectively 'on location' as they'd done in the kitchen without the need for a full studio.

Taylor Stanton did have to be there, of course, and, other than the tides, she had been the most difficult part of the complicated jigsaw for the film schedule, because she had a back-to-back workload, but Poppy had finally managed to co-ordinate everyone.

It felt like the crack of dawn, although it was actually 6.30 a.m. Poppy frowned as she looked at the call sheet. 'It'll be fine if everyone follows the schedule to the absolute letter. Including the weather, the sea and the horses,' she grumbled to Dave as they loaded up her Jeep with technical equipment on the appointed day. Alice's clothes swung in suit carriers hung from hooks in the back. Three changes of clothes for three events – riding, hiking down to Durdle Door for the picnic, and a glamorous evening outfit – not to mention shoes, a riding hat and spares of everything in case they needed them. Alice had said she'd wear her wetsuit over in the speedboat.

'Don't think about it,' Dave said. 'Let's just concentrate on us getting to Studland.'

'Yes. You're right.' She got in the driving seat, wondering if he was as calm as he sounded. He didn't say much as she drove them through the waking-up town. Poppy guessed that the prospect of filming the woman he had a soft spot for cavorting around with his rival for the day wasn't filling him with glee.

At the ferry, there was no queue, so she drove the Jeep straight on. The crossing took less than five minutes and, while Dave read through some paperwork on his lap, Poppy decided to use the time to gather her thoughts.

She wasn't the type who put much stock in meditation, but she had found that deep breathing and a spot of visualisation could help hugely. As the ferry clanked its way on to the chains that propelled its journey, she lowered the driver's window and took a lungful of the fresh sea air. There was a slight sea mist and the sky was a hazy, milky blue. It promised to be a beautiful day, just as the forecasters had predicted. She pictured the speedboat skimming across a sparkly sea with a blue sky and a faint sun shining down on the waterskier it towed.

After this, she got slightly sidetracked by the image of Phil in a wetsuit – that was a sight that could get a girl's blood pressure rocketing up. Lucky old Alice, spending the day with him – not that he'd be in a wetsuit for the whole day of course but...

'Wakey-wakey.' Dave's voice jolted her back to the present. 'We're here, boss.'

Poppy gave herself a little shake. She had to stop this. Drooling after her stepsister's prospective boyfriend was bad. Very bad. She restarted the Jeep's engine. 'We'll need plenty of wetsuit shots,' she said before she'd got her brain fully in gear again. 'And, um, shots of bare feet in the sand.' Feet were better. Wetsuits were sexy. Feet were not. Concentrate on feet.

'I have done this before,' Dave said mildly. 'Once or twice.'

'Sorry.'

She shut up swiftly. The less said about wetsuits the better.

* * *

To Poppy's relief, everyone was on time. Mike and Si were already at Jo's café, drinking coffee at a picnic bench. Mike had just got a bacon roll, which she saw Dave eyeing enviously.

'There's time to get one,' Poppy said to Dave. 'If you want one.'

As she spoke, Mike stood up. 'My shout, mate. I think I owe you one.' He put his bacon roll on the bench table and headed back towards the café's serving hatch.

Before anyone else could speak, there was a flurry of movement and the sound of wings and a giant white bird swooped in and was gone again before anyone could move.

Si yelled and swore loudly.

Poppy blinked. 'What the hell just happened?'

'That bloody great seagull just nicked Mike's roll.'

'It bloody better not have done!' Mike spun around and looked outraged. He shielded his eyes and stared at the sky. 'I'll flaming kill it.'

The seagull was nowhere to be seen as Mike paced about furiously on the wooden decking and then Poppy spotted it, perched up on the roof of Jo's café, clearly enjoying its stolen booty.

Poppy had a sudden vivid flashback of Foxy stealing Dave's bacon butty at the Bluebell and, clearly, she wasn't the only one because Dave said mildly, 'If you can't get a bacon butty off a three-legged dog, I can't see you getting one back from a seagull.'

Poppy snorted and then clapped her hand over her mouth.

Si had given into mirth too and was now choked up with laughter.

After a few seconds even Mike saw the funny side.

'I'll get you another one,' Dave said and went back to the hatch, where Jo – if indeed it was Jo – wisely made no comment.

* * *

Phil turned up with a kitbag just as they finished their butties. He was already in a wetsuit. The rest of his clothes had to be in his car. Poppy sneaked a look at his Lycra-clad torso before noticing that Dave was watching her and swiftly averting her eyes again. It was actually a shock to realise she was slightly disappointed. In her fantasies on the ferry, Phil had looked a fair bit hotter than he did in reality.

He actually looked quite tired today – there were shadows beneath his eyes. Good job they had make-up on hand, or they would do when the boat got here. Alice had just texted to say that she, Mandy and Matt had just left Poole Quay and would be with them very shortly.

Poppy went to talk to Phil. 'Lovely to see you. How are things?'

'I've had quite a bit on. But things are good.'

'The Bluebell Cliff must be getting very busy,' she enquired politely.

'I've been busy there, yes. I've also been doing some work with an independent theatre company.'

'Great stuff.' She felt pleased he was doing what he had pronounced was his heart's desire.

'I've been very much looking forward to filming with Beauty Spot again.' He nodded as if to underline his point.

'You must be looking forward to seeing Alice,' she hedged.

'I am. I think today will be great. I have to say I think you've chosen the perfect spot. I'm really impressed.'

It was only as Poppy was turning away from Phil that it struck her the chemistry that she'd come to expect was no longer there.

She was quite relieved. Maybe common sense had finally kicked in. Also, why had she never noticed that most of Phil's sentences began with the word 'I'?

* * *

A few minutes later, the drone of the speedboat heralded the arrival of Alice, Mandy and Matt. Matt got the boat in as close as he could to the shore and the two women splashed out through the frill of the tide, Alice wearing neoprene boots and Mandy in shorts and flip-flops. They were both carrying bags and smiling.

Phil went to greet Alice and the two of them exchanged air kisses. They didn't look like prospective lovers, or maybe she was reading too much into that. Poppy shook her head. They were probably a bit on edge. They both knew how important today was.

Very soon, the beach became a hive of activity. Poppy had contemplated using two boats, but to save money she'd decided on just the one – one cameraman would be in the boat, and one on the shore.

She'd also given serious consideration to using a drone, but then they'd have needed a pilot and civil aviation clearances and it was just another person to pay, so she'd reluctantly abandoned that idea too. Instead, they were using GoPros, which would be attached to mounts on Alice and Phil's chests. Phil, who was familiar with them, had just fixed his into place and Dave was helping Alice with hers.

He said something to Alice as he adjusted it, his close-cropped head close to her blonde one, and they both laughed. Poppy felt a stab of pain so sharp in her heart that she gasped aloud and touched her chest. Mandy, who was standing the closest to her, looked at her in alarm.

'Are you all right, Poppy?'

She realised that she still had her hand over her heart and she rubbed her chest self-consciously. 'I'm fine. I think I've got a touch of indigestion.'

'Are you sure? We don't want you keeling over with a heart attack.'

'It's definitely indigestion. I often get it if I eat breakfast too early.'

Mandy was still looking at her in concern. 'I think I've got some antacid tablets in my bag. Just a sec.'

'Thanks. Perfect,' Poppy agreed. Anything to cut short this conversation, because she knew with a sudden clarity exactly what that pain had been. It certainly wasn't indigestion. She'd never had indigestion in her life. It wasn't physical at all. It was familiar, but it was the kind of pain she hadn't felt for a very long time. It was the pain of knowing that the man she cared deeply about was actually more interested in another woman.

She blinked a few times. Hang on a minute. Dave was her friend. Only her friend.

But you didn't feel how she'd just felt about a friend.

She tested her theory by looking back at the couple who were still talking, their heads bent close, intimate and familiar. No one else seemed to have noticed them. Mike was chatting to Si and Phil was standing in the sea with his back to the shore, talking to Matt on the boat.

Poppy's breath caught in her throat. For a few seconds, standing there on one of the most beautiful beaches on earth, her head swum with conflicting emotions. It didn't make sense. She wasn't in love with Dave. He was her colleague and her best friend. She didn't even find him attractive.

Her heart gave a hard thump of disagreement. That wasn't true. She'd wanted to kiss him at Rose's party. She'd blamed that on having too much to drink, but in some deep-down part of herself she knew now with utter certainty that she hadn't been wearing wine goggles, the wine had just whipped away her inhibitions. She might have been denying it with every ounce of self-will that she had, but she'd been falling for Dave, slowly but surely, for a very long time, she now realised.

But all that stuff about Phil – all that chemistry she'd felt – had she just been kidding herself where he was concerned too? Had she just been responding to the flirting of an attractive man? A man for whom flirting was second nature. No wonder he was such an accomplished maître d'. Flirting was practically a qualification for that job. Oh my God, how had she been so blind? And how had she not known how she felt about Dave?

But Dave was unaware. Dave had eyes only for Alice. Before today, Poppy was pretty sure that Alice had eyes only for Phil. If anyone had asked her an hour ago if Phil and Alice would make a good couple, she'd have said, 'Yes.' But the chemistry that had always buzzed between them hadn't seemed much in evidence today. Since Alice had arrived and they'd exchanged air kisses, they'd barely glanced at each other. Was that shyness because they hadn't seen each other for a few weeks? Or was it possible that Phil had only fought to get this far so he'd have maximum television exposure that he hoped would further his acting career? Did he really want to go out with her stepsister or had he just been acting all along?

Poppy felt cold at the thought. Oh, what a tangle. To use one of Dave's own phrases, 'you couldn't make it up.'

She glanced at Phil once more. She could hear him talking to Matt, but his deep actor's voice no longer sounded sexy.

'I've always wanted a boat,' Phil was saying. 'I don't know much about them. I do like the idea, though. I can't wait to get out on the water.'

It was all I, I, I...

In the last twenty seconds, Poppy felt as though her whole world had shifted on its axis. She needed to shift it back. She forced herself back to the present and clapped her hands to get everyone's attention. 'Right then, you lot. We can't stand around chatting all day. We'd better get started. Let's crack on.'

25

Whether Phil did or didn't fancy Alice didn't affect the filming. The waterskiing sequences went like a dream. The sea glittered, the sky sparkled, the sun shone so it was pleasantly warm, even though it wasn't yet ten, and after a couple of spectacular crashes, Phil picked up the art of waterskiing surprisingly quickly. He even got cocky once and let go with one hand to punch the sky with a fist, which had Alice clapping impulsively and cheering him on. It would make great television.

There was a lot of laughter and Dave pronounced they had plenty of action shots and plenty of sand, sea and coastline, ahead of their schedule.

'That couldn't have gone better, could it?' he told Poppy, sounding pleased as they said their goodbyes to Matt and headed back up towards the car park in chattering groups.

'That's what I thought.' She walked alongside him on the sun-dappled footpath beneath the canopy of leafy trees. She was still trying to adjust to the lightning bolt of realisation that she had feelings for him. The pain that had heralded it had eased off, swept aside by the distraction of work and the concentration required to get things perfect. But the awareness of him hadn't gone. She was suddenly acutely aware of every movement he made and she was conscious of how far apart they were at any given moment, and every time they touched or brushed against each other, her skin felt supercharged. It was making her jumpy. She was relieved when they got back to the car park.

Once there, Alice and Phil went off to get changed back into dry clothes, Alice to the Jeep and Phil to his own car. When they emerged again, Mandy would work her magic with hair and make-up. She was already unpacking her mobile hair kit, which involved an enormous colourful towel.

Poppy was in mid-conversation with her crew, all of them standing in the morning sunshine a little way from the parked cars to give Alice and Phil some privacy, when there was a loud bellow from behind them. This was followed by the sound of a door banging open. When Poppy spun around in surprise, she saw Phil, naked but for a pair of skimpy Superman briefs with a big red S on a bright blue background, running away from his car at top speed.

'What the fuck?' said Dave as they all turned to stare at Phil, who was barefoot on the stony ground (as well as bare pretty much everything else), which had slowed him down somewhat. He was now hopping from foot to foot on the scrubby grassed edge of the car park, staring back in the direction of his car, his face the picture of horror.

But for his expression of revulsion, it could have been funny, and some of the crew were smiling uncertainly. Was this another of Phil's theatrical attention-seeking stunts?

Si, who had a camera in his hand, had already started filming.

'Stop that immediately,' Dave told him, before turning towards Poppy. 'Do you want me to go?'

'Um, yes. That's probably best. If you don't mind?' She wasn't sure that it was appropriate for her to race after a practically naked Phil. She certainly didn't want to – hell, if she'd needed any confirmation that she didn't fancy Phil Grimshaw one iota, here it was. Even so, it was almost impossible for the eye not to be drawn to the big red S on the tight-fitting blue fabric of his underwear.

Blinking rapidly, she glanced around, hunting frantically for a towel or something that Dave could take with him, but the only one in sight was Mandy's beach towel, which Poppy had just realised was emblazoned with a picture of Wonder Woman. Oh God no. That would be worse than nothing.

Dave must have come to the same conclusion because he was empty-handed as he strode across to Phil.

Poppy glanced in the direction of her Jeep. Alice, now dressed again in shorts and a gorgeous T-shirt, her damp blonde hair tendrilling prettily around her shoulders, was getting out. Her face was concerned.

She came towards Poppy. 'Is he OK? What happened?'

'Dave's just finding out.'

The two men were conversing urgently and then Phil was pointing back towards the door of his car, which was wide open, its blue paintwork gleaming in the sunlight, and shaking his head. He seemed completely oblivious to the fact he was wearing nothing but his pants and had drawn the attention of the whole car park.

With a little shrug, Dave headed purposefully over to Phil's car, clearly on a mission. They all watched as he leaned into the passenger seat. He seemed to be picking up items of clothing, one at a time, and then shaking them out in front of him. Then suddenly he jumped back as something black fell from a pair of shorts on to the car park. Whatever it was, it was big, almost golf-ball size – they could all see it from several feet away – with leg-like appendages.

'Sweet Jesus,' said Mandy, giving a little shudder. 'That's one humungous spider. No wonder the poor bloke ran like the clappers. It must be one of those foreign ones. You hear about them sometimes coming over in bunches of bananas and ending up in supermarkets. Don't touch it, Dave,' she shouted.

Dave was already bending over for a closer look. Then he picked up the spider, dangled it from one leg so that it wriggled vigorously, and started walking back towards them. 'It's not real,' he called as he got closer. 'It's a very authentic-looking fake, though.'

'You mean someone put it there?' Si was incredulous. 'In his clothes?'

'How cruel,' Mandy said.

'I bet I can guess who it was,' Mike remarked, his lips twitching a little. 'And his name begins with Mr and ends with B.'

'Yes.' Alice was hugging her arms around herself. 'This has that crazy chef written all over it. He knows Phil has arachnophobia. Don't bring it any closer, please, Dave. Are you absolutely sure it's not real?'

'Hundred per cent.'

Poppy went to meet him. 'It's very hard to tell. I'd have fallen for it. Phil must have got the shock of his life.'

'Yeah. It's a good job he wasn't driving when he spotted it. They really need to get that feud of theirs sorted out before someone gets hurt.'

'I couldn't agree more.' She looked across at Phil, who was still standing miserably at the edge of the car park in just his pants. 'I think you've been the victim of a practical joke,' she called.

He came slowly towards them, his face grim. 'I swear I'll kill that man. One of these days, I won't be responsible for my actions.'

'Cool jockeys,' Alice called, which was clearly supposed to

lighten the mood but didn't work, at least not where Phil was concerned.

He stared at the ground, biting his lip.

'I'll get dressed,' he said, going back to his car and picking up his shorts, which were still lying on the ground where Dave had dropped them. He tugged them on and got back into the passenger seat and slammed the door.

Poppy was glad he'd shut the door. She could hear snorts of laughter coming from her team, all of whom were struggling to control themselves. Suddenly, she had an almost overwhelming urge to laugh herself. What was it about knowing you must not laugh because it was completely inappropriate that made you want to laugh even more?

She swallowed it down. *Think sad thoughts. Think about funerals. No. Not funerals.* She would never be able to think about undertakers again without remembering Auntie Sheila's mouth opening and closing like a goldfish. She coughed to cover a splutter of mirth.

'Can you do something with that spider?' she said to Dave, forcing herself to focus. 'We'd probably better not leave it here in case it gives some nervous member of the public a heart attack.'

'Please don't put it anywhere near me either,' said Alice with feeling. 'And if it's going in your car, Poppy, may I request that I sit as far away as possible?'

'I'll put it in the back pocket of my camera bag,' Dave said. 'I don't use that much.'

* * *

Fortunately, they'd been slightly ahead of schedule, so by the time they had driven in convoy to Durdle Door, Alice and Mandy with her and Dave, and the rest of the crew crammed into the other car, they were still on track, rather than late.

This didn't stop Poppy from feeling stressed. The spider shenanigans could have wrecked today. She dreaded to think what would have happened if Phil had stormed off to get his revenge on his tormentor. Several times on the way to Durdle Door, she'd checked her rear-view mirror to make sure Phil's car was still behind them.

'Don't look so worried, boss.' As they unloaded kit, Dave gave her arm a companiable pat, which caused her to jump out of her skin. 'Sorry – I didn't mean to startle you...'

'I must still be – er – feeling jumpy over that bloody spider.'

'Well, that's enough to make anyone jumpy. They don't bother me, and I still jumped.'

'Exactly,' she said, avoiding his eyes. 'Whose idea was it to bring the old-fashioned picnic basket?' She felt the need to keep things professional.

'Yours. You said they were incredibly romantic.'

'I didn't realise how heavy they were when I said that,' she murmured, heaving it out of the back.

'I'll carry it.' Dave reached past her and she leaned back quickly to get out of his way and bashed her head on the Jeep's roof. She was aware of his curious gaze, but there was no way she could give him an explanation. She could hardly say, 'It's you. Every time you touch me, it's like putting my hand on an electric fence, except that I don't want to jump away, I want to jump towards you.' The feeling was so new, she scarcely understood it herself.

'Can I carry anything?' Alice's question brought Poppy back to reality.

'No, sweetheart,' said Mandy before Poppy could reply. 'You

have another appointment with make-up – you can't have a romantic picnic with mascara streaks all down your face.'

'Have I? I thought it was waterproof.'

'Turn of phrase,' Mandy said, 'But beautiful as you are, we do need to get you television-ready. Shiny faces are a no-no.'

'Sorry. That'll be my sunblock.'

'We can cover that up.'

* * *

By the time they had all trekked down to the beach where Alice and Phil were having their lunchtime picnic beside the iconic arch, Poppy was beginning to relax again. The familiarity of working with her team, not to mention the sheer hard work of lugging heavy kit around, was helping. The spectacular scenery was a good distraction too. Even the ever-cynical Mike was impressed by the beauty of their surroundings – the vast arch worn through the rock, the towering cliffs and the turquoise sea that stretched out to meet the only slightly lighter turquoise sky.

Poppy was also incredibly relieved that Phil's experience with the spider hadn't affected his mood for too long. He seemed to have recovered his good humour, despite the fact he'd been made to look ridiculous in public. He wasn't quite up to joking about it yet, though. When Si had made a sly crack about his Superman shreddies, Phil had scowled at him and Si had shut up hastily. This didn't stop Si cracking spider jokes when Phil was out of earshot, though.

'What do you call a spider with no legs?' he asked Mike as they set up the picnic on the beach.

'A raisin,' Mike said, raising his eyebrows. 'The old ones are the best ones.'

'OK then, you'll like this one. What do spiders eat in Paris?'

'No idea. What do spiders eat in Paris?'

'French flies.' Si smirked and both Mike and Mandy sniggered.

'Don't let Phil hear you,' Poppy warned. 'And no cracks about Superman either.'

The last thing she needed was her leading man taking umbrage. Stern and brooding might be incredibly attractive on camera, but sulky and furious weren't so good and if he decided he'd had enough of this altogether and abandoned ship, they would all be in trouble.

Luckily, Phil was every inch the solicitous gentlemen as he and Alice picnicked on a tartan blanket on the golden sand with the famous great arch of limestone rock behind them. He and Alice touched frequently, Poppy noticed, but it was much more evident when the cameras were rolling. Curiously, from both of them. Were they both putting on a show? Surely not. The heat must be getting to her, she thought – the temperatures had climbed as they'd got closer to midday. The cove was sheltered, so even the sea air didn't cool it much.

There were a lot more people on Durdle Door beach and Poppy was busy in crowd-control mode, answering questions from curious members of the public and generally being incredibly nice to everyone while keeping them out of shots so that the cameramen could work. As usual, she was finding that most of the general public were very helpful and happy to give the film crew plenty of space.

'We couldn't have picked more perfect weather if we'd planned it,' Mike said when they finally broke for lunch. He retrieved a jumbo pack of Doritos from his bag as they set off back up the steep cliff path. 'What?' he said when Si commented. 'Watching other people eat makes you flaming hungry.'

* * *

By two, they were finished at Durdle Door and climbing back into their respective cars.

The third location was the horse ride along the beach at Shell Bay. This involved another trip in convoy through the Dorset countryside.

'How's your ankle holding up?' Dave asked Alice as they drove. 'You're not getting any twinges at all, are you?'

Poppy had asked Alice the same question herself earlier, but it was nice of Dave to be so considerate, despite the fact his obvious affection for Alice caused her a pinprick of pain.

'Good as new, thanks, Dave. I told you I was a tough cookie.'

'How are you feeling now, Poppy?' Mandy asked from the back. 'Did that indigestion settle?'

'Yes, thank you.' Poppy hoped she wasn't blushing.

'Indigestion? When did you start getting that, angel?' Poppy met Alice's eyes in the rear-view mirror. 'Are you sure it's indigestion?'

'I think so. Anyway, it's gone now.' Poppy searched frantically for a diversion. 'Are you looking forward to riding along a sunset beach?'

'I am and so's Phil, although he did ask me about that earlier. It's not going to be sunset at 3 p.m., is it? Are you doing something clever with the editing?'

To Poppy's relief, Dave stepped in. 'It's not that clever,' he said. 'It's just the use of filters. As you say, we're a little early for sunset, but we can get quite a dramatic moody feel.'

There was a bit more talk about special effects and then Mandy said idly, 'Are we allowed to do spider jokes now?'

'Go for it,' Dave prompted.

'What do you call an undercover spider?'

'I don't know. What do you call an undercover spider?'

'A spy-duh.' Mandy laughed loudly at her own joke as everyone in the car groaned.

'Where do spiders meet their partners?' Alice asked. 'On the web.' Alice had always had a near photographic memory for jokes and she loved puns. She was away now. 'What does a cross spider do? Go up the wall.'

'Did you hear about the spider love triangle?' Mandy interrupted. 'It was a tangled web.'

There were more groans, but the laughter was infectious.

When the two women ran out of jokes, Dave said, 'My turn. What's a spider's favourite TV show?'

'What?' they all chorused.

'The Newlyweb Game. The Newlywed Game,' he prompted, emphasising the last part of the word.

'You're too young to remember that,' Alice told Mandy, who looked nonplussed. 'It was an American game show. Massively successful. It ran for years.'

'So will Date for a Day,' Dave said, and then half-turned to speak to Alice. 'Are you looking forward to your beach ride?'

'Very much.' She caught Poppy's gaze in the rear-view mirror. 'Nothing like a good gallop along a beach to blow away the cobwebs.'

26

Alice looked stunning in jodhpurs. The stretchy fawn material clung to every inch of her endless legs and Poppy was aware that more than one of the men standing around her on the beach was casting admiring glances her way. Dave was amongst them.

Phil was too busy adjusting his own riding outfit to be looking. He wore grey breeches that moulded around his muscular thighs and bottom, teamed with a very stylish grey and white shirt, which was open at the neck. He looked the perfect moody, brooding Poldark, even down to his hair, which had gone a little curly since the sea.

Poppy knew she'd have found this whole ensemble much sexier if she hadn't known he was wearing Superman briefs underneath it. She forced the image out of her head. This was no time to slip back into giggle mode. Holy guacamole, how had she ever found him attractive? She found herself comparing Phil with Dave and finding the maître d' couldn't match up. She had to shake this disconcerting thought away.

The owner of the horses and a lad who didn't look much older than sixteen had led the two gorgeous chestnuts on to the beach. The horses' coats gleamed and the brass buckles on their tacks glinted as they caught the afternoon sun.

One of the chestnuts had just done what horses tend to do best at inappropriate moments and there was a pile of steaming dung on the sand.

That was a reality they certainly wouldn't be focusing on, Poppy thought, reminded of what Lennox had said about horses, as the lad cleared up with a shovel and bucket.

Alice moved towards the lead chestnut and stroked his neck and he pricked his ears and blew on her fingers.

'Hello, gorgeous,' she said.

'I thought you were talking to me for a minute,' said the lad with a wistful expression and Alice laughed. 'Do you need a hand to get on?'

'I think I can manage.' While he held the reins, Alice sprung into the saddle with a practised ease.

To Poppy's relief, Phil did the same on the other chestnut. Clearly, he hadn't lied about being able to ride then.

They were already gathering a small crowd of onlookers, drawn by the horses and the presence of the cameras and boom.

'Do you two just want to have a trot up and down and get the feel of the horses?' Poppy said. 'Make sure you're happy.'

Both riders set off, trotting side by side up the beach.

Poppy looked at Dave and he nodded approvingly.

'I must admit I had my reservations,' he said. 'But this is going to look spectacular.'

'We're lucky that we've got such nice weather. And that we've got exactly the right amount of beach.' She gestured to the wide strip of hard sand.

'That wasn't luck. It was planning. Give yourself a big pat on the back, boss.'

'Don't tempt fate. We're not done yet.' Although his words had warmed her. Or maybe that was the sun?

'Fair comment. Shall we get a few "general views" before we start?' He shielded his eyes to look in the direction of the riders, who were now small specks in the distance. 'Looks like they're going to canter back.'

'Let's do it,' Poppy said and the crew swung into action. A few moments later, the horses flashed past them in a streak of fiery gold and thunder of hooves on hard sand. Both Phil and Alice looked perfectly at home; both of them, to Poppy's relief, also looked reassuringly in control. They pulled up a short distance away and Poppy waved them over. 'It makes me want to ride again,' she said to her crew as they waited for the riders to head back.

'I wouldn't get on a horse if you paid me a million pounds,' Mike said.

'A lucky reprieve for the equine world,' Si quipped, sticking his belly out in an imitation of Mike and waddling a few steps up and down the beach.

'I'll ignore that, you cheeky bloody bugger.'

'I'd love to try it,' Mandy said. 'It's one of those things on my bucket list. How about you, Dave?'

'I can ride, as it happens. An uncle of mine had a farm we used to visit when I was a kid. He had an old hunter.'

Poppy looked at him in surprise. 'You've never said.'

He clicked his tongue. 'You've never asked.'

She had a brief moment's fantasy in which she and Dave were cantering through the surf, but fortunately Alice and Phil arrived back before she got too carried away. They were laughing and puffing almost as much as the chestnuts. 'That was such brilliant fun,' Alice said. 'But I'm not as fit as I thought.'

'Me neither. But I don't think there's any other sport that uses the same muscles as riding.' Phil's face was alight. The chemistry was back between them. Maybe Poppy had imagined the fact that it had ever gone.

'Right then,' she said. 'Let's get started properly.'

It couldn't have gone more perfectly. It would have been hard to find a better way of showing off Dorset's beautiful beaches or the romance of a couple on their first-ever date than having them canter two showy chestnuts along the golden sands of Studland Beach. It was obvious that both Phil and Alice were having the time of their lives as they splashed back and forth through the surf.

When Poppy stood close to Dave as he played back some of what he'd taken, she felt a rising sense of excitement. 'This is utterly brilliant.'

'I only taped what was there, boss.'

'Don't put yourself down. Big pat on the back.'

When Poppy declared they were done with the riding sequences, she felt as high as if she'd just completed a parade of triumph around the winner's enclosure at Ascot. She'd forgotten how much she loved location shooting. It was so different to being cooped up in a studio doing take after take. It was so natural and fluid. She loved the adrenaline, the sheer nervous energy and focus, fuelled by little more than caffeine and excitement, or at least that's how it had been today. She'd not eaten more than a handful of grapes from the Durdle Door picnic since breakfast.

Having called it a wrap, she and her crew and the horses clip-clopped back to the car park with their entourage of onlookers, a couple of whom were busy interrogating Si and Mandy. Poppy overhead the odd line from a distance.

'What programme is it going to be on?'

'Is it *Poldark*? Was that Aidan Turner? He's even better-looking in the flesh.'

'Taller too – I thought he was a short-arse.'

Poppy made a mental note to tell Phil. He'd be thrilled. It might help to soothe the humiliation of the spider episode.

'Last stop, the Bluebell,' she said, as they all got into their respective cars once more.

* * *

Technically, a crew shouldn't be working for more than twelve hours, although in practice this did sometimes happen. It was unavoidable occasionally. Poppy's schedule had been carefully worked out so they didn't go over today, but it was always going to be a close-run thing. None of her crew had wanted to step down. They had all insisted they wanted to see out the whole day and, slightly against her better judgement, Poppy had let them. But this did mean they were working against the clock.

The filming of the romantic evening meal was scheduled for six. Alice and Phil had both made the metamorphosis from jodhpur-clad rider to glamorous dinner date in record time with the help of wardrobe and make-up and were now seated ready at their table in the Bluebell Cliff's restaurant. The silver cutlery gleamed, the candlelight flickered, even though it was still very much daylight outside, and Alice in a beautifully cut magenta dress and costume jewellery and Phil in a suit that made him look even more like Poldark faced each other across the table.

Poppy had been relieved to learn that Mr B was not on duty tonight, so there would be no punch-ups in retaliation for the spider stunt. Or any further practical – or rather impractical – jokes from Mr B. Neither Alice nor Phil would be eating much on camera – that never looked good – the emphasis was on the wine and the chat.

For simplicity's sake, Poppy had handed over the directing to Dave. She was aware that he was focusing on long shots while another cameraman did the more intimate shots of the couple. She wondered if he was trying to avoid being at close proximity to what was clearly a very successful date. She didn't interfere – Dave was more than capable of directing and she felt for him, having had a taste herself today of the pain of unrequited feelings.

The only thing that was now slightly worrying her was that Taylor Stanton was running behind schedule. She'd just had a message to say she had been held up. The routes to the Bluebell, both via ferry and road, were gridlocked. 'I'll be there as soon as I can,' Taylor had told Poppy via her Bluetooth car phone, 'but unless I can find a passing helicopter, I'm a little stuck.'

'It's fine,' Poppy had reassured, because there was really nothing else she could say.

Taylor finally arrived half an hour after they should have finished shooting and, after a quick confab with the crew, they unanimously decided to go ahead with the reveal in the lighthouse.

'We can sleep for a week when we're done,' Mike said.

'Yeah, boss, sleep's overrated,' Dave said, suppressing a yawn.

They were probably all running on adrenaline, Poppy thought as they headed up the steep spiral staircase of the light-house. She knew she was. For the last hour, she'd been feeling slightly light-headed, having still not eaten, but she certainly wasn't sleepy. She wasn't hungry either. She'd gone past it.

The filming of the reveal would take place in the honeymoon suite that was at the very top of the lighthouse and she had to admit the room was spectacular. A circular space with a floor-to-ceiling window overlooking the sea, this was where the great light would originally have sat. It was now hired out for special occasions and had bespoke circular furniture, including a bench that nestled against the window, and it was here that Taylor would ask the all-important question of the couple.

Poppy had deliberately avoided asking Alice or Phil what they were going to say. Since the beginning of the day, she had changed her own mind over and over. In programme terms, the outcome didn't matter really – although, in an ideal world, it would be lovely if they were to wax lyrical about each other and announce that they definitely had a future. She knew that wasn't going to happen in every show, but it would be nice if it happened on the pilot.

She was about to find out. They were all crammed into the relatively small space. The lighting had been set up at the same time as they'd done the risk assessment earlier, which was just as well as they weren't far off sunset.

'Three, two, one... action,' Poppy said, for what she fervently hoped was the last time that day.

'Now then, my darlings,' Taylor began. 'We've reached the final hurdle. And it's been quite a day, hasn't it? You've got to know each other a little better – you've watched each other in action – so to speak. At times with very little kit on.' She winked at the camera and turned back to Alice. 'So did Phil impress you with his waterskiing then, Alice?'

'I was very impressed,' Alice replied. 'He picked it up really quickly.'

'And he looked a fine figure of a man in his riding gear, didn't he? In fact, I'd describe him as a proper action hero, as I'm sure our viewers will back home. But it's not up to the viewers to decide, is it? It's up to you, Alice. Is he the Dorset gentleman you said you were looking for yesterday morning?' She put a finger to her lips. 'Before you say anything, let's ask Phil how he thinks your date went.' Taylor turned towards Phil. 'How about you, Phil? Do you like Alice more or less than you did before you spent the day with her?'

'Definitely more,' Phil said, his eyes flashing dark. 'How could I not? She's utterly gorgeous.'

Alice looked radiant at his praise.

Taylor turned back to Alice. 'So it's all down to you, Alice. Do you feel the same way about Phil? Tell me... And tell the viewers at home. Are you going to see Phil again or has this just been a Date for a Day?'

Alice opened her mouth, but she didn't speak straight away. 'Well, Taylor, I...'

Poppy held her breath. Her head span a little more. She was suddenly very hot and the lights seemed ultra-bright and then brighter and then muted and then the whole room was swirling and spinning and she was slipping away into darkness.

27

Reality came back in fragments. Sound was first. Poppy could hear voices.

'Is she OK?'

'What happened? I thought...'

'Stand back. Give her some air.'

'It's flaming hot in here.'

It was flaming hot. Poppy agreed wholeheartedly with whoever had said that.

'Has anyone called an ambulance?'

It was the mention of an ambulance that galvanised her into a reaction. She became aware that she was lying on something hard. The floor maybe. She could feel carpet under her fingers.

She opened her eyes but swiftly shut them again when she felt sick.

'I don't need an ambulance,' she said as firmly as she could in the circumstances.

'Poppy, angel, don't try to move.' Alice's concerned voice was close to her ear.

She opened her eyes again, this time with more success

because the room stayed still. Alice was kneeling on the floor next to her.

'I think I must have fainted.'

She could see Dave holding a mobile phone. He was hunkered down on her other side. 'We should probably just get you checked over.'

'No.' She remembered suddenly where she was as she saw the studio lights above her head. 'Shit, did I just ruin the reveal? Have we got to—'

'Don't worry, we've got a wrap.' Dave was still looking at her with concern. 'How do you feel? You keeled over like a felled tree.'

'I was too hot. It's no biggie.'

'She doesn't usually faint.' That was Alice again. 'She said she had indigestion this morning, but she doesn't usually get indigestion either. Or at least she's never mentioned getting it to me.'

Bloody hell. How much longer was that indigestion going to come back to haunt her?

'Is she as anti-hospitals as you are?' Dave asked Alice.

'No, she's not normally anti them at all – at least no more than anyone is.'

'I am here, you know,' Poppy said. She tried to sit up again and this time it was more of a success. The sickness was passing. 'I'm perfectly fine. Really I am,' she said as she got into a sitting position on the floor. Her head was throbbing and she could now see several other concerned faces, including Phil and Taylor, all looking in her direction. 'Get lost, please, you lot, I don't need an audience.'

'You heard the lady,' Dave said. 'We're done here anyway. Go and get some sleep or a drink or something. We'll catch you up in a minute.'

Poppy had given them the option to stay overnight at the Bluebell or go home depending on where they lived. Taylor had opted to stay – she came from the furthest away. Alice, Poppy and Dave were all staying. Phil wasn't staying as he was local and Beauty Spot Productions hadn't offered to fund it. She couldn't remember what Mandy, Mike and Si were doing. The thoughts ran around in her head and she closed her eyes. When she opened them again, only Alice and Dave were left in the circular room. They were both still sitting on the floor, but now Alice was holding out a glass of water.

'Thanks.' She took it gratefully and drank.

'I bet you haven't eaten, have you?' Alice said. 'You've been too busy tearing around trying to do three jobs at once.'

'Busted,' Poppy said, feeling better now she didn't have such a big audience. 'I just went past it, you know how you do. And it's hot, isn't it?'

Dave was holding something out in a paper wrapper that said 'Bluebell Cliff' on the front. 'Chocolate shortbread from the room. It's the best I can do. Although they are good. Mr B might be a pain in the butt, but I don't think I've ever tasted such melt-in-the-mouth biscuits.'

'I bet *you* haven't eaten either,' Poppy accused, looking at the packet longingly.

'Yeah, but I didn't just faint,' he retorted.

'Share them,' Alice said in an affectionate, exasperated tone. 'Are you sure that's all it was, angel? How are you feeling now?'

'Much better,' Poppy said, taking a biscuit and returning the remaining one to Dave. He was right. They did melt in your mouth. She turned her attention back to Alice. 'Don't keep me in suspense. What did you say to Phil? I never heard your answer. Are you guys going to see each other again?'

'Yes,' said Dave.

'No,' said Alice.

'But you said yes on the show.' Dave was now looking at Alice with genuine surprise.

'I know we did, but that's because we both felt that would be the best outcome and, don't get me wrong, we do like each other, but there's not really any chemistry there. Also, Phil's seeing someone else.'

'What? You're kidding me.' Poppy let out a deep breath. She was starting to feel sick again for an entirely different reason. 'He said he was single on his application form. That was part of the deal.'

'Oh, he *was* single back then. He wasn't lying, but he's met someone since we did the filming. He told me yesterday. She's also an actor and they've fallen for each other. He kept saying how sorry he was, but he didn't do it on purpose.'

Alice sounded incredibly cheerful for someone who'd just found out they'd been ditched before they'd even properly got going.

'How bloody annoying,' Dave said. 'Are you OK with that?' He leaned forward to touch Alice's shoulder and she looked at him happily.

'I'm fine with it.' Her eyes were sparkling. 'More than fine.' She shot a sideways glance at Poppy. 'But that's because I've got my eye on someone else too.'

Of course she had. It was Dave. Poppy was beginning to wish she'd stayed oblivious – in more ways than one. But it was slowly dawning on her that actually this could be the best outcome for everyone, particularly for Dave, who'd been looking quite depressed since Alice's announcement that she had her eye on someone else. It was obvious he had no idea that Alice meant him.

She should put that right. 'I'm thrilled,' Poppy said, looking from one to the other. She had no intention of standing in their way. Maybe them being a couple would snap her out of whatever crazy feelings she'd been bombarded with today. 'I think you two are a really good match.' Phil wasn't the only one who could put on quite a good act when the situation demanded it, she thought, pleased with herself.

'Oh, it's not Dave,' Alice said quickly.

'Isn't it? But I thought...' Her traitorous heart leapt, although she dared not look at Dave. It would hurt too much to witness his disappointment.

'It's Alistair,' Alice clarified. 'Don't worry, no one else knows and we've both said that we'll keep it quiet until after *Date for a Day* has aired, if necessary.'

'Do you mean Alistair as in... the other guy who was in the final?' Poppy felt as though she was trying to get on a merry-go-round that wouldn't stay still. No sooner did she think she'd caught up with the situation than it moved on again.

'The human rights lawyer?' Dave echoed. Several emotions had flitted across his face in the last few seconds. Relief, disappointment, surprise, but now he shook his head and gave a rueful smile. 'Finishing in second place is the story of my life,' he said to them both. 'I'm used to it.'

Poppy felt for him.

'He's being gentlemanly,' Alice said, looking at him pointedly. 'Aren't you, Dave?'

For the first time since this crazy roundabout conversation had begun, he looked vulnerable.

'Oh, for goodness sake.' Alice looked from one to the other. 'Surely you two can see what's been obvious to everyone else for weeks?' She gathered the folds of the magenta dress around her and got up slowly from the floor where they were all still sitting. 'You two are made for each other. And, on that note, I think I'll leave you guys to it and go and catch up with Taylor and Phil. I promised them both a massive drink.' When she was halfway to the door, she glanced back over her shoulder. 'By the way, there's an absolutely stunning sunset over the sea. It's incredibly romantic. You two should get off the floor and take a look.'

Then she was gone and they could hear her heels tip-tapping into the distance as she ran down the spiral staircase.

Poppy wondered if Dave was feeling as flabbergasted as she was. He hadn't moved throughout Alice's little speech. Now they looked at each other.

'My sister's always had an overactive imagination,' Poppy said quickly, not wanting him to feel sorry for her.

'Is that so?' He was sitting very close, which was doing disturbing things to her insides. 'Is she imagining that you want more than friendship with me?'

'No,' Poppy blurted. 'She's not imagining that bit, but if you don't...'

Before she could say anything else, he bent his head a little closer and touched her face. 'She isn't imagining it from my end either.'

'I thought you liked Alice.' If she hadn't already been on the floor she might have keeled over again.

'I do. She's lovely. But I'm not attracted to her.' He paused. 'To be honest, I thought you liked Phil.'

'I thought there was some chemistry there myself for a while. But it's definitely gone.' She looked into Dave's eyes, which were still close to hers. She'd always thought they were brown, but there were tiny gold flecks in their depths. Or maybe that was the sunset. The whole room was bathed in golden light.

He stroked her cheek very gently with his index finger. 'Are you still feeling giddy? Do you need a hand to get up, honey?'

'Actually, I'm quite happy down here.' She leaned forward and kissed him and after a fraction of a second he put his arms around her and kissed her back and for a long time that was all they did: tender, gentle, 'getting to know you' kisses. *This is so lovely*, she thought. *How did I not realise it would be so lovely?*

When they finally drew apart, he said, 'I've wanted to do that for as long as I can remember.'

And even though there was some part of her, some tiny locked-away part, that knew this was true, she needed to be sure. It had been such a long time since she'd trusted a man. Or even trusted herself, come to that.

'Then why haven't you?' she asked him, and then she remembered that time at Rose's party when she'd tried to kiss him and he'd resisted. 'Why didn't you kiss me at Rose's party?'

'Because I wanted you to remember it too – I didn't want you to wake up in the morning and not remember what had happened the night before. And I certainly didn't want you to regret it.' A beat. 'Call me old-fashioned.' He smiled at her.

'Fair enough.'

'And I was right, wasn't I, because when you phoned the next morning, you told me that you couldn't have regretted it more.'

'I know I said that, but that's because I thought it wasn't what you wanted. I was embarrassed. I'd convinced myself you turned me down because you fancied Alice.'

'I didn't. It's always been you.'

She could see the truth of this in his eyes and hear the depth of his feelings in his voice.

'I know we joke about it, Poppy, but the fact of the matter is, you've had your heart under lock and key ever since I've known you.'

He was right about that. She had locked it away after Stephen because it had been the only way to survive. In fact, she hadn't just locked her heart away, she had packed it in ice.

Before she could answer, he went on, 'I've always hoped that one day that might change.'

She met his eyes again, loving the way he was looking at her. That kiss had thawed much of the ice and his words were melting the rest. She could feel a warmth spreading up through her that had nothing to do with the heat of the room and everything to do with that zinging chemistry that had made itself known so violently this morning and had been fighting to be heard ever since.

'But I wasn't in a rush,' Dave added quietly. 'I thought I'd wait and see what happened.'

'How long would you have waited?'

'I'm not sure.' His eyes glinted with amusement. 'Not forever. Although there is that saying, isn't there? All the best things in life are worth waiting for.' He tilted his head in a question. 'This is all about me. How about you? How do you feel? Do you want a relationship with your director of photography? Romance, dating, kissing, all that schmaltzy stuff? Or shall we forget this conversation ever happened and go back to being friends and colleagues? I can do that, if that's what you want?' His voice dropped a bit.

'No,' she said swiftly. 'That's not what I want. You're right about me locking away my feelings. But that didn't mean they weren't there. I guess that if I didn't believe in love a bit, I wouldn't have pushed so hard for this show.' She rubbed her eyes. 'But you know that, don't you?'

He gave her a half-smile.

'The truth is I've just been in denial. I'm totally up for schmaltz and dating and romance, especially if there's more kissing involved. In fact, I think we've got a lot of catching up to do on that front.' She caught his hand and tugged him to his feet.

'But first of all, while we're on romance, do you think we should check out this sunset?'

'I thought you said sunsets were for softies.' There was laughter in his eyes. Laughter and passion – oh my goodness, that was such a potent mix.

'I was in denial about sunsets too,' she said, dragging her gaze from his and looking out of the window. 'Oh wow...'

Now they were standing up, there was no denying the beauty of this one. The great, glass floor-to-ceiling windows gave an unhindered view across the sea to a peach-stained sky. Their timing was perfect. The sun was balanced on the very edge of the horizon. The sky around it was alight with gold and the sea was touched with fire. It was breathtakingly beautiful.

Poppy felt as though they were standing in a golden room. A couple at the end of an epic romance, in the seconds before they stroll away into a sunset holding hands, as the credits roll.

For a moment, neither of them spoke. She was aware of their breathing and the scent of him – a mix of this morning's faded aftershave and sea. She was aware of the steady thrum of her own heartbeat, of warmth and of a quiet and deep happiness.

Poppy knew she was going to remember this moment forever. Not the moment when she fell in love, because she was pretty sure that had been happening for a long time, increment by increment, but the moment when she finally let herself believe in it again, the moment when she gave love a fighting chance.

28

When Poppy woke up the next day beneath the Egyptian-cotton luxury duvet of one of the Bluebell Cliffs beautiful boutique rooms, her first thought was that she'd imagined the previous night's events.

Her second thought was that this was not her room. She was pretty sure the en-suite bathroom door was in a different place.

Her third thought was that she was not alone.

She gave a deep sigh of contentment as she realised she hadn't imagined any of it. Dave was beside her, eyes closed, breathing peacefully. She took the opportunity to study him in the dawn light that filtered through the heavy curtains which they hadn't quite closed last night. He had a tiny mole on his shoulder. A lightly muscled, lightly tanned shoulder. He had beautiful shoulders. He had a beautiful body.

Fragments of memory came back to her thick and fast. Their brief foray to the bar to let the crew who were staying over know that she was OK, that the fainting had been nothing but a combination of not eating and exhaustion.

Then they had gone to his room and ordered room service

and they had carried on talking and kissing – in fact, kissing had featured rather heavily. Room service had come but she didn't remember them eating very much. A quick glance at the dressing table on the other side of the room revealed the remains of their meal. Had they eaten anything at all? She had never in her life missed two meals in a day and barely noticed – was this what love did?

Her mind raced on, past the neglected room service, to the part where they had decided to rip off each other's clothes. Not that this had been so much of a decision, as such, but more a slow-growing realisation, culminating at exactly the same time for both of them, that they couldn't bear to wait another moment to get naked.

Holy guacamole, how had she ever thought that Dave was staid and reserved? She had never known lovemaking like it, and it had felt exactly like that – lovemaking – not just mind-blowing sex. Although it had certainly been that too. It had put every past experience she'd ever had into the shade. Made her experiences with Stephen look like clumsy, immature fumbling – as though they'd been two children role playing at being adults.

For years she had held the memory of Stephen in some idealised glass case. Last night it had been shattered, irrevocably. How had she ever imagined that her ex was her soulmate? How had she ever confused flirting with Phil as chemistry? What on earth had she been thinking?

She had never known that lovemaking could be like it had been last night with Dave: tender, urgent, amazing, ecstatic, delicious, unselfish and beyond her wildest dreams. She had no idea what time they had finally fallen asleep, but oddly she didn't feel tired now either.

Dave opened his eyes. 'Hey, you.' He propped himself up on one elbow. 'Last night wasn't just a wonderful dream then?'

'That's what I was lying here wondering.'

'Maybe we did dream it.' He ran his fingertips across her bare shoulder and then in an exploratory foray along the curve of her breast.

She gasped, as every sense she had sprung into alertness at the memory of his touch. 'Maybe we should refresh our memories,' she said. 'What do you think?'

'I think that you're insatiable, Poppy Allen. And I like it.'

She giggled. 'We have got a lot of catching up to do, I mean, that is if you needed an excuse.'

'I don't need an excuse.' He peeled the duvet down, very slowly, his eyes locked on to hers. 'Catching up sounds good to me. Bring it on.'

* * *

When they finally made it into the dining room, just before the Bluebell stopped serving breakfast at 9 a.m., they were met by a round of applause from Mike, Si, Alice, Mandy and Corinna.

'What?' Poppy said, sliding into the seat beside Alice.

'Oh, nothing.' Alice exchanged glances with Mandy, who smirked. 'We're just impressed you actually made it downstairs. Taylor said to say goodbye, she had to get back to London.'

'Thanks. She mentioned she'd have to go early. Sorry I'm late. It was a long day yesterday.'

'A very long day.' Dave reached for a piece of cold toast.

'And a very long night,' Mike quipped, with a salacious wink. 'For some people staying in the hotel, present company excepted, of course.' He shook his head. 'Take the buggers in the room next door to me. They weren't sleeping at all – not by the sound of it. Very thin walls in this place. I think I might put in a complaint to the management.'

'What room were you in?' Poppy asked anxiously, and Mike beamed from ear to ear.

'Hook, line and sinker.' He met her gaze and she felt her face heat up to furnace level. 'It's all right, boss. Just joshing with you. It's none of my business what consenting adults do under cover of darkness. Even if they don't do it very quietly.'

Si gave a snort of laughter.

Dave kept diplomatically quiet. But as soon as everyone else was chatting again, Poppy hissed to Alice, 'Am I just being paranoid, or does everyone know?'

'It's written all over your faces,' Alice said. 'You have that glow. The one people get when they've just figured out they're in love. You're as shiny and sparkly as a couple of teenagers. And everyone is really pleased for you both. As I think I might have mentioned yesterday, it's obvious to everyone around you that you're made for each other.'

'Oh.' Poppy helped herself to a croissant from the basket on the table. Her appetite seemed to have come back with a vengeance. 'Do you think it matters – you know, mixing business with pleasure?'

'No, angel, I do not. I think it's absolutely brilliant. Dave is lovely. You're lovely. It's bloody fantastic.'

As she finished speaking, Poppy was aware that a stillness had come over the table and everyone was looking at her, and Mike said, 'Hear hear.'

'I echo that,' Si muttered, lifting up his coffee mug in a toast.

And suddenly everyone was clapping again.

* * *

It felt quite sad packing up to leave the Bluebell Cliff. Poppy didn't want to go. Even when she was at reception paying their bill and Clara was smiling at her.

'Were you pleased with how it all went in the end?' the manager asked her. 'I know we had a slightly shaky start, but I hear yesterday went off very well.'

'It's been wonderful,' Poppy said. 'Thank you so much.'

'And you will let us know if the series gets full approval, won't you?'

'You will be the first to know,' Poppy confirmed, holding out her hand to shake Clara's and then, on impulse, leaning forward and kissing her cheek instead. 'You and your staff have been amazing.'

'With one or two notable exceptions.' Clara clasped her hands in front of her. 'Although I do believe that Phil and Mr B may have finally resolved their differences.'

Poppy wondered if she knew about the spider incident. She decided not to mention it and she was glad she hadn't because Mr B chose that moment to stroll into reception.

'Are you lot on your way?' He didn't wait for an answer. 'I'm glad I caught you. I wanted to extend my apologies for the minor hitches that occurred. So unfortunate. Mix-ups with ingredients! They're the bane of a chef's life. And a producer's – even one of your calibre, I'm sure.'

'Quite,' Poppy said. Luckily for him, she was in a very good mood. Even an unrepentant chef wasn't going to be able to change that.

* * *

The next week would have seemed flat if it wasn't for the steadily growing joy of her new relationship with Dave. On the surface, things were much the same. They still saw each other a lot at work. But now they saw each other outside work too.

Although the boundaries had blurred irrevocably between them, they managed to stay on an entirely professional footing at work. But outside of work they spent every spare moment doing the things that couples do: talking about their hopes and dreams, making love, going out on dates, sending dozens of schmaltzy WhatsApp messages and falling more deeply for each other day by day. Poppy had worried that she might find it too difficult spending so much more time with him. But she found she couldn't get enough of him. It was as though the man who'd always been her best friend had suddenly become her lover too and it was wonderful.

When they were strolling along Poole Quay one evening at the end of May, she invited him to the June curry night.

'Are you sure?' he said. 'Isn't that a family gathering?'

'It's family and partners,' she said, grabbing his hand and pulling him to a temporary halt on the quay so that a couple of tourists had to sidestep sharply past them. 'I know you've met most of my family anyway, but I want to introduce you properly as my man. My soulmate, the person I'm head over heels in love with.'

'I would be honoured, Poppy.' His eyes were dark in the dusky blue sky. 'I'm head over heels in love with you too.'

'I know. You tell me every night on WhatsApp.'

'Do I? Sorry. Is it too much?'

'No. You can never tell me enough.'

'You are the love of my life,' he said and they kissed, right there in the middle of the quay.

Poppy was aware of the lapping of the water at the edges of the quay, the squawks of seagulls, the buzz of voices – someone had just yelled, 'Get a room' – and the muted music coming from one of the pubs on the quay. But mostly she was aware of Dave and how perfect it felt to be in his arms.

* * *

The evening before the June curry night, Poppy had an odd text from her mother. She hadn't had one for a while, but this one said:

Really looking forward to seeing you on Friday. Kenny and I are thinking of going to your pope.

Poppy forwarded it to Alice and Rose with a couple of question marks. Rose sent back a text that said:

I got one too, but I don't have a clue what she means.

Alice sent back a one liner:

Received same. Mystified.

Poppy put it out of her head. She was certain their mother's news had nothing to do with any pope. But it didn't sound too worrying.

* * *

It was odd but also lovely going to curry night as a couple. Dave arrived to collect her wearing smart cords and a shirt and a dark jacket. He was freshly shaved.

'You've dressed up,' she said, studying him. 'Have you actually polished your shoes?'

'Um, yeah. I have. Is it too much?' He took his jacket off. 'Is this too formal? I've got my leather one in the car. I could wear that instead.'

'You look great. Don't look so worried.' She was touched that he'd made so much effort.

'I don't want to let you down.'

'You've never let me down, Dave. Not in all the time I've known you.' As she spoke, she realised it was true. He'd always been reliable, gentlemanly, kind – is that why she hadn't ever thought of him as boyfriend material? Because her previous experience of boyfriends had been quite the opposite.

'What?' Dave asked.

'I was just thinking that I want to spend the rest of my life with you.' Holy guacamole, had she just said that out loud?

It seemed she had, because he was now looking at her with an astounded expression.

It was Poppy's turn to feel nervous. 'Um, I probably should have edited that.'

'Because you didn't mean it?' There was a lightness to his question, which was at odds with the seriousness in his eyes that she usually only saw when he was intently focused behind a camera.

'I meant it,' she said. 'It's just taken me a long time to realise it.' She was suddenly very conscious that he might not feel the same at all and she was getting deeper in by the second. Who needed a shovel? 'Anyway,' she said brusquely, glancing at her watch and hoping her flushed face wasn't too obvious. They were still standing in the dim light of her hall. 'We'd better get going. Or we'll be late. Are you OK to carry this?' She thrust the bag containing the desserts at him and rushed off.

Downstairs in the car park, they transferred the desserts to the back seat of his car.

'You'll need to make sure you don't brake too hard,' she said, trying to divert him from what she'd said upstairs. 'Or there'll be Eton Mess, um, mess all over your car. It's a nightmare getting cream out of car seats. Maybe I should carry that one on my lap. Maybe I should—'

'Maybe you should stop talking for a second, Poppy, because I want to say something. Shall we get in the car?'

'Sure. Right.' Shit. Here it came. All that stuff about not wanting a serious relationship. About it being difficult to trust again. All the stuff he'd said when they'd had that Italian meal – had that only been a couple of months ago? The night when it had started to change, although she hadn't even properly been aware of it then. The night when she'd begun to realise that it was possible to trust a man again. That it may even be possible to love one.

But she still shouldn't have said it. Everyone knew men hated commitment, that they ran a mile at the first sign of the word. Especially when it was mooted in cold blood on a doorstep when you were already doing something ultra-scary like taking him to a family meal. Oh, crap.

She was so tangled in self-doubt that she almost missed what he said completely.

'Remember when I said that I wouldn't wait forever, Poppy?'

'Yes.' Of course he wouldn't. No one in their right mind would hang about waiting for a romance that might never happen, just on the off-chance. There were plenty more fish in the sea.

'Well, I lied about that. I'd have carried on waiting.' He had rested his hands on the steering wheel but now he turned to meet her gaze. 'I've loved you pretty much from day one, Poppy. The truth is, the only thing that's changed across the last five years is the intensity of my feelings.'

She looked at him. 'But now you've got to know me in a

biblical sense, you've realised your feelings aren't as strong as you'd thought?'

'No, you muppet. They're stronger than they've ever been.' He leaned closer. 'If I can call the woman I want to spend the rest of my life with a muppet, can I?'

'I think that on this occasion it may be perfectly justified,' she said, feeling a wonderful warmth spreading through her entire body as she kissed him.

29

It was Poppy's turn to be the focus of the curry night. Everyone wanted to talk to Dave. And everyone wanted to congratulate her on the completion of the filming of *Date for a Day*. And, as usual, everyone wanted to talk at the same time.

'When will it be on?'

'Alice said she can't tell us the outcome of the date until it's aired. Is that true?'

'Is there any possibility that I can be in the next one?' That was Micky.

Poppy looked at him in amazement. 'I thought you liked being single, honey?'

'No takers at the dinner-date club then?' Lennox said slyly. 'Did they find out you can't cook?'

'I can cook perfectly well, I'll have you know.'

'But they got bored of your cheese on toast masquerading as Welsh rarebit. Can't say I blame them.'

Micky threw a cushion at Lennox, narrowly missing knocking a fragile pink orchid flying, and Lennox laughed.

'Lighten up, little brother. I'm joking.'

'Stop behaving like children, we've got guests,' Eleanor chided.

'Please don't stop on my account,' Dave said, grinning.

Poppy, who was sitting beside him, squeezed his hand. She already knew her family loved him. He'd won over her mother by producing a tiny tub of yellow patio roses that he said he'd bought from his local farm shop – no supermarket cut flowers here – and he'd won over Kenny when they'd got into a discussion about old Mercedes cars and Dave had promised him a spin in his at the earliest opportunity. Not to mention the fact that he'd got major brownie points for saying he would love to have a look at the flatbed truck and see all the photos of its progress.

In fact, with the exception of Eleanor, they had all trooped out to the garage while they were waiting for the curry and Kenny had stood there, prouder than a new father while Dave had admired the truck.

'It's cracking, that,' Dave had said, running his hands over the baby blue paintwork. 'How long did it take?'

'Decades,' Lennox had answered.

'Four years,' Kenny had said, ignoring him. 'I bought it for two thousand pounds and I've just advertised it in *Classic Truck* for offers around thirty-five.'

'Thirty-five quid. You're taking a loss on that,' Lennox had taunted.

'Thirty-five thousand,' Kenny had said without a trace of smugness. 'It's what they're worth. I had an enquiry today. I might take you all out for a meal if I sell it.'

There was a stunned silence in the oil-scented coolness of the concrete garage as everyone gaped at the vintage truck.

'Bloody hell,' Micky had said. 'That's good going.'

'You're a genius,' Rose had gushed.

'Our superstar dad,' Alice had said, putting her arm around him. 'You've always been brilliant with cars.'

That had set the tone for the rest of the evening.

By the time they had eaten the curries, toasted Kenny's success, several times, and started on desserts, Poppy was beginning to feel warm and full of bonhomie. She'd forgotten about Eleanor's cryptic text until Rose brought it up.

'Mum, what was that text you sent about the pope?' She raised her perfect half-moon eyebrows.

So did Eleanor. 'The pope?' she queried.

'You sent a text. I kind of assumed you didn't mean you were going to see the pope, but he was definitely mentioned.'

'I got that too,' Lennox said. 'I assumed you were having a midlife crisis. Again. That is why you've been signing up for all those weird activities you've been doing lately, isn't it? Some kind of madcap menopausal mission.'

'Don't be so rude,' Dana said, prodding him in the ribs.

Eleanor gave Lennox a hard stare. 'He can't help himself, Dana,' she said, 'But I don't need to tell you that. You're married to him.'

'Sorry,' Lennox said with uncharacteristic contrition.

Poppy looked at their mother who, despite her defensiveness, did actually look quite worried. And then, to Poppy's surprise and concern, Eleanor lowered her gaze and said, 'No, actually he's right. That's exactly what I've been doing. I've been on a menopausal mission, sparked off by feeling like I'd been thrown on the scrapheap.'

Alice was the first to spring to her defence. 'You're definitely not on the scrapheap. Fifty-eight is not old.'

'You're still young,' Poppy added.

'Youngish,' Rose said.

'Sixty is the new seventy,' Lennox said. 'Everyone knows that.'

'He means sixty is the new fifty,' Micky corrected.

'That's right, I did.' Lennox looked mortified. 'Sorry.'

'Stop apologising, it doesn't suit you,' Eleanor told him at the same moment that Kenny, who'd been silent all this time – he always had trouble getting a word in edgeways – shifted along the sofa and put his arm around his wife.

It was this little gesture of solidarity that solidified the feeling of slightly anxious concern towards Eleanor into one of whole-hearted empathy. Kenny never said a lot – he usually let the family banter wash over his head like a short summer shower – but if he thought his wife needed a hug, then everybody sat up and took notice.

'What is it, Mum?' Poppy asked gently, and the room fell quiet as the focus was suddenly firmly on the matriarch.

'I'm probably being silly.'

There was a chorus of disagreement.

When it was quiet again, Eleanor continued, 'It's just that... It's just – well, I look around at you all – all so successful in your own lives, all following your dreams – Poppy with her television show, Rose with her own personal-trainer business, Alice a high-flyer in her dream job, Micky doing law... Lennox...' She paused.

'Drifting from one job to the next and wearing ridiculous socks?' Lennox offered.

'Lennox making everyone laugh and about to start his own family,' Eleanor said loyally, and got a look of such pure love from her eldest son that Poppy wondered if their mother knew something the rest of them didn't.

'And, of course, my lovely Kenny restoring beautiful old vehicles,' Eleanor continued, squeezing his arm. She sounded slightly choked. 'And, well, I feel as though I've never achieved anything or done anything worthy of an accolade in my entire life. I feel as though I'm a very boring middle-aged woman who's had the most tedious, mouse-brown life ever. It was all right when you were all young because you were my focus. And it was all right when I was at the library because I felt valued there and I spent so much time around books and reading them that I didn't really notice I hadn't achieved anything else. But then when the library made me redundant, it hit me that I had done very little with my life outside of the family. And then suddenly I didn't even have the distraction of books any more. I'm sorry. This is all very "woe is me", isn't it?' She tailed off and looked at her hands and Poppy saw to her horror that a tear had just rolled down her nose and dripped on to her wedding ring.

'Oh, Mum, that's nonsense. You are the most wonderfully bright, eloquent, erudite woman I've ever met. You've spent your whole life supporting others. And I know everyone's going to agree with me when I say we all love you totally.'

'That's right,' Rose said. 'You're a brilliant mum. And none of us would be where we are today if you hadn't supported us 100 per cent.'

'Absolutely,' said Alice.

'You're the best,' said Micky.

'You're not mouse-brown either,' said Lennox. 'More grey. A really nice grey. I mean, people would pay to be that shade of grey.'

'You see, love,' Kenny said, his eyes gentle and patient, as though this wasn't the first time they'd had this conversation. 'What did I tell you! Listen to your family.'

'They're just saying that to cheer me up. I knew they would. They're just being lovely.' But she did look slightly appeased.

There was a little silence and Dave cleared his throat. 'I know I'm an outsider, but I suspect they're being lovely because they learned it from you. That speaks volumes.'

'He's right,' Jack murmured.

'Hear hear,' Dana said. 'You're at the very centre of an amazing bunch of people. They wouldn't be here without you and I don't just mean on this earth, although most of them wouldn't! I mean at this curry night and at all the other curry nights that have ever happened. We never miss them, do we? And that's down to you, and the way you have of making everyone feel welcome and included, month after month, year after year.'

Poppy thought that was the most she had ever heard Dana say, with the possible exception of the night they'd sat outside her house in Poppy's car. 'Thank you, Dana,' she said. 'That's spot on.'

'I'd still like to shine at something,' Eleanor said. 'Achieve something in my own right, like you all have. Do something that's just for me.'

'Maybe you could write a novel?' Rose suggested. 'Instead of reading them...'

'Although we have noticed you're not reading as much as you used to,' Micky said. 'Is that because you're off books?'

'No, darling,' Eleanor said. 'It's because my eyesight's not as good as it was... that's another thing that's been bothering me.'

'Have you seen the optician lately?' Rose asked.

'Yes. Yes, I have. I've got the beginnings of glaucoma.' Eleanor gave a small sigh. 'They can treat it, but it's harder to read.'

'But why didn't you say, Mum?' Rose, who was closest, leant across to pat Eleanor's hand. 'Why didn't you tell us? You must have been worried sick.'

'I kept thinking it wasn't as bad as all that. But it is really. It's one of the reasons I've been sending you all nonsensical texts. I've been dictating them lately because it's easier. But my phone doesn't always get it right. The translation from voice to text isn't perfect and I have trouble reading what it puts. Usually, I get Kenny to check. But when he isn't around... I sometimes don't bother.' She tailed off again.

It made so much sense. Poppy ached for her. 'I guess that's why you haven't been doing so much reading either, Mum?'

'It is, yes.'

'I keep telling her she should use an electronic reader,' Kenny said. 'You can change the text size. Make it bigger. That's right, isn't it, Micky?'

'Yeah, it is,' Micky said. 'I think you can do that on your phone too.'

'I like proper books,' Eleanor said. 'I like the smell of them, the feel of them, the weight of them. But even the large-print ones are tricky to read lately.'

'What about a magnifier?' Dana asked. 'We have some at school for reading. They're quite cheap, these days. That way you could stick to proper books.'

'I've seen those,' Jack said. 'My grandad had one for the racing pages of the newspaper. I think it had a light in it.'

Eleanor was looking much more cheerful than she'd been when this conversation had started. 'I don't know why I didn't tell you all sooner.'

'You still haven't told us about the pope, Mother,' Lennox said, getting out his phone and waving it about. 'Are you going to enlighten us? Is there any news about Pope Francis or any other religious leader we should know about? I mean, personally, I'm always keen to keep abreast of ecclesiastical announcements. Can I say abreast and ecclesiastical in the same sentence? Or is that totally inappropriate?'

Eleanor glanced at him with affection. 'I meant what I said earlier. You do always make me smile, darling. That's a gift.'

'I wish I did it on purpose, more often.' But he looked pleased, nonetheless.

'Well, as you've already surmised,' Eleanor continued, 'my news has nothing to do with the pope and possibly a bit to do with a menopausal mission.' She took a deep breath and looked at Kenny. 'Shall I tell them what we've been planning?'

'Go for it, love.'

'Kenny and I have decided we'd like to go travelling. We want to do it in style, but also fairly cheaply – if that makes sense. Once we've sold the truck, fingers crossed, we're thinking of buying a motorhome and just setting off. That probably sounds completely crazy at our age, but actually we would both like to see a bit more of the world. We thought we might start with some famous literary places to give us a focus.'

'It's been on our bucket list for a while,' Kenny put in and rubbed his beard. 'Well, the travelling has.'

'Sounds great, Mum,' said Rose and Poppy simultaneously.

'I still don't get the pope reference,' Lennox pressed. 'Are you visiting churches or something?'

'No – as I said, I dictate all my messages. That text was supposed to say, Kenny and I were thinking of going to Europe... Europe and your pope probably sound quite similar to a computer, don't they?' She shook her head and stared into the distance. 'I've always wanted to go to the American Library in Paris – it's one of the largest English-language lending libraries in Europe. Phew, that's a tongue-twister. I wonder what my phone would have made of that! I'd also love to see Livraria Bertrand, which is the oldest operating bookstore in the world. That's in Lisbon. And there's the National Museum of Romanian Literature in Bucharest.'

As she'd been speaking, Eleanor's face had taken on a glow and passion had coloured her voice. Poppy felt hugely relieved that her mum was going to be all right now, or at least was on the way to being all right.

'I wasted all that time, trying to find a new interest,' Eleanor continued, 'something I could feel passionate about – that's why I started the string art and the piano lessons – and all those other crazy things. But really my passion is, and always has been, literature.' She paused for breath. 'Travelling around Europe is something I wanted to do when I was younger. I was going to take a year out, but then I met your father, and I got pregnant with you, Lennox.' She glanced with affection at her eldest son. 'And the rest, as they say, is history.'

'That sounds brilliant, Mum.' Micky was leaning forward enthusiastically. 'You two will have a great time.'

'And it will be very handy having a mechanic with you,' Alice said. 'What will you do about the garage, Dad? Have you told them?'

'I have and they're happy to hold my job open for when we get back. If I still want it.' It was his turn to flush slightly in the rosy warmth of the conservatory. 'We may get bitten with the travel bug. Europe first – and then the world.'

'But our first trip will just be a couple of months,' Eleanor said quickly. 'Don't worry, we'll only miss one curry night. We want to keep up with all of your news. Baby-making, television shows, romances – and we'll need to come back for my eye appointments.'

'We could always host the curry nights at ours for one month,' Dana offered.

'Or ours,' Jack said. 'We could take it in turns.'

Everyone started talking at once again and, in the end, it was Micky banging a teaspoon against a glass who shut them up.

'I want to propose a toast,' he shouted. 'Listen up.'

'Can I suggest breasts and ecclesiastical journeys?' Lennox shouted, in an overexaggerated, silly voice. He was clearly on a high.

'No, you can't,' Micky said. 'Fine subjects as they may be. I'd like to propose a toast to our amazing parents. And to families, past and present, and to all those who are yet to come.' He, too, glanced at Dana and Lennox, who both looked pleased as punch. Poppy would have put money on the fact that they had some news of their own.

'Hey, Micky,' Rose shouted. 'Can we simplify it a bit and just say, "to amazing families"?'

'Yeah, good idea,' he said, and everyone raised their glasses.

Poppy squeezed Dave's fingers with her free hand. She couldn't remember a time when she'd felt so gloriously contented and happy.

'To amazing families,' Micky said, holding his glass high.

'To amazing families,' they echoed.

EPILOGUE

At the July curry night, Lennox and Dana announced they were expecting a baby, and that actually their first scan had just showed that Dana was expecting twins. It looked as though Lennox would get his wish for a big family before he was too old, after all.

Kenny announced that the flatbed truck had sold for 37,000 pounds. He'd had two enthusiasts bidding against each other.

Fortunately, none of them had been eating at the time otherwise some of them may have choked on their food. Poppy knew they wouldn't mock his hobby again, although there would always be jokes about big ends.

* * *

At the August curry night, Rose and Jack announced that they too were having a baby, just the one in their case, and the cousins would be born within three months of each other.

Also, just before the August curry night, Netflix got in touch with Poppy to tell her that they loved the pilot and they green-lit the series the following month. Beauty Spot Productions, and all of Poppy's dedicated crew, are currently working on the next episode.

* * *

To Poppy's relief, Micky met Sasha, a fellow legal eagle, at work so didn't have to rely on meeting his soulmate on *Date for a Day* – which meant she was under a little less pressure. Micky and Sasha are planning to move in with each other very soon.

* * *

Alice and Alistair proved to be the perfect match. They have taught each other to be less work-focused and have made a pact to go riding along sunset beaches as often as possible.

* * *

Phil and his actor girlfriend are currently rehearsing for a Shakespearean production to be performed at Brownsea Island and Alice, Alistair, Poppy and Dave have booked front-row seats. Clara and her husband also have front-row seats and apparently dogs are welcome, so Foxy will be accompanying them. There's even a rumour that Mr B might be going. But no one knows whether this is actually true!

* * *

After a lot of careful research, Eleanor and Kenny bought a twenty-five-foot motorhome, which they adore. They are about to set off on their literary-location tour – first stop, Paris. But they will be back at regular intervals.

* * *

Poppy and Dave are now equal partners in Beauty Spot Productions, just as they are equal partners in every other aspect of their lives. It turned out Dave had dabbled with stocks and shares since he was a teenager and had been rather good at it so he had built up quite a nest egg.

They took their families and the rest of the crew to the Bluebell Cliff to toast the success of *Date for a Day*. Clara gave them a case of complimentary champagne and a riotous evening was had by all.

Phil Grimshaw and Mr B both came to the table to raise a glass with them and the two feuding men managed to get through an entire evening without so much as a cross word. Although when Alice asked Phil if the situation between him and the eccentric chef was now fully resolved, Phil just smiled enigmatically and didn't commit himself either way.

* * *

Poppy and Dave are planning their wedding at the Bluebell Cliff Hotel. They decided they wouldn't waste another second of their lives being apart. It will take place in the spring and they are already thinking about a coastal theme.

This will involve lighthouses and the bluebell woods and very possibly a boat trip. They are considering how they could incorporate a lifeboat.

There will also be some wedding photographs of a beautiful

bride and a gorgeous groom, strolling hand in hand into a golden sunset, which is, as everyone knows, the way that all wonderful fairy-tale romances should finish.

ACKNOWLEDGMENTS

Thank you, as always, to Judith Murdoch. Thank you to Caroline Ridding, my fab editor, and the rest of the brilliant Boldwood team. Thank you to the lovely Jade Craddock. Thank you to Gordon Rawsthorne for his endless support. A particularly big thank you must also go to Karen Gilchrist for her expert knowledge on what it's like to be a TV producer. This novel is very much the better thanks to your generosity of spirit, Karen.

Thank you also to Jonathan Evans for being so inspiring and Ingrid Duffell for her technical know-how. Thank you to Tony Millward, Adam Millward and Pam Lant. I'd also like to say a massive thank you to my readers. Thank you for all the lovely messages and emails you send me. It means the world to know that you love reading my novels as much as I love writing them.

MORE FROM DELLA GALTON

We hope you enjoyed reading *Shooting Starts Over Bluebell Cliff*. If you did, please leave a review.

If you'd like to gift a copy, this book is also available as an ebook, digital audio download and audiobook CD.

Sign up to Della Galton's mailing list for news, competitions and updates on future books:

http://bit.ly/DellaGaltonNewsletter

Explore more glorious escapist reads from Della Galton.

ABOUT THE AUTHOR

Della Galton is the author of over 15 books, including *Ice and a Slice*. She writes short stories, teaches writing groups and is Agony Aunt for Writers Forum Magazine. She lives in Dorset.

Visit Della's website: www.dellagalton.co.uk

Follow Della on social media:

- facebook.com/DailyDella
- twitter.com/DellaGalton
- instagram.com/Dellagalton
- bookbub.com/authors/della-galton

ABOUT BOLDWOOD BOOKS

Boldwood Books is a fiction publishing company seeking out the best stories from around the world.

Find out more at www.boldwoodbooks.com

Sign up to the Book and Tonic newsletter for news, offers and competitions from Boldwood Books!

http://www.bit.ly/bookandtonic

We'd love to hear from you, follow us on social media:

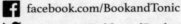 facebook.com/BookandTonic
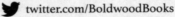 twitter.com/BoldwoodBooks
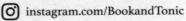 instagram.com/BookandTonic